JANE BETTANY is the author of the DI Isabel Blood crime series, set in the fictional Derbyshire town of Bainbridge. The first book in the series – In Cold Blood – won the 2019 Gransnet and HQ writing competition, which was for women writers over the age of 40 who had written a novel with a protagonist in the same age range.

Before turning to novel writing, Jane had been writing short stories and non-fiction articles for over twenty years, many of which have appeared in women's magazines, literary magazines, newspapers and online.

Jane has an MA in Creative Writing and lives in Derby.

Also by Jane Bettany

The Detective Isabel Blood series
In Cold Blood
Without a Trace
Last Seen Alive

Murder in Merrywell

JANE BETTANY

ONE PLACE. MANY STORIES

HQ
An imprint of HarperCollins*Publishers* Ltd
1 London Bridge Street
London SE1 9GF

www.harpercollins.co.uk

HarperCollins*Publishers*
Macken House, 39/40 Mayor Street Upper,
Dublin 1 D01 C9W8
Ireland

This paperback edition 2023

1

First published in Great Britain by
HQ, an imprint of HarperCollins*Publishers* Ltd 2023

MIX
Paper | Supporting
responsible forestry
FSC™ C007454

This book is produced from independently certified FSC™ paper
to ensure responsible forest management.

For more information visit: www.harpercollins.co.uk/green

Printed and Bound in the UK using
100% Renewable Electricity at CPI Group (UK) Ltd

For my sister, Dawn
with love

Prologue

This whole, unfortunate state of affairs could have been avoided . . . would have been, if she hadn't been so persistent, so determined to get what she wanted, no matter what the cost.

It's regrettable, but the problem can't be allowed to continue. It must be resolved, and quickly. The tiresome conversations, her relentless questions and absurd assumptions . . . all of it has to stop.

Quite frankly, her presence in the village is becoming intolerable. There's an irritating naivety about her that verges on recklessness. She doesn't seem to understand that actions have consequences: that for everything taken, something has to give.

The current impasse must end today. The time has come to take action, before the situation spirals out of control and everything implodes.

This will be a day of reckoning: a chance to rectify mistakes and protect the future.

Chapter 1

Violet Brewster was in the lobby of Merrywell village hall, sitting on a rickety and very uncomfortable wooden chair. As instructed, she had arrived at eleven o'clock precisely, and it was now twenty past. She didn't like to be kept waiting – it made her anxious and irritable in equal measure.

To her right, in the main hall, a playgroup session was underway. Usually, she relished the sound of children playing happily, but today their raucous shouts and squeals were making her jumpy. It wasn't in her nature to be so on edge, but then it wasn't every day she got to pitch for an important contract with Merrywell parish council. Her fledgling business, *The Memory Box*, was barely three weeks old, and she desperately needed to secure her first commission. This was her big chance to bid for a lucrative project, and she couldn't afford to mess it up.

Perhaps some deep breathing exercises would calm her nerves. She inhaled through her nose, filling her lungs to capacity before exhaling slowly and mindfully.

In.

Out.

In.

Out.

Repeat.

By twenty-five past, she was getting fidgety again. She straightened the collar of her blouse, twiddled with the plain gold chain that hung around her neck, and wondered how much longer they were going to keep her waiting.

Pressing her damp palms together, she shuffled restlessly. What if the councillors didn't like her ideas for the project? What if they didn't like *her*? After all, it wasn't just Violet's business that was new – *she* was also a newcomer to Merrywell. Would they trust an outsider to engage with local residents and ask the right questions for the film of community memories they were planning?

As she pulled back her cuff and frowned at her watch, a young woman came bounding into the lobby.

'Violet Brewster?' she said. 'Sorry to have kept you waiting. The committee is ready for you now.'

Finally, she thought. *Let's get this show on the road. Come on, Violet, you can do this.*

'I'm Molly, by the way,' the woman said, as she tucked her long blonde hair behind her ears.

Violet smoothed out her skirt before standing up. 'Pleased to meet you,' she said, smiling effusively. 'I take it you're one of the councillors?'

'Me?' Molly threw back her head and laughed. 'No, I just take the minutes of the meetings. You wouldn't catch me standing for election to the parish council. I wouldn't have the patience to deal with Merrywell's whinge bags.'

Violet smiled politely at Molly's indiscretion.

'There's a small but very vocal group of residents who are constantly complaining about something,' Molly confided. 'Litter, dog mess, the state of the local playground . . . I'm sure you can guess who I'm talking about.'

'Not really,' said Violet. 'I only moved to the village three weeks ago.'

'You'll find out who I mean soon enough.' Molly nodded

meaningfully. 'Although, don't get me wrong – despite the moans and groans of the local cynics, Merrywell is a lovely place to live.'

Violet followed her along a narrow corridor towards the rear of the building.

'This is where the parish council holds its meetings,' Molly said, pointing to a door marked *Small Events Room*. 'Come on in. They don't bite . . . well, not all of them, anyway.'

Inside the sparsely furnished room, two women and three men were sitting behind a long row of desks, their faces dour and serious. The set-up seemed overly officious, almost inquisitorial – and the single chair placed in the centre of the room did nothing to dispel that impression. Violet was invited to sit in it.

She crossed her legs and waited to be interrogated, half-expecting someone to switch on a dazzling light and shine it in her face.

The woman sitting at the centre of the interview panel was in her sixties, with silvery-grey hair and flamboyant, red-framed glasses. She leaned forward and offered Violet a tight, lipsticked smile.

'I'm Judith Talbot, leader of the parish council,' she said. 'Thank you for coming here today, Mrs Brewster, and for submitting your written proposal for producing our community film. We've all had an opportunity to read through it, and it's fair to say we like your ideas. Our objective is to create an interesting and lasting record of living memories, and your vision for the project appears to deliver on all of our goals.'

Violet released a stealthy sigh of relief and began to relax. *Thank goodness for that*, she thought. The brief she'd been given for the project had been vague and lacking in any detail – so it was reassuring to know the concept she'd come up with had hit the spot. Maybe she wouldn't need to give the councillors the hard sell after all. It sounded as though they'd already made up their minds, and this meeting was merely a formality – a chance to award the contract and instruct her to get on with things.

Judith Talbot cleared her throat. 'Whilst we were impressed with your proposal, Mrs Brewster,' she said, 'we do have a few queries.'

The councillor's words pricked Violet's bubble of optimism, bursting it instantly. *Don't get ahead of yourself, Brewster*, she told herself. *You can't afford to be complacent. It's not in the bag yet.*

'I'll be happy to answer your questions,' she said. 'And do please call me Violet. Mrs Brewster makes me sound like my mother-in-law . . . *ex* mother-in-law.'

Was it her imagination, or was the guy at the end of the table stifling a smile? Violet knew his name was Matthew Collis, but only because he was a fellow tenant at Merrywell Shopping Village. He was a joiner and maker of bespoke furniture, which he manufactured in the workshop at the back of his shop. She'd seen him around a few times, but they hadn't been formally introduced.

Judith Talbot glanced at her notes before continuing. 'As I understand it, your business . . . *The Memory Box* . . . is a new venture. *Very* new, in fact.'

'That's right,' Violet replied. 'I started trading a few weeks ago. As I'm sure you're aware, I've taken over the tenancy of a small unit at the shopping village. That will be my base, although naturally I'll spend a lot of time out and about, depending on where my projects take me.'

'And what *projects* are you working on at the moment?' Judith asked, fixing Violet with a steely gaze.

So far, Violet hadn't had so much as a sniff of a paying customer – but she wasn't going to admit that. If she did, she'd almost certainly blow her chances with the council. She knew how lucky she was to have this opportunity to pitch for work, and she was determined to capitalise on it. The Merrywell community film was the catalyst she needed to get her business off the ground.

'I've been focusing on marketing my services and setting up a website,' she said, evasively. 'And following up enquiries, of course.'

That wasn't strictly true. There had been no enquiries. So

far, the expensive online advertising campaign Violet had been running had produced absolutely nothing.

Zero. Nada. Zilch.

While waiting for the non-existent enquiries to flood in, she'd filled her time by perfecting her pitch for the community film. She must have read through the written proposal a dozen times before she'd finally emailed it to the council.

'So you haven't actually undertaken any work yet?' Judith frowned. 'You've no track record, as such? No satisfied clients who can vouch for you?'

Clearly, there was no pulling the wool over Judith Talbot's eyes.

'I hope that won't be a stumbling block,' Violet said. 'My business may be new, but *I* have decades of relevant career experience. If it's references you want, I can arrange that.'

Before Judith had a chance to respond, Matthew Collis cut in. 'That won't be necessary,' he said. 'Chasing up references takes time. This film is being funded by a lottery grant, and we're keen to get things underway as soon as possible. Perhaps you can tell us a little more about yourself and *The Memory Box* to help us decide whether or not you'll be a good fit for the project.'

Violet was grateful for his intervention. She wondered where to begin, and how much to tell the committee about herself and her new business venture. Maybe she should start with the basics.

'After graduating, I started out as a journalist, and later moved into corporate communications,' she said, summarising her twenty-five-year career as succinctly as possible. It was important to establish her credentials, but she didn't want to bore them with the humdrum details of her working life. It was information about *The Memory Box* they were after, not her life story.

'My move to Merrywell seemed like the perfect time to set up a business of my own,' she continued. 'Through *The Memory Box*, I'll be offering a variety of services, harnessing the skills I've learned over the years. As well as working with communities to create living memories and village histories, I'll be helping

7

individuals tell their personal and family histories, so that they can be preserved for future generations. Through the medium of film, I'll record house, school and business histories; anniversary, memorial and birthday tributes; even living wills and last wishes. In short, I'm planning to capture on video whatever people feel compelled to talk about or want to share with others.'

Judith looked sceptical. 'It's an interesting business concept,' she said. 'But also rather an unusual one . . . I don't think you'll find many customers here in Merrywell. It's a small, traditional village. We've managed to get funding for our community film, but it could be years . . . decades before we undertake another similar project.'

Violet smiled. 'I don't intend to restrict myself to Merrywell. My business is based here because it's where I live, but I'll be offering my services to a much wider target market. The Peak District is ideally placed for easy access to Sheffield, Derby, Nottingham and Manchester. I can pack up my camera and recording equipment, and go almost anywhere.'

'I hear you've bought Greengage Cottage,' Judith said.

'That's right,' Violet replied, wondering what that had to do with anything.

'And you live alone?'

'I do, yes.'

'And can I ask why you chose Merrywell?' Judith persisted. 'You're obviously not from around here. What drew you to the village?'

Was it her imagination, or were the questions becoming increasingly irrelevant to the business in hand? It would appear that Judith Talbot was either a naturally inquisitive person, or – more likely – a shameless snoop. Violet didn't like it when people pried so brazenly into her personal life – especially now, when she was still smarting from the emotional upheaval of her recent break-up. She had no intention of telling the committee that her divorce had necessitated selling her marital home. Nor was she

8

willing to divulge that the breakdown of her marriage had forced her to take a long, hard look at her life and make some radical, and much-needed changes.

Violet's immediate reaction to Judith's barrage of questions was to tell her to mind her own business – but then she remembered how much she and *The Memory Box* needed this commission. The Merrywell film would be a major coup – something to add to her portfolio and establish her reputation in the community. So, even though Judith's blatant prying was making Violet's toes curl, she felt obliged to respond. As council leader, Judith would have the casting vote when it came to awarding contracts. She couldn't risk rubbing her up the wrong way.

Forcing a smile, Violet pointed her thumb over her shoulder, towards the window behind her. 'You only have to look at the view out there to see what drew me to Merrywell,' she said. 'I first got to know this area when I was a student in Sheffield. I joined a walking club, and a group of us used to head into the Peak District most weekends. I've held on to those memories, and visited Derbyshire on and off ever since.' She shrugged. 'When I decided to move away from London, the Peak District was the obvious choice for my relocation.'

Judith opened her mouth to ask another question, but the white-haired man on her left got in first.

'I'm Lionel Pilkington, parish councillor and former head teacher of Merrywell Primary School. You've said you plan to harness the skills you've acquired during your career. What are those skills, exactly? Tell us why we should put our faith in you to produce our community film.'

'Over the course of my career, I've worked in several communications roles . . . for charities and educational establishments, as well as huge corporations,' Violet said. 'During that time, I've interviewed people from all walks of life. I'm a good listener, and I've learned how to ask the right questions . . . to encourage interviewees to confide and share their experiences.' She smiled.

9

'I believe everyone has a story to tell, and through *The Memory Box* I'll be giving people the chance to pass on their knowledge and wisdom.'

'That sounds very commendable,' Lionel said. 'And in my experience, the most interesting stories are often told by the humblest of people.'

'What about the technical side of things?' Matthew Collis said. 'I assume you're proficient in video production and sound editing?'

'Of course,' Violet replied, 'and I also have some experience of graphic design.'

She decided not to mention that these were skills she had only recently acquired. Whenever she'd been called upon to do any filming in her employed roles, there had always been someone alongside her to operate the cameras, lighting and recording equipment. Before committing to her business idea, Violet had enrolled on a series of fast-track courses to learn the technical skills she would need to run *The Memory Box*. Each course had thrown up some challenging hands-on exercises, and Violet had practised tirelessly at home, but she had yet to test her film-making skills in a real-life, bona fide, paying situation. It was this aspect of her business that she was least confident about, but she wasn't going to tell Matthew Collis that.

What she did instead was launch into her pitch. She ran through her ideas for engaging with local residents, outlined the areas she proposed to cover in the film, and summarised what the committee could expect from her, and what the timescales would be.

With her speech over, and the rest of the committee's questions answered, Violet sat back as Judith Talbot conferred quietly with her colleagues.

'Thank you for sharing your ideas and answering our questions, Mrs Brewster . . . Violet,' Judith said eventually. 'We're going to spend some more time discussing what you've told us, and I'll be in touch with you tomorrow to let you know our decision.'

Violet smiled at the councillors and stood up. She had done her best. All she could do now was keep her fingers crossed and hope for a positive outcome.

As she headed for the door, she tried not to think about what would happen if they said 'no'.

Chapter 2

Violet was woken the next morning by the machine-gun rattle of a marauding magpie. Even though it was three weeks since she'd moved into Greengage Cottage, she still wasn't used to the ever-present sound of birdcalls outside her windows. Before their divorce, she and Paul had been married for twenty-four years, and the last twenty of those had been spent in a terraced house in Fulham, which was on a noisy, traffic-clogged road. Violet was far more accustomed to the wail of sirens and revving engines than the sweet song of a robin or the chatter of blackbirds.

Pulling back her bedroom curtains, she gazed down at her flower-filled garden and the lush green fields beyond. If she stood on her tiptoes and peered to the right, past the curve in the road near St Luke's church, she could just make out the entrance to her place of work – Merrywell Shopping Village. It was a courtyard of converted barns, outbuildings and workshops that had once been part of the local manor house. The shopping village had been developed to offer artisan and creative retail opportunities, along with studios, galleries and meeting spaces. Located on the main tourist route to Buxton, it was a popular stop-off point for holidaymakers.

Violet stood at the window and savoured the view for a few moments before heading downstairs to her sunny kitchen. With its flagstone floor and limewashed beams, it was her favourite room in the house. While she waited for the kettle to boil, she gazed out of the mullioned window above the sink, feeling grateful that the failure of her marriage had resulted in at least one positive thing – her move to Greengage Cottage. Being here was definitely something to be thankful for.

At eight-thirty, having downed a mug of strong tea, she pulled on a lightweight jacket and set off for work. In London, her daily commute had involved an early start and a crammed thirty-five-minute journey on the tube. Here in Merrywell, it was a mere three-minute pleasant stroll to *The Memory Box*.

A fresh breeze was blowing from the west as she wandered through the village. Spring flowers were blooming in every front garden: primulas, pansies and aubretia, a few late daffodils, grape hyacinths and tulips. Several trees were also bursting into blossom, their pale blooms delicate against the clear blue sky.

As Violet passed the village shop, a tall, elderly man emerged carrying a newspaper and a plastic bottle of milk. He nodded briefly and uttered a single, gruff word.

'Morning.'

When first accosted in this manner, Violet had felt spurned, certain she was being cold-shouldered as an incomer. When she'd mentioned this to a neighbour, she was relieved to discover this was the standard greeting in Merrywell. Apparently, a simple *morning, afternoon,* or *evening* was deemed sufficient when acknowledging a fellow villager.

Smiling at the man, Violet nodded and replied in a similar vein.

As she passed the White Hart, the smell of stale beer mingled with the fresh spring air. She hadn't visited the pub yet, but that was something she intended to remedy soon. Thursday nights were quiz nights, so perhaps that would be the best time to put in an appearance.

Rounding the bend in the road, she peered over the wall at St Luke's church. It was small and squat, built in the Norman style, with a plain tiled roof and a side porch. As churches went, it was architecturally unremarkable, but Violet knew it was supported by a loyal congregation.

A couple of hundred yards beyond the church was the entrance to Merrywell Shopping Village. *The Memory Box* was nestled in the far corner of its courtyard, in the smallest unit in the development. Next door was a shop selling arts and craft supplies and jigsaw puzzles. On the other side of that was *The Antiques Emporium*, which was packed with dark furniture and cabinets filled with curios and collectibles. On the second side of the quadrangle *Collis Fine Furniture* was flanked on one side by a yarn, wool and fabric shop called *Sew-in' to Knitting*, and on the other by an outdoor clothing store. On the third side was a shop called *The Epicurious*, which sold locally produced jams, chutneys, pickles, biscuits and handcrafted chocolates. Alongside that was a studio area, with space available for hire. It was used for arts and crafts workshops, cookery demonstrations and yoga sessions, and regularly served as a meeting place for local hobby groups.

The whole of the fourth side of the courtyard was occupied by *Books, Bakes and Cakes* (known locally as 'the BBC'). In Violet's opinion, it was the finest shop in Derbyshire. Housed in a converted barn, it was the largest building in the shopping village. As its name suggested, it provided a bookshop, bakery and café all under one roof, and was run by three members of the Nash family.

It was to the bakery that Violet headed now, having foregone breakfast at home in favour of a takeaway cappuccino and one of Fiona Nash's mouth-watering muffins.

The bell above the door jangled as she entered. Even though it was still early, Fiona was already dealing with a queue of locals, there to buy their favourite loaves, buns, tarts and pies. As she breathed in the yeasty smell of fresh bread, Violet's stomach rumbled. This shop was her happy place – combining, as it did, three of her favourite things: books, cakes and coffee. As far as Violet was concerned, *Books, Bakes and Cakes* offered a winning combination.

Fiona Nash was a tall, red-haired fifty-year-old, who exuded energy and bonhomie. She and Violet shared the same quirky sense of humour, which is probably why they had quickly struck up a friendship. Fiona was originally from Nottingham, but she'd lived in Merrywell for ten years and was the go-to person for information about the local area. Her husband, Eric, ran the bookshop side of the business, and their daughter, Sophie, managed the café.

'Cappuccino?' Fiona said, when Violet reached the head of the queue.

'Yes, please, and I'd also like one of your fabulous muffins.'

'Blueberry, banoffee or chocolate?'

'Blueberry, please,' said Violet. 'Purely on the basis that it sounds like the healthiest option.'

Fiona laughed. 'I probably shouldn't say this, but there's nothing remotely healthy about the muffins we sell in here. However, they are delicious . . . and quite addictive.'

'Tell me about it.' Violet patted her waist guiltily. 'I've gained three pounds since I moved to Merrywell – and I'm blaming every one of them on your bakery.'

'How was your meeting with the parish council?' Fiona asked, as she prepared Violet's coffee.

'It went OK . . . I think.' Violet joggled her head from side to side. 'They'll let me know their decision sometime today.'

'You don't sound very confident.'

Violet pulled a face. 'They liked my ideas, but the fact that my business is so new may be a problem.'

'Surely they can't hold that against you?' Fiona said. 'Everyone has to start somewhere.'

'True. I'm just not convinced they want me to start with *their* project. They asked a lot of questions, most of which I was happy to answer – although for some reason, Judith Talbot was *very* curious about why I'd moved to Merrywell.'

Fiona rolled her eyes. 'That's Judith for you. On the face of it, she's a pillar of the community, but she's also a barefaced busybody.'

'That was definitely the impression I got,' Violet said.

'In fairness to her,' Fiona added, 'Judith does have the best interests of the village at heart. She can be difficult sometimes, but she's the ideal person to lead the council. I'm sure she'll make the right decision and get you on board for the filming project.'

Violet held up both hands, fingers crossed.

'Will you let me know what happens?' Fiona asked.

'Of course.' Violet handed over a five-pound note and picked up the bag in which Fiona had placed a still-warm muffin.

'When you get the go-ahead,' said Fiona, 'and notice I said *when* and not *if* – because I have every faith in you – then you must come over and talk to me.' She handed Violet her change and her takeaway coffee. 'I'll give you a heads-up on who to speak to. There are loads of interesting characters in Merrywell. You'll be spoilt for choice.'

'I hope so,' Violet said. 'Although it doesn't necessarily follow that all of them will want to speak to me or be involved in the community film.'

Fiona smiled. 'I'm sure you'll be able to persuade them.'

'I must confess, I do have a knack for getting people to share their secrets,' Violet said. 'But I haven't got the contract yet, so I mustn't count my chickens. For now, I'm going to sit at my desk, make some phone calls and focus on drumming up some other business leads. I can't put all my eggs in one basket.'

'Are those the eggs that the chickens you haven't counted yet have laid?'

Violet laughed. 'Something like that.'

The first thing Violet did after she'd let herself into *The Memory Box* was drink her coffee and devour the muffin. Only then did she draw up a 'to-do' list and make a plan for the day. Her website was already completed and had gone live, as had the online mailing list – although, so far, only five people had subscribed to it, one of whom was her mother.

When she logged in to check on the click-through rate for her online advertising campaign, she grimaced. The results didn't look promising. Maybe she'd been naïve to assume that a few social media ads would bring in a flurry of customers. So far, she'd shied away from old-fashioned print advertising, but maybe it was time to produce a few flyers and posters to distribute to anyone willing to display them. She was sure Fiona would put some on the bakery counter, and Eric was a kind bloke. He'd stick a poster up in the bookshop if she asked him nicely.

As she added DESIGN FLYERS AND POSTERS to her 'to-do' list, the door opened. The sound made her heart leap momentarily, but the resulting flash of anticipation was extinguished when she saw who was coming into the shop. Instead of a potential customer, the person entering was Matthew Collis. Outside of his role as a councillor, it seemed unlikely he would want to engage the services of The Memory Box.

Then again, maybe he was here on official business, delivering the council's verdict on the filming contract.

'Good morning,' Matthew said. 'I thought I'd pop over and introduce myself properly. I really should have called in before now, but better late than never.'

'I'm sure you're a busy man.' Violet smiled. 'What with running your business and being a councillor.'

Matthew grinned. 'Yes, parish council duties do have a way of swallowing up my spare time. Between you and me, it's a pain in the backside sometimes. I'm not entirely sure how I got roped into it. I hate committees.'

Violet laughed. 'It wouldn't be my scene – although, obviously, I hope I can work with the council on the filming project.' She raised her eyebrows. 'Any news on that front?'

Matthew screwed up his face, prevaricating. 'There is,' he said, 'but my life wouldn't be worth living if I told you what it was . . . Judith wants to speak to you herself.'

'On the basis that most people shy away from delivering

bad news,' said Violet, 'I find it reassuring that Judith wants to break the news herself. I'll take that as a positive sign.'

Matthew smiled at her and winked conspiratorially. 'I couldn't possibly comment.'

Violet felt her spirits lift. The signs were encouraging. Very encouraging indeed.

She watched as Matthew turned around, taking in the layout of *The Memory Box*. 'There's not much room in here,' he said. 'It's more like a matchbox than a memory box.'

'I don't need much space. As long as I've got room for my desk and my Mac, I'm happy. There's a storeroom at the back, and a small room I can use for interviewing, if I need to – but I'm expecting most of the filming I do to be carried out on location.'

'On location, eh? That sounds very glamorous.'

'Trust me,' Violet said. 'It's not.'

He grinned. 'Have you recovered from yesterday's encounter with the parish council?'

'Just about. There were a few tough questions, but that's understandable. You needed to establish whether I'm the best person for the project, right?'

'The fact that your business is based in the shopping village gave you an instant head start. We councillors like to support local businesses wherever possible.'

'In that case, my timing couldn't have been better . . . establishing *The Memory Box* at the same time as the council was commissioning a community film.' She smiled. 'How lucky is that?'

'Pure serendipity,' Matthew agreed.

'Any idea when Judith is likely to get in touch?'

'I'm certain you'll hear from her sometime today,' Matthew replied. 'I should probably warn you . . . Judith can be a tough taskmaster. She's expecting great things from this community film.'

'I'd better work hard then,' Violet said. 'Assuming I get the commission.'

'Exactly.' Matthew winked again. 'Anyway, I'll leave you to it. I only came over to welcome you to the shopping village and say a proper hello.'

'Thanks,' Violet said. 'I appreciate it.'

'Feel free to drop into my workshop sometime. I'd be happy to show you around, and I'm also fairly clued up on local history. I'd be glad to help with information for the film . . . assuming you're asked to make it, that is.'

'Thanks,' she said. 'I'll remember that.'

Giving her a covert smile, Matthew turned and opened the door. As it closed behind him, Violet slipped into the back room and executed a restrained, mustn't-jump-the-gun happy dance.

It was three o'clock when Judith Talbot finally conveyed the council's decision. She chose to do so in person, turning up at *The Memory Box* unannounced, while Violet was in the back room, making herself a cup of tea.

'Judith!' she said, as she carried her steaming mug back into the main shop. 'I didn't hear you come in.'

'You'd be wise to get a bell fitted above the door,' Judith said. 'You can't be too careful, you know.'

'Please, take a seat. Can I get you a tea, or a coffee? The kettle's just boiled.'

'No. Thank you all the same,' she said, sitting down and folding her hands in her lap.

Violet had observed that Judith liked to dress conservatively, usually in muted shades of grey or brown. Today, she was wearing a shin-length, loose-fitting dress that was the colour of thunderclouds. Paradoxically, the council leader also appeared to have a penchant for brightly coloured accessories and matching spectacles. The red glasses from yesterday had been replaced by a pair with square lenses and bubble-gum pink frames, which co-ordinated perfectly with the chunky pink necklace that hung around her neck.

'I come bearing good news,' Judith said. 'Having considered your proposal carefully, I'm pleased to say we'd like to appoint you as our community film-maker.'

Violet gripped her desk, feeling her knees buckle as she sat down. Matthew's less than subtle hints had given her every reason to hope, but hearing Judith's official confirmation of the council's decision came as a huge relief.

A wave of gratitude was welling up inside her. She wanted to laugh with joy – laugh and laugh and laugh until she cried – but Judith Talbot was observing her from the other side of the desk, her expression serious. Ignoring the gleeful giggle in the back of her throat, Violet bit her lips and forced them into a controlled and professional smile – one she hoped would convey a suitable balance of surprise and pleasure.

'That's wonderful news. Thank you, Judith.'

'I'm sorry it's taken so long to get back to you with our decision,' Judith added. 'I've been waiting for the legal team to draw up the paperwork. I thought it would be a nice idea to deliver the good news in person, and bring the contract with me at the same time.'

She extracted a printed document from a voluminous pink handbag and handed it to Violet.

'We can both sign the contract now if you're happy to do so, or you might want to take some time to read through it first. It's up to you.'

After scanning each page and checking the salient points, Violet agreed that the contract could be signed right then and there. She didn't want to give the council any time to change its mind.

'We were rather hoping you'd start work on the project immediately,' Judith said.

'It'll be my pleasure,' Violet replied, as she added her signature to the paperwork. 'I'll begin first thing tomorrow.'

Chapter 3

'I hope you know what you're letting yourself in for, young lady.'

As a forty-six-year-old, Violet was no longer accustomed to being referred to as a *young lady*. Then again, age was relative, and Nigel Slingsby was at least thirty years her senior. She mustn't take him too literally.

'Merrywell might look like a nice, quiet place,' Nigel continued, 'but scratch beneath the surface and you'll find all sorts of shenanigans going on.'

Violet smiled. 'I'm not sure the parish council will want me to include *that* kind of thing in the community video. My remit is to include a brief history of Merrywell and interview local residents to capture their memories of the village, and their experiences of living here.'

'Did they ask you to talk to us oldies first?' Nigel raised an eyebrow. 'So that you can record our memories before we croak?'

Violet shook her head and laughed. 'You look as fit as a fiddle to me . . . you're hardly ancient, are you?'

'I'm seventy-six,' Nigel said. 'But you're right. I don't feel my age. There's life in the old dog yet.'

On Fiona's recommendation, Violet was starting the project by interviewing three of Merrywell's long-standing residents:

Martha Andrews, an octogenarian who had been born in the village; eighty-seven-year-old Damian Rushcliffe, who – after being evacuated to Merrywell during the Second World War – ended up being adopted by the couple who looked after him; and Nigel Slingsby, a retired engineer and chair of Merrywell's bowls club.

She had chosen to begin with Nigel, who had agreed she could interview him at home. They were currently in his living room, where he was sitting in an overstuffed armchair next to an unlit fireplace. A yellow Labrador dog lay on a multi-coloured rug at his feet.

The cluttered room wasn't the ideal setting for filming. The mantelpiece was packed with knick-knacks and gewgaws, and the walls were covered with assorted prints and paintings. The one consolation was that the sun's rays were beaming through the front window, directly onto Nigel's face, providing perfect natural lighting.

'Thanks for agreeing to talk to me at short notice,' Violet said, as she set up her camera and recording equipment. 'You have the honour of being my first interviewee.'

'Is that right?' Nigel said, sounding unimpressed. 'I'm the guinea pig, am I?'

'Hardly,' Violet said, giving him a mock frown. 'I do know what I'm doing, you know.'

'Are you sure about that? The way you're wrangling with that camera suggests otherwise.'

He was right. She was feeling ridiculously nervous, and consequently she was fiddling and fussing, terrified that she'd come to the end of a terrific interview, only to discover she'd forgotten to switch the camera on.

'I'm just making sure everything's working properly before we start,' she said, trying not to sound too defensive. 'Checking the lighting and sound levels . . . that sort of thing.'

Nigel looked unconvinced by her bravado.

'I'm reliably informed that you know almost everyone in

22

the village,' Violet said, to distract him from her double-checking procedures.

Nigel nodded. 'That's right, I do. I was born in Matlock, but my parents moved to Merrywell when I was nine and I've lived here ever since. Everybody knows everyone in this village. That's just the way it is.'

Worried he'd get into his flow before she had her equipment set up, Violet stalled him with a more general question.

'Do you live alone?' she asked.

'No, I have a live-in lover.'

Violet laughed, assuming he was joking.

'I'm not pulling your leg,' Nigel said, sounding affronted. 'Really, I do. Her name's Sandra Feddingborough, and she and I have lived together for the last eighteen months. Like I say, there's life in the old dog yet.'

Violet straightened her mouth to stop herself from smiling. 'Is Sandra here? I can interview her as well, if you think she'd be willing to talk to me.'

'I'm sure she'd be happy to,' Nigel said. 'She's down at her keep-fit class at the moment, but she'll be back presently. You can ask her yourself.'

Violet nodded as she assessed the camera angle one last time.

'How did you get into this line of work?' Nigel asked, watching as she adjusted one of the tripod legs.

'I started my career as a journalist and then moved into communications,' Violet told him, as she inspected the viewfinder display. 'I've lost count of how many people I've interviewed over the years.'

'Sounds like you're an old hand, then.'

She grinned. 'Yes, you could say that – although I'm having to learn a few new tricks, now that I'm running my own business.'

'You must be bonkers,' Nigel said. 'I've never understood why anyone would want to give up a steady job and a pension to work for themselves.'

23

'I'm sure everyone has their own reasons,' said Violet. 'But you're right . . . it is a big step, and a risky one.'

'So why did *you* do it?' Nigel asked.

'It's complicated,' she replied. 'Too complicated to explain with a glib answer. I'll tell you another time, yeah? For now, sit back and let me ask the questions.'

Once the camera was rolling and he began to reminisce, Nigel's grouchiness melted away. Prompted by Violet, he talked fondly of his family's move to Merrywell in the mid-1950s.

'We came to live here when my father went to work at Merrywell railway station,' he said. 'Dad loved it there . . . thought he'd got a job for life . . . but unfortunately, the line closed in 1967 and the station shut down. It was all a consequence of the Beeching Report. There were so many rural railway services lost back then. Those cuts had a devastating impact on communities like ours.

'After the station closed, my father had no choice but to find work elsewhere. He took a job in a foundry in Matlock, and he wanted to up sticks and move back to the town – but my mother wouldn't hear of it. She loved being in Merrywell. She told Dad if he wanted to go back to Matlock, he'd be on his own. Needless to say, they stayed. In fact, they're still here, buried side by side in St Luke's churchyard.'

When she asked about Nigel's own experiences as a youth, he became surprisingly emotional. His eyes welled with unshed tears as he recalled his time helping out on the local farm during harvest time.

'All the young lads and lasses would get involved, especially with the haymaking.' He smiled wistfully. 'Many a romance blossomed as a result of those sunny summer days.'

Nigel spoke eloquently and enthusiastically, and the stories he told were interesting and authentic. His words painted a picture of a simpler, bygone era. Not everything he said would make the final cut, but Violet already knew she would be including several of Nigel's anecdotes in the film.

In all, he chatted for almost twenty minutes. When the interview was over, Violet thanked him and switched off the camera, pleased with how it had gone. This was an excellent start to the project.

As she packed away her equipment, she noticed that Nigel was absent-mindedly stroking the dog's ears and staring into the empty fireplace. His far-away expression was absorbed and melancholy.

'Are you OK?' she asked. 'I hope it's not upset you . . . talking about the past.'

He turned to her and smiled, rousing himself.

'Not at all,' he said. 'As a matter of fact, it's done my soul good to recall some of the people and places I knew long ago. I tend not to examine the past, see. I prefer to keep my old memories in a box marked *"ANCIENT HISTORY – DO NOT REVISIT"*. Fact is, I should reminisce more often. Talking to you now has made me realise how happy I've been here in Merrywell . . . for the most part anyway.'

'You didn't look very happy a moment ago,' Violet said.

'Ah, now . . . that's because I was remembering my wife. You recall I said that romance often blossomed during those haymaking days?'

'I do.'

'What I failed to mention is that I met my wife, Helen, during haymaking. We were seventeen when we started courting. Married by the time we were twenty.'

'I take it Helen has passed away?' Violet said, assuming that was why Nigel was looking so pensive.

'No.' He shook his head. 'She left me. Packed a case and walked out in 1982. I haven't seen or heard from her since.'

It was the last thing Violet had expected him to say.

'I'm sorry to hear that,' she said, not knowing how else to

respond. 'I've just been through a marriage break-up myself, so I understand how difficult it must have been for you.'

'I was devastated,' Nigel said. 'Even now, the memory of that time still has the power to hurt me, which is why I choose not to think about it. Having said that, I wasn't totally surprised when she cleared off. We were married for sixteen years, and the last five or six of those weren't what you'd call happy. We'd hoped to have a family by then, but it wasn't to be, and I don't think Helen ever came to terms with that. She'd set her sights on becoming a mother, and when it didn't happen, she became restless. During our last year together, we pretty much led separate lives. Looking back, I see now the split was inevitable . . . it was just a matter of time.'

Violet nodded sympathetically. She could sense his pain, see it in his eyes.

'Of course, the local gossips had a field day,' Nigel continued. 'There were rumours in the village that Helen had been seeing someone else.'

'And had she?'

He shrugged. 'Not that I know of. If she was having an affair, I had no inkling of it.'

'She would have told you, wouldn't she, if she was leaving you for another man?'

'Maybe,' said Nigel. 'Maybe not. Perhaps she didn't want to hurt me by telling me the truth. She did leave a note, a *Dear John*, but there was no mention of anyone else. The letter just confirmed what we both already knew – that our marriage was over. Helen said she wanted a new life . . . that she was going away, and she was sorry for the way things had turned out.'

The dog stood up and rested its head on Nigel's knee, as though sensing his need for comfort.

'After she'd gone, I stopped going out . . . became depressed. I felt I'd failed, you know? Failed her. Failed myself. It saddened me that a relationship that had started so promisingly . . .

so beautifully, could have ended so abruptly. No matter what the circumstances, it's always hard when love dies.'

Violet thought of her own failed marriage. Her divorce from Paul had been relatively civil – both of them agreeing it was the best thing – but it certainly hadn't been easy. Overall, the experience had felt like a bereavement. Distressing and unpleasant.

'Things have a way of working out,' she said, in an effort to cheer Nigel up. 'And you have Sandra now . . . someone new to love. That must make you happy.'

'It does,' he said. 'But it also makes me frustrated. You see, I'd like to ask Sandra to marry me, but I can't.'

'Whyever not?'

'Because, technically, I'm still married to Helen. We never got divorced.'

Violet frowned. 'Why don't you get in touch with her? Surely she'd have no objection to bringing things to an end, legally?'

'If only it were that simple.' Nigel folded his arms. 'Problem is, I have no idea where she is. I've made a few enquiries, but they've all drawn a blank. Sandra has tried to help too . . . She's searched for Helen on Facebook – but no joy. It's as though my wife has disappeared . . . vanished into thin air.'

'Someone must know where she is. Doesn't she have any relatives you can talk to?'

Nigel shook his head. 'Helen's parents died a few years after we were wed, and she was an only child. There used to be a great-aunt who lived over in Baslow, but she died the year before Helen left.'

Against her better judgement, Violet found herself intrigued by Nigel's quest. Drawn to it.

'You said she left you in 1982?'

'That's correct,' Nigel said. 'June 1982. Almost forty years ago.'

Violet raised her eyebrows. 'In that case, there must be an easy way to resolve this. I'm no legal expert, but as you've been separated and living apart for so long, I'd imagine you'd be able to get a divorce even without your wife's agreement.'

'She'd still have to be involved in the process though,' Nigel said. 'I'd have to prove to the court that she'd been served divorce papers. How can I do that if I don't know where she is?'

'Doesn't your lawyer have any way of finding her?'

Nigel sighed. 'The truth is, I haven't spoken to a solicitor yet. The whole divorce thing has never been an issue until recently. It was only after Sandra moved in with me that I began to think about sorting things out properly.'

'If I were you, I'd get some professional legal advice. There's bound to be a way around it.'

'I'm sure there is. I do wonder where Helen is though . . . where she's been all these years. It crossed my mind that maybe she's changed her name or got wed again.'

'If she's got married again while she's still married to you, she's committed bigamy,' Violet said.

He nodded. 'I realise that, but I wouldn't put anything past Helen.'

'Have you considered the possibility . . .' Violet paused, loath to put forward the most obvious explanation. 'Well . . . that maybe Helen has passed away?'

Nigel frowned. 'Yes, that is something I've thought about, although obviously I hope it's not the case.' He narrowed his eyes, assessing her. 'You said you were a journalist, didn't you? I bet you know how to ferret out information. Would you be willing to ask a few questions for me? Do some digging?'

'Digging? Me?'

She shuffled uncomfortably, wondering how to politely but swiftly rebuff Nigel's appeal for help. She needed to say something quickly, *anything* to nip this in the bud. If she said nothing, her silence might be interpreted as tacit agreement.

The trouble was, the prospect of disappointing Nigel made her feel horribly guilty. Only a few minutes ago she'd been sympathising with the man. How could she now justify turning down his request for help? She could find a spare hour to look into things on his behalf, couldn't she?

It's out of the question, said a stern voice in her head, the one she thought of as 'serious' Violet. *You have a film to make, and that has to be your priority. Focus, woman. Don't get sidetracked. You can't afford to botch this.*

But another voice, the bolshie one she called 'wild' Violet, was heckling loudly. *Hang on a minute*, 'wild' said, her interest piqued by the prospect of (to quote Nigel) ferreting out some information. *Let's not make any hasty decisions.*

Leaving her internal voices to argue among themselves, Violet sat back and reflected on the fact that, as a journalist, she had never been given the chance to flex her investigative muscles. After graduating, she'd worked for a provincial newspaper, where she'd been assigned to report on court cases. If there had been the odd juicy murder once in a while, it might have relieved the boredom, but she'd only ever covered petty thefts, breaches of the peace and driving offences. On the very week she'd finally gained a promotion and the opportunity to work on some meatier news stories, Paul had announced he was transferring to London. Violet immediately resigned her junior reporter role and, a month later, followed him to the capital, feeling fully stoked and determined to get a job on Fleet Street – but that dream had to be abandoned when she'd found herself unexpectedly pregnant.

Impending motherhood had forced her to totally rethink her career plans. Realising she wouldn't be able to commit to the irregular hours of a journalist, she'd opted instead for a steady position in corporate communications. The intention had been to return to journalism later on, when her daughter, Amelia, was older – but somehow that had never happened.

'I hate to tell you this, Nigel, but it's twenty-three years since I worked on a newspaper. And I'll be honest with you, I was never what you'd call an intrepid investigative reporter.'

'Bet you would have liked to have been though.' Nigel tilted his head. 'You have an intrinsic sense of curiosity; I can see it in your eyes.'

Violet wasn't sure whether to be flattered or offended by Nigel's assessment. Although accurate, it made her acutely aware that she had a lot more in common with Judith Talbot than she cared to admit.

'I'm right, aren't I?' Nigel insisted. 'You're inquisitive . . . you enjoy uncovering the truth.'

Give him his due, Nigel Slingsby had her well and truly sussed. Even so, she wasn't willing to make a promise she might not be able to keep.

'I do like uncovering the facts of a story,' Violet replied, feeling her resolve weakening. 'However, I've just launched a new business and I have a community film to make. Plus, I've recently moved house. I've still got some unpacking to do, and some decorating. I'm sorry, but I don't have any spare time at the moment.'

Nigel's hopeful expression crumpled into one of disappointment.

'It's not that I don't *want* to help,' she added. 'This just isn't the best time.'

Even though he looked utterly crestfallen, Nigel appeared to accept her decision. 'I understand, lass,' he said. 'And I know what a stickler Judith Talbot can be. I don't suppose she'd be too thrilled if she found out you were helping me instead of working like a Trojan on her precious film. I'll do as you've suggested . . . I'll find myself a good solicitor and get some proper advice.'

'I think that would be for the best.' Violet stood up. 'Thanks for a great interview, Nigel. I appreciate it.'

He walked with her into the hallway.

'Don't go just yet,' he said. 'Hang on a tick . . .'

Pulling open the door to the cupboard under the stairs, he stuck his head inside and emerged a few seconds later, holding an old shoebox.

'What have you got there?' Violet asked, hoping it might be old photographs of the village.

'Just a few bits and bobs Helen left behind,' he said, blowing dust off the box lid. 'I got rid of most of her stuff, but I held on to these . . . Lord knows why. Anyway, you might want to take a gleg . . . There are a couple of old black-and-white snaps and some other stuff. You never know, you might find a clue as to where she went after she left the village.'

Violet frowned. 'Like I say, I really can't spare the time. Besides, I'm assuming you've already checked the contents of the box? If *you* haven't spotted any clues, there's not much chance that I will.'

Nigel shrugged. 'I've looked through everything countless times, and I'll admit I'm none the wiser. Summat might strike a chord with you though . . . a fresh pair of eyes, and all that.'

Violet grimaced. 'Nigel,' she said, trying to sound firm. 'I'm not going to investigate.'

'I know, I know . . . but, please, take it anyway.' He thrust the box into her hands and then stepped back. 'Who knows? You might get a few minutes to look through it. If not, just drop it back when you're next passing.'

Violet considered placing the box on the stairs and making a swift exit, but Nigel's stubborn persistence was slowly paying off. She didn't like giving in to pressure, but she had to admit, the prospect of photographs was intriguing. Silently, she tucked the box under her arm, telling herself that taking possession of it put her under no obligation to examine the contents.

'I'm not making any promises,' she said. 'Your best course of action is to contact a solicitor. That's the way to move things forward and free yourself up to tie the knot with Sandra.'

Nigel cleared his throat. 'Ah, now . . . with regards to me and Sandra getting wed, I'd appreciate you keeping that bit of information under your hat. The thing is, I haven't actually proposed to her yet. Who knows? She might say "no".'

From behind them came the sound of someone sliding a key into the front door lock.

'That's her now,' Nigel said. 'Remember, say nowt.'

Violet pulled an imaginary zip across her lips and smiled.

Chapter 4

Despite having a perfectly valid reason for refusing Nigel's request, Violet felt excessively guilty as she left his house. She put the shoebox in the boot of her car alongside her camera bag, and drove the short journey back to the shopping village. On top of her feelings of guilt, she was also experiencing pangs of disappointment. She couldn't deny it: at any other time, she would have welcomed the chance to track down the whereabouts of the mysterious Helen Slingsby.

But onwards and upwards. This afternoon she had lined up an interview with eighty-three-year-old Martha Andrews. First though, she would call in at the bakery to buy a late lunch.

'How did your first interview go?' Fiona asked, as she prepared Violet's order: a smoked salmon and cream cheese bagel and a cappuccino to go.

'Exceptionally well,' Violet said. 'Nigel was a good choice . . . thanks for recommending him.'

'If you'd asked me a few years ago, I would never have put his name forward. He was painfully shy back then . . . there's no way he would have agreed to appear on camera. You've Sandra to thank for bringing him out of his shell.'

'She arrived just as I was leaving,' Violet said. 'I only spoke to her briefly, but she seems lovely, and she obviously thinks the world of Nigel. She's also promised me an interview.'

'They do make a nice couple.' Fiona smiled. 'I'm pleased for him. From what I've heard, Nigel had more than his share of unhappiness in his younger days. It's nice that he's found love in his twilight years.'

After checking over her shoulder to make sure there was no one within earshot, Violet leaned closer to the counter.

'Do you know anything about Nigel's wife?'

Fiona shook her head. 'She left long before I moved to Merrywell. What makes you ask? Are you hoping to interview her for the film?'

'No, nothing like that,' Violet said. 'Nigel wants to make contact with her, that's all.'

Fiona yanked her head back. 'Really? Why does he want to reconnect with her, after all this time?'

'I'm sure he has his reasons,' Violet said. She trusted Fiona implicitly, but she wasn't going to betray Nigel's trust by revealing his secret proposal plans. 'He's not having much luck finding her,' she added. 'He asked if I'd help track her down.'

Fiona raised an eyebrow as she handed over the cappuccino. 'Did he now? He must have taken a liking to you then?'

Violet grinned. 'He was quite frosty at first, but I think he warmed to me in the end.'

'And are you going to help him?'

'I'd love to, but unfortunately, I can't spare the time. I felt awful having to turn him down, but he seemed to understand.'

Fiona folded her arms and gave Violet an old-fashioned look. 'I've only known you for a few weeks, so I could be wrong, but I suspect you'll change your mind before too long. You won't be able to resist. You have an inquiring mind and you like mysteries.'

Violet laughed. 'It's funny you should say that . . . Nigel

Slingsby described me in very similar terms. What is it with me? Do I give off some kind of snooping vibe?'

Fiona grinned. 'Not exactly. But there is something about you. An aura, maybe. You have a flair for getting to the bottom of things.'

'The only thing I intend to get to the bottom of today is my to-do list,' Violet replied. 'And next on that list is interviewing Martha Andrews, so wish me luck.'

When she left the bakery, Violet was carrying an extra bag containing a chocolate choux bun. Fiona had assured her it was Martha Andrews' favourite cake, and was guaranteed to sweeten her up. The news that she might need sweetening was slightly alarming, but forewarned was forearmed.

Violet told herself she was taking the cake along to thank Martha for agreeing to take part in the film, but the truth was, it was a bribe – pure and simple. A way of ingratiating herself with one of Merrywell's oldest and potentially grouchiest residents.

Martha Andrews lived on the western outskirts of the village, in a house on a row of terraced properties close to the school. Her front garden was well tended and bursting with colourful spring bulbs, including a glorious display of deep purple hyacinths. Their cloying perfume filled Violet's nostrils as she made her way up the path and rang the front doorbell.

Martha looked nothing like Violet had expected. Apart from her snow-white hair, she showed few signs of her true age. She was tall and willowy, with sharply defined cheekbones, and a short pixie hairstyle that suited her face perfectly. She must have been stunningly beautiful when she was a young woman. Still was for that matter.

'Please, come in,' Martha said, once Violet had introduced herself. 'Let's go and sit in the dining room.'

As Violet followed along a narrow passageway, she took in her host's attire. Martha was dressed on trend in a pair of Diesel slim-fit jeans, and a finely knit, cobalt blue jumper that looked as if it was made from the softest cashmere. On her feet, she wore a pair of sporty white trainers with silver side stripes, which Violet knew for a fact were from Whistles, because she had an identical pair herself.

The dining room occupied the centre portion of the long, narrow house. It was beautifully furnished with a modern table and chairs, and a metal-legged console, which was topped with a vase full of powerfully scented white lilies. Bookshelves had been fitted in the alcoves either side of the fireplace, and there was a large and very healthy-looking parlour palm in the corner. The armchair by the window was occupied by a sleeping tortoise-shell cat.

Martha offered tea, and while she went into the kitchen to make it, Violet set up her camera.

'Thanks for agreeing to this,' she said, when Martha returned carrying a tray of tea things. 'I called at the bakery earlier and bought you a choux bun. Fiona told me they're your favourite.'

Martha accepted the proffered bag with a smile. 'That's kind of you. I usually restrict myself to one of these a week, but in view of your generosity, I'll make an exception. However, I will save it until later, if that's OK . . . until after the interview.'

She poured tea from a cosied teapot and, while they drank it, Violet explained about the community film and outlined what would happen during the interview.

'It's an excellent initiative,' Martha said. 'It's about time the village did something like this. I hope you're getting plenty of co-operation from members of the community.'

'So far, so good,' said Violet. 'In my experience, people love the idea of being interviewed . . . most of them, anyway. This is a chance for residents to get involved in creating a permanent record of life in the village – past and present. I'm sure they'll see the merits of the project.'

'Who have you spoken to so far?' Martha asked.

'I'm working my way through a long list of people, but I only started today. You're my second interviewee. I spoke to Nigel Slingsby earlier, and in the morning, I'm going to talk to Damian Rushcliffe.'

Martha sipped her tea. 'I'm surprised Nigel agreed to get involved. He's not known for seeking out the limelight . . . quite the opposite, in fact.'

'He gave an excellent interview,' Violet said. 'Like you, he's lived in the village a long time, so he was an obvious person to talk to.'

'I remember his family arriving in Merrywell in the Fifties,' Martha said. 'They moved into the house opposite ours, and I started to hang out with Nigel's older sister, Pamela. Pammy was like me . . . a wild child. She moved away after she got married, and we lost touch. I knew Nigel's wife too . . . but that was later, of course. Helen and I worked together at Merrywell Primary . . . I was a teacher and she was the school secretary.'

Violet pricked up her ears. 'When was that?'

Martha thought for a moment. 'The Seventies into the early Eighties?'

'What was she like?' Violet said, unable to suppress her curiosity. 'Nigel's wife, I mean.'

'Very good at her job.' Martha paused before continuing, as though choosing her words carefully. 'But she wasn't exactly the most popular person in the staffroom. Helen could be moody. Volatile. Nice one minute, snapping your head off the next. To be honest, I kept out of her way as much as I could.'

'I understand she upped and left?'

'You're very well informed,' Martha said, her tone instantly icy.

'Nigel told me.'

'Did he now? I find that hard to believe. He never talks about Helen.'

'He talked to me about her,' Violet said, feeling the need to defend herself.

Martha scrutinised Violet carefully, as if assessing whether she could trust her. She must have concluded that she could, because when she spoke again, her voice was a lot less frosty.

'I do know that Nigel was gutted when Helen left him,' she said. 'To be frank, we were all taken aback by the suddenness of her departure. No one at the school knew she was planning to leave, except the head . . . and I gather she only gave him a few days' notice. Things fell apart in the office, after that. The attendance records weren't kept up to date, the school dinner money didn't get paid into the bank . . . It was utter chaos for a while. A complete shambles. As I say, Helen was good at her job. Very efficient.'

'Nigel asked me to help find out where she is,' Violet said. 'Do you know if she had another job lined up when she left?'

'Haven't a clue, my dear. Helen and I weren't what you'd call friends. On the contrary, we had more than our share of run-ins. I was the last person she would have confided in.'

Even though Violet longed to ask more about the enigmatic Helen, she knew the clock was ticking. It was time to get the interview with Martha underway.

Chapter 5

Violet left Martha's house forty minutes later. The interview had gone well, if not as expected. Martha had spent the first twenty minutes talking about her time as a teacher in Merrywell – a career that had begun in the Sixties. Clearly, she'd been a forward-thinking individual, always seeking out new ways to help the children who struggled with conventional learning styles. Martha confessed that some of her ideas had been controversially ahead of their time, and admitted they hadn't always been well received at the school.

During the rest of the interview, she had recounted an interesting and avant-garde personal life. She had never married, but had conducted several love affairs over the years, most of which had blossomed during her extensive trips abroad. Martha had travelled widely and often. Initially, her overseas jaunts had taken place during the school holidays, but later – after taking early retirement – she had gone away for longer periods, always returning to Merrywell eventually.

'This village is far from perfect,' Martha said. 'And it could never be described as exciting . . . but it's in my blood. There's something about this place that draws me back . . . I've been to some fascinating countries, but I can honestly say there's nowhere in the world quite like Merrywell. I suppose that's because it's my home. It's the place I will always return to.'

Violet was reassured by such a ringing endorsement of the village. Uprooting herself from London and coming to Derbyshire had been a leap of faith – and there were times when she wondered whether she'd done the right thing. But this afternoon, with Martha's words still fresh in her mind, she felt extremely upbeat about her move.

As she walked past the school and back towards the centre of the village, she stopped to admire the verdant front garden of a sprawling, stone-built house. Its flower borders were lush and vibrant, and a neat, stripy lawn was giving off the sweet smell of freshly cut grass. The River Wye curved alongside the house, rushing beneath the trailing branches of a large weeping willow as it flowed towards the Derwent. In the distance were rolling hills that today looked soft and welcoming in the haze of the unseasonably warm afternoon. Violet knew that in the winter, those hills would be covered in snow and appear much more forbidding – and she vowed then and there to make the most of the good weather and the summer that lay ahead. In a few weeks, when things were less busy, she would pull on her hiking boots and head off on a long, exploratory walk.

Now though, she turned in the direction of Greengage Cottage. It was almost four o'clock, and she decided to go straight home, rather than head back to *The Memory Box*.

As she opened the front door, her phone began to ring. She smiled as she pulled it out of her pocket and looked at the screen. It was her daughter, Amelia.

'Hi, Mum.'

'Hi, sweetheart,' Violet replied. 'How are you?'

'Good, thanks. I've been out at a conference and I'm on my way back to the office . . . thought I'd give you a quick call. Anything to report?'

'Quite a lot, actually.' Violet flopped into the armchair by the front window and told her daughter about the community film.

'That's brilliant news,' Amelia said. 'The first of many lucrative contracts, I'm sure.'

'I bloomin' well hope so,' Violet said. 'What about you? How are things? Keeping busy?'

'Yes. Never a dull moment at this end. Having said that, I'm hoping to get a week off next month. I thought I might come and stay with you for a few days, if that's OK. I can't wait to see what you've done with the cottage.'

'Other than unpack my stuff, I've done very little,' Violet said. 'But don't let that stop you. I'd love you to come. You're welcome any time, you know that. Text me the dates.'

'Will do.'

They lapsed into silence, one second stretching into another.

'Darling? Are you still there?'

Just as Violet was beginning to think they'd been cut off, Amelia spoke again.

'Have you heard from Dad?' she said.

The question took Violet by surprise. 'No,' she replied. 'Why would I?'

'No reason. I just thought he might have rung.'

'Sweetheart, your dad and I haven't yet reached the stage of ringing each other up for a friendly chat. Quite honestly, I'm not sure we ever will. There isn't a lot left for us to talk about – it's one of the reasons we're no longer married.'

'OK, Mum. No need to go off on one . . . I was only asking.'

'I'm not *going off on one*,' Violet said, keeping her voice level. 'I'm just stating the facts.'

'Has Granny visited yet?' Amelia asked, changing the subject.

'Not yet,' Violet replied. 'She's skiing at the moment.'

'Skiing! Granny?'

'As in *spending the kids' inheritance*.' Violet laughed. 'She's in the Caribbean, on a last-minute cruise, but she's hoping to visit in June. No doubt she'll turn up looking tanned and healthy, and put me to shame.'

'*You* should take a holiday, Mum. After the stress of moving house and setting up your business, you deserve a break.'

'Maybe I will, later in the year. Right now, I've got too much on with this community film to take any time off. But . . . hey, I'm not knocking it. Believe you me, I couldn't be happier. Being busy is what I need right now.'

For her dinner that evening, Violet grilled a breast of chicken, which she served with a mixed salad and buttered Jersey potatoes. She also poured herself a large, chilled glass of Sauvignon Blanc.

She set a place at the kitchen table next to her open MacBook and, as she tucked into her meal, she logged on to her social media accounts. As she opened Facebook, Violet thought again about Nigel and his failed attempts to locate his wife. It had been hard to ignore his appeal for help, knowing how desperate he was to propose to Sandra. The couple's joint efforts to find Helen on Facebook had been unsuccessful, but maybe Violet would have more luck. As a starting point, she looked up Sandra, thankful she had an unusual name.

The search results produced only one Sandra Feddingborough. As she took a sip of wine, Violet clicked onto the profile picture, and read the post that was pinned to the top of the page.

Can you help my partner? He's trying to track down Helen Millicent Slingsby, née Grogan (born 8.7.46) who lived in Merrywell, Derbyshire, until 1982. If you know Helen, please DM me or pass on this message and ask her to get in touch. Thank you.

The post was accompanied by a photograph of a smiling, dark-haired woman in her thirties. This, then, must be the enigmatic Helen. Despite a wide smile, there was something sad and inscrutable about her face. As Violet studied the photograph, she wondered when it had been taken. Before the Slingsbys' marriage had turned sour, or after?

Sandra's Facebook post had been shared by fourteen people, and forty-two people had reacted to it. The majority of the reactions used the 'sad' or 'care' emoji. There were only two comments, but neither was from anyone local. One woman said she remembered Helen, but hadn't seen her for decades. Someone else suggested that Sandra get in touch with the Salvation Army, whose family tracing service might be of help. Other than that, the pinned post had generated very little information – useful or otherwise.

Her meal finished, Violet pushed her plate aside, pulled the MacBook closer, and rested her fingers on the keyboard. Using Helen's full name and date of birth (as posted by Sandra), she decided to make a few quick searches to see if she could find any clues to her whereabouts.

An hour and a half later, she sat back, straightened her shoulders and rubbed the back of her neck. She'd completed a fruitless search of all the major social media channels, checked directory enquiries, and even bought credits for a genealogy site so that she could conduct a search of the births, deaths and marriage records, and the electoral roll. She'd found a record of Helen Millicent Grogan's birth in 1946, and her marriage to Nigel Slingsby in 1966, but apart from that . . . nothing. Despite a thorough search for Helen using both her married and maiden names, Violet had found absolutely no trace of her.

She stood up, retrieved her dirty plate and went over to the kitchen sink to wash up. As she rinsed her wine glass, she thought through the possibilities. Perhaps Nigel was right, and – for some reason – Helen had changed her name. But why on earth would she do that? What would be the point? If, as Helen had said in her *Dear John* letter to Nigel, she wanted to start a new life, why choose to begin again under a completely different name? It made no sense.

More troublingly, why was there no record of Helen after her marriage to Nigel in 1966? A thorough search of the internet

42

usually found mention of even the most scrupulous of techno-phobes. The absence of any kind of online presence for Helen was baffling.

Violet stared out of the kitchen window and let two of the most tantalising, thought-inducing words in the English language roll around in her mind: *what if*?

The words fired her imagination and conjured all manner of questions and possibilities.

What if something had happened to Helen after she left Merrywell? She had packed a suitcase and left a note for Nigel, and she'd told her boss she was leaving . . . so she'd obviously planned to go somewhere – but *where*? And what if those plans had gone awry? What if the rumour about her having an affair was true? Who might the 'other person' in her life have been? Had Helen left Nigel to be with him? Was she with him now?

Or perhaps Helen's plans had been scuppered by someone else? Someone who didn't want her to start a new life? What if something had happened to Helen *before* she left Merrywell? What if the reason Helen couldn't be found was because she had never left the village at all?

Chapter 6

At six-thirty the following morning, Violet threw off her duvet and got out of bed. Random thoughts had been swirling around in her mind all night, causing broken sleep and weird dreams. Rather than waking up refreshed, she was starting the day with a muzzy head and eyes that felt gritty.

Thankfully a large mug of strong tea perked her up no end. She drank it outside, sitting at the bottom of the garden, looking out over the low, dry-stone wall to the fields beyond. Apart from a cacophony of chirps from a gang of sparrows, the scene was quiet and calming. Eventually, the reviving triad of tea, fresh air and a few arm stretches cleared her head – so much so that she resolved to go into work early.

Her arrival at the shopping village was one whole hour before the bakery opened, which ruled out the possibility of topping up her caffeine intake with a cappuccino. Wrinkling her nose at the prospect of making do with instant coffee from the jar in her office, she fished around in her bag for the key to *The Memory Box*. Before she'd had a chance to unlock the door, she heard someone call her name.

'Violet!'

She turned and saw Matthew Collis smiling at her from the other side of the courtyard.

'You're in early today,' he said. 'Is everything OK?'

'Yes, I'm fine,' she said. 'I just didn't sleep very well . . . thought I may as well come in to work.'

'Trouble sleeping? That doesn't sound good. You're not having problems with the film, are you?'

'No, everything's fine with the film. I recorded the first two interviews yesterday and they went really well. It's something else . . . something someone asked me about yesterday. The question's been crawling around in my head ever since, like an earworm.'

Matthew pulled a face. 'Sounds horrific. I'm about to make a pot of coffee. Do you want to come in and talk about it?'

Violet narrowed her eyes. 'What kind of coffee?'

'Ground,' he replied. 'As I recall, it's a Brazilian blend. It will be strong, aromatic and made in a cafetière.'

'In that case,' Violet said, smiling for the first time that day, 'lead the way.'

The interior of *Collis Fine Furniture* was like Dr Who's TARDIS, in that it appeared much bigger on the inside than it looked from the outside. The front portion of the shop was laid out as a showroom, sporting a collection of classy and very elegant pieces of furniture. A pale beech chest of drawers caught Violet's attention. As she paused to run a speculative hand across its smooth surface, she noticed the price tag. *Blimey*, she thought. There was no disputing it was a gorgeous piece of furniture, but it was well out of her price range.

Matthew had disappeared into the back to make the coffee. On her way to join him, she inspected a circular table and a tall bookcase, breathing in the spicy, teaky smell of wood . . . and something else. Linseed oil, maybe?

A glass partition separated the shop into two distinct areas. On the other side of the glass was a spacious workshop, which contained three workbenches of varying sizes, plus two large pieces of machinery, which she guessed must be for cutting, turning or sanding wood. There was also a collection of hand tools on the workbenches, with many more hanging in neat rows on the walls. Apart from a few stray wood shavings on the floor, and a pair of part-finished dining chairs in one corner, the workshop was remarkably tidy.

'What do you think of the place?' Matthew said, as he reappeared carrying two mugs of coffee.

'I'm impressed with the shop,' Violet said, as she accepted one of the mugs. 'And your workshop looks extremely organised and surprisingly neat.'

Matthew laughed. 'I try to keep everything in order ... not always successfully. I do have a place for everything, but not everything is where it's supposed to be.'

She sipped the coffee, which was strong and very hot.

'There's milk and sugar, if you want it,' he said.

'I don't take sugar,' Violet said. 'And today, I'll drink it black. It'll help keep me awake.'

'So, are you going to tell me why you had a sleepless night?'

Violet lifted the mug to her lips and blew on the coffee, wondering how best to answer. As a councillor, Matthew might not approve of her being inadvertently drawn into Nigel Slingsby's dilemma and the mystery of his wife's whereabouts. On the other hand, she'd already secured the council contract – why worry about making the right impression? Helping a fellow villager was nothing to be ashamed of, and the online searches she'd made had all been done in her own time. It wasn't as if she was neglecting her real work – the community film was progressing nicely.

Even so, she decided to swerve Matthew's question by asking one of her own.

'Have you always lived in Merrywell?'

Her query was far from arbitrary. If Matthew was a long-time resident, there was every chance he'd known Helen Slingsby. At a guess, he was about fifty: so, if he'd attended Merrywell Primary

School, it would have been around the time Helen worked there as the school secretary.

'Yes, all my life,' Matthew replied, sounding surprised at the conversation's sudden change of direction. 'Apart from the three years I spent at university.'

'University?' It was Violet's turn to sound surprised.

'Is that so hard to believe?'

'No, of course not,' she said. 'What did you study?'

'Psychology.'

'*Psychology?*'

Matthew cupped a hand around his right ear. 'Is it me, or is there an echo in here?'

She laughed. 'Sorry. I just didn't expect you to say that. How does someone with a degree in psychology end up making furniture?'

'It's a long and complicated story,' Matthew replied. 'The short version is that I was never cut out to be a psychologist. And, let's be honest, not many people pursue careers in their chosen field of study, do they? The leap from psychology degree to furniture maker isn't much bigger than say . . . someone with a degree in journalism becoming a maker of community films.'

'Touché,' said Violet. 'Although I did work as a journalist, albeit briefly.'

Matthew shrugged. 'Careers . . . like life, don't always turn out as we expect, or hope. Having said that, I chose to become a joiner. I love making furniture, and I'm happy in my work.'

'I'm glad to hear it,' Violet said. 'And based on what I've seen in the showroom, I'd say you're very good at what you do.'

'Why, thank you. Now, are you going to tell me what's been keeping you awake, or are you going to avoid answering my question altogether?'

Violet took a deep breath. 'I interviewed Nigel Slingsby yesterday,' she said, electing to tell the truth. 'He talked to me about his wife and mentioned that he was trying to trace her. He tried to recruit my help. I turned him down, of course. I told him I couldn't spare the time . . . not while I'm working on the community film.'

'But?' said Matthew. 'I take it there's a *but* coming?'

She smiled. 'Last night, after dinner, I logged on to my social media accounts and, while I was there, I thought I'd do a quick search for Helen Slingsby . . . purely as a favour to Nigel, you understand.'

'Oh, I understand,' Matthew said, giving her an anxious smile. 'I think I understand perfectly. And did you manage to find her?'

Violet lowered herself onto a stool and placed her mug on the adjacent workbench.

'No, I didn't, and I suppose that's what kept me awake. There's no mention of Helen anywhere on social media, and there's no recent record of her on any electoral roll or the births, deaths and marriages register.'

'Births, death and marriages?' Matthew said. 'It sounds to me like you did a lot more than a *quick check*.'

Violet smiled sheepishly. 'I was intrigued, and when faced with a challenge, I don't give up easily.'

'Is that why you couldn't sleep?' said Matthew. 'Because you failed to crack the mystery?'

'I'll admit I was disappointed with myself. I assumed I'd run a few quick searches and find Helen immediately – but the thing that bothered me the most was *why* I couldn't find her. I got to thinking . . .'

She hesitated, wondering how wise it was to voice her concerns.

'Go on,' Matthew said.

'What if . . .' Violet began, sounding uncharacteristically timorous. 'What if she never left the village?'

Matthew gave a half-frown. 'How do you mean? What are you suggesting?'

Violet could sense from his tone that she had said too much . . . taken her idle speculating a few strides too far.

'Ignore me,' she said, laughing nervously. 'Forget I said

anything. I'd had a large glass of wine with dinner. I was letting my imagination run away with me . . . I realise that now.'

'Tell me where your imagination was taking you,' Matthew said.

Violet shook her head. 'I'll only make myself look foolish. I'd like to ask *you* something though . . .'

He smiled. 'Do you make a habit of this? Someone asks you a question you don't want to answer, so you parry with one of your own?'

She hesitated.

'Go on,' Matthew said. 'I'll humour you. What's the question?'

'Did *you* know Helen Slingsby?' she said.

He frowned. 'I'm not sure we should be having this conversation. I don't think Nigel would be happy if he knew you were talking to me about his wife.'

'On the contrary, he told me to ask questions,' Violet said. 'He asked me to do some digging. So, tell me. Did you know Helen?'

Matthew drained his coffee mug and moved around to the other side of the workbench.

'Yes, I knew her,' he said. 'But I was only a kid back then. She worked at the school, and she had a reputation.'

'For what?'

'Being unapproachable,' he said. 'And she could be nasty. Most of the kids were scared of her.'

'Scared? How come?'

He pulled a face. 'She was strict . . . crabby and impatient. I remember my friend forgot to bring his dinner money once, and he was sent to see Mrs Slingsby in the office. He hadn't done it on purpose, obviously, but that didn't wash with her. She belittled him, made him feel stupid. A nicer person would have told him not to worry, but Mrs Slingsby gave my friend a long and unnecessary lecture on taking responsibility . . . ranting about how he'd wasted her time. He was trembling when he came back to the classroom. She'd frightened him half to death. He was a kid, for pity's sake. There was no need for her to behave like that.'

'Perhaps she didn't like children,' Violet suggested.

'She shouldn't have been working in a school then, should she?' Matthew said, an odd look passing across his face. 'Anyway, it wasn't children she didn't like – it was human beings in general. I suspect she was deeply unhappy, and she chose to unleash her misery on the people around her. It meant she wasn't well liked – at the school or in the village. Most people were glad to see the back of her when she left.'

'Do you know where she moved to?' Violet asked.

'I've no idea.'

'Nigel said there were rumours she'd been having an affair. Do you think there's any truth in that?'

'You're asking the wrong person,' Matthew replied. 'I was only ten when Mrs Slingsby left. I barely knew her.'

'But she lived in the village . . . you must have known her outside of school? I thought everyone knew everyone here in Merrywell.'

He moved his feet apart and folded his arms. 'My family weren't friendly with the Slingsbys. Our paths rarely crossed.'

'Did your parents have a view on why Helen left, or where she might have gone?'

He held up his hands. 'As I said . . . they didn't socialise with Mr or Mrs Slingsby.'

He'd become reticent. Irritated. Was there something he wasn't telling her?

'Sorry . . . but where are you going with this?' Matthew asked. 'What's with all the questions?'

Violet smiled. 'I guess I'm just curious.'

'You can say that again.' He laughed half-heartedly. 'You could give Judith Talbot a run for her money.'

'I'm not being nosy,' Violet said, folding her arms defensively. 'I'm trying to help Nigel.'

'I thought you told him you couldn't spare the time. If he's that desperate to find his wife, why doesn't he pay for some professional help, or get the police involved? They'd be able to find her.'

'Do you think they'd contact Mrs Slingsby on Nigel's behalf?' Violet asked.

He shrugged. 'I'm sure they could . . . whether or not they *would*, is anyone's guess. I doubt the local police have time to pursue those kinds of inquiries. Like you, they have far more important priorities.'

Matthew's words tugged at Violet's conscience. His meaning was clear. *Focus on the community film and don't get sidetracked by Nigel Slingsby.*

She sighed. 'You're right. I mustn't let myself get distracted . . . but I can't help feeling sorry for Nigel.'

'Why don't you suggest he hires a private investigator?'

Violet dismissed that idea with a shake of her head. 'He wouldn't have asked for my help if he could afford one of those.'

'I guess not,' Matthew said, as he hooked a finger around the handle of his empty mug. 'He must be feeling pretty desperate.'

'*What*? Because he asked me to help, you mean? Charming!'

'Sorry . . .' Matthew smiled apologetically. 'That came out wrong. From what you've told me, you've already done a sterling job on Nigel's behalf. A private investigator would have charged a small fortune for the online searches you've done.'

'Not that they've been of any use,' Violet said. 'I've drawn a complete blank. I only wish I could do more.'

Matthew scratched the side of his jaw. 'There's nothing else you can do – unless of course you've got a magic wand, or a contact in the police force.'

'I have, actually,' Violet said. 'Got a contact in the police, that is. Not a magic wand.'

Matthew's eyes widened. 'The local police?'

'No, in the Met. He's a chief superintendent.'

'Wow! How well do you know this guy? Well enough to ask for a favour?'

'I know him almost as well as I know myself,' Violet said. 'But I'm no longer in a position to ask for any favours. You see . . . the person I'm talking about is my ex-husband.'

Chapter 7

Violet had politely declined Matthew's offer of a second cup of coffee, excusing herself on the basis that she needed to prepare for her interview with Damian Rushcliffe later that morning.

The real reason for turning him down was more complex. The truth was, having mentioned Paul's name, she didn't want to get dragged into *that* conversation – the one where she felt obliged to discuss her marriage and explain why it had ended in divorce. It was a subject she preferred to avoid – definitely not something she was comfortable talking to Matthew Collis about. She didn't know him well enough.

Instead, she'd scurried out of his workshop, crossed the courtyard and escaped to the sanctuary of *The Memory Box*, where she'd spent the last two hours editing the previous day's interviews. At eleven o'clock, she picked up her camera bag, locked up the studio and set off for her appointment with Damian Rushcliffe.

The modern, assisted-living bungalow he lived in was located in a small cul-de-sac in a quiet corner of the village. Violet was invited into the 'lounge', which had a deep red carpet, custard-yellow walls, and a brilliant white ceiling. The colour scheme made her feel as though she'd landed in the centre of an enormous bowl of trifle.

The room was surprisingly uncluttered. The only ornaments on show were displayed on what appeared to be a genuine, G-Plan, teak sideboard. A Murano glass fish took pride of place in the centre, positioned between a large fruit bowl and a silver-framed photograph.

Violet paused to study the woman in the photo frame. She had dark, twinkling eyes, and hair that was swept into a stylish up-do, exposing a long, elegant neck, around which hung a striking pendant.

'That's my Zelda,' Damian said, nodding towards the photo. 'She died three years ago.'

'She looks lovely,' Violet said. 'She was a very chic lady, and she has a beautiful smile.'

'Aye, she always scrubbed up well.' Damian smiled. 'That photo was taken at my retirement party. Zelda had bought herself a new frock, and she looked stunning. It was a grand do. Fancy restaurant, champagne, the works.'

'Sounds very posh,' Violet said, as she began to open up her tripod.

Damian sat down. 'You know, I'm not sure I'll be any good at this,' he said, cringing nervously. 'Talking into a camera isn't something I've done before.'

'You'll be fine,' Violet reassured him. 'Try to ignore the camera . . . pretend it isn't there. Just sit back and relax and be yourself. If it's OK with you, I'll start by asking about the past . . . I'd love to hear about your memories of wartime Merrywell.'

Damian smiled. 'The past I can cope with,' he said. 'I remember my childhood as though it were yesterday. But if you were to ask me what I had for breakfast this morning, or where I've put my reading glasses, I might struggle.'

'Let's keep the main focus of the interview on your arrival in Merrywell as an evacuee then. I'm sure people will be interested to hear about that.'

Violet sat down, positioned the camera and switched it on. As Damian responded to her questions, it struck her that

– although the things he was talking about were still within living memory – that wouldn't be the case for much longer. As Damian's generation dwindled, their first-hand wartime memories were disappearing forever. It was vitally important to record their stories, which was one of the reasons Violet was so passionate about the community film project.

Damian had been evacuated from Coventry in the summer of 1940 and, on arrival in Merrywell, had been billeted with Mr and Mrs Rushcliffe. Less than three months later, he'd received the news that his mother had been killed during the devastating raid on Coventry on the 14th of November. A year after that, his father had been killed fighting in the North African campaign.

'As you can imagine, it was a tough time,' he said. 'But Mr and Mrs Rushcliffe were good to me. They told me I'd always have a home with them, even after the war was over.'

'How did you feel about that?' Violet asked.

'Relieved, I suppose. I was young. Resilient. I had to get on with life. What choice did I have?'

'It sounds as though your mother did the right thing ... sending you away,' said Violet. 'If you'd stayed in Coventry, you might not have survived the raid. At least your mother died knowing you were safe, in Merrywell.'

'Aye,' Damian said. 'You're right, I was safe enough here – although this area wasn't without a few dramas of its own. There was one time when St Luke's was damaged by a German bomb. It happened one night, during a raid on a factory in Bakewell. People became nervous after that. There was a growing sense of unease ... concerns that the whole country was turning into one vast battlefield.'

Violet listened silently. These were exactly the kind of memories she was keen to record.

'The incident prompted the vicar to approach the authorities about building a communal shelter in Merrywell,' Damian continued. 'The reverend wanted something big enough to accommodate all the residents. Up to that point, no one had thought there was any real danger here in the village . . . but after the church was damaged, a few people built dugouts in their back gardens. Some of the houses had a cellar they could use, and there was talk of sheltering in the railway cutting over by the station, should the need arise. No one had expected there to be raids, but the damage to the church caused panic. We began to think that nowhere was safe from stray bombs, not even Merrywell.'

'And was the vicar successful?' Violet said. 'Did the village get its shelter?'

'Aye, give him his due . . . he got approval for a proper under-ground structure. Before you could say Jack Robinson, a huge trench had been dug in the school playing field and a concrete shelter was lowered inside it. At the time, I was too young to understand the concept of irony, but I remember thinking how peculiar it was . . . me – an evacuee – watching them construct an air raid shelter in Merrywell, in what was supposed to be a safe haven.'

'Was it used much?' Violet asked.

Damian shook his head. 'Not a lot,' he said. 'Although there were a couple of occasions when the locals were extremely grateful for it. I recall a surprise raid one summer evening in 1942. We learned later that two German planes had come in low from the west coast and dropped bombs at New Mills, and then moved on to Eyam quarries. According to reports, the pilots flew so low, people expected them to hit the trees. It was the same planes that machine-gunned Chatsworth House and damaged its stonework. After that, they flew over to Chesterfield . . . Clay Cross way. But aside from that one incident, I'm not sure the village could fully justify the cost of building a shelter – although we were glad of it, nonetheless.'

Damian told her that, after the war, he'd been officially adopted by the Rushcliffes.

'I met Zelda in 1956, at a dance in Bakewell,' he said. 'We got married in 1958, and our lad was born in 1960.'

'Does your son still live in the village?'

'No,' Damian said, shaking his head. 'He moved away years ago. Lives down south now. I'd prefer him to be closer to home, but we each have to follow our own destiny, don't we? Mine led me to this village, and I've been content to stay here ever since. I'm one of the oldest residents now, so I suppose you could say I'm part of the history of the place . . . and it's definitely a part of mine. The circumstances that brought me here weren't the best, but everything worked out all right in the end. I have no regrets. Merrywell's a grand village, and I've had a good life here.'

He'd spoken for almost half an hour without flagging, telling his story quietly and reflectively, and carefully describing the things that had happened during the war years. But now that the interview had drawn to a close, he rubbed his eyes, looking tired.

'Would you like a cup of tea, before you go?' he asked, as he rested his head against the back of his armchair.

'I'm OK, thanks,' Violet said. Then, noticing the look of disappointment on his face, she added: 'But I could make one for you before I go, if you'd like me to.'

Damian smiled. 'That would be wonderful,' he said. 'It would save my old legs a trip to the kitchen.'

Violet left him sipping a cup of tea and munching on a ginger biscuit. She had been both fascinated and moved by the poignancy of Damian's story. As part of her proposal for the community film, she had agreed to provide transcripts of key interviews, which the parish council would use to create a written record for future generations. Damian's childhood memories of wartime Merrywell definitely merited inclusion in that archive.

Violet walked back through the village, ruminating on some of the things Damian had told her. It was hard to imagine how different and difficult life must have been for people eighty years ago.

As she rounded the corner near the shop, she spotted Nigel Slingsby and Sandra Feddingborough in the distance. They were walking towards her, arm in arm, leaning into each other and laughing. When Nigel saw Violet, he raised his right hand in greeting.

'How are you?' Sandra asked, as Violet drew level with them.

'I'm good, thanks,' she said. 'I've just finished interviewing Damian Rushcliffe. He's been telling me what life was like in Merrywell during the war.'

'Ooh, I love a bit of nostalgia, me,' said Sandra. 'I can't wait to see the film, once it's finished.'

'I'm afraid that won't be for a while yet,' Violet said.

'But worth the wait, eh?' Sandra patted Violet's arm before swiftly changing the subject. 'Isn't it a lovely day? We're going to get a nice bottle of white wine from the shop to have with our dinner this evening.'

'Sounds lovely,' said Violet, thinking about the half-finished bottle of Sauvignon Blanc in her own fridge. 'Actually, Nigel, I'm glad I've seen you . . . Can you spare me a minute? I'd like a quick word.'

'I'll pop into the shop and get the wine while you two have a chat,' Sandra said.

'I wanted to talk to you about Helen,' Violet said, once she and Nigel were alone. 'I wasn't sure I should say anything in front of Sandra.'

Nigel smiled. 'The only thing you have to keep quiet about in Sandra's presence is that I'm planning to propose. Other than that, she and I have very few secrets.'

'My lips are sealed about the proposal,' Violet reassured him. 'Regarding Helen . . . I know I told you I couldn't spare the time to help, but I was at a loose end last night, and I was intrigued . . . so I did a quick search online, to see if I could trace her.'

Nigel's face brightened. 'That was kind of you. Any luck?'

'Unfortunately not,' Violet said, regretting having raised his hopes. 'I found no mention of her and . . . to be honest, I find that surprising. Worrying, even.'

'Worrying?' said Nigel. 'In what way? Do you think she might have died?'

Violet nodded. 'It seems likely. I wondered if you'd thought about contacting the police? They might be able to help.'

Nigel wrinkled his nose. 'I doubt they'd want to get involved,' he said. 'They're hard pressed enough as it is. Besides, it's hardly a police matter, is it? No . . . I'm better off making an appointment with a solicitor, to find out how, or if, I can file for divorce. Thanks for your help, though, Violet. I'm grateful.'

'I'm only sorry I couldn't find any answers for you.'

'What about the box I gave you? Have you had a chance to look through it?'

Violet squirmed as she remembered the shoebox, which was still languishing in the boot of her car.

'No. Sorry, Nigel. I haven't had time.'

'Don't worry,' he said. 'I know you're a busy lady.'

Sandra chose that moment to reappear, brandishing a bottle of Chardonnay.

'Come on, Nigel, love,' she said. 'Let's stick this in the fridge so it's nicely chilled by the time we eat our dinner.'

Violet waved as the contented pair strolled back along the road, their peals of laughter ringing out as they made their way home.

As the midday sky was clear and bright, Violet decided to spend an hour wandering the village with her camera, capturing some general infill footage that would be useful for the film. She started in the main street, and then moved on to get exterior shots of the village hall, the church, and the war memorial. By the time she'd finished, her stomach was rumbling.

When she arrived at the bakery to buy lunch, she was surprised to see no sign of Fiona. Instead, her daughter, Sophie, was behind the counter.

'Where's your mum today?' Violet asked.

'Gone off for a meeting with one of her suppliers,' Sophie said, with a roll of her eyes. 'Leaving me stuck with running the shop, as well as overseeing the café. She promised to be back before the lunchtime rush, but here we are . . . one o'clock, and there's still no sign of her.'

'You're not on your own, are you?'

Sophie smiled. 'No, thankfully not. My two trusty assistants are looking after the café. I can rely on them.'

As Sophie wrapped Violet's sandwich, she asked about the community film.

'Mum said you'd been talking to some of the oldies,' she said. 'I hope you're going to speak to some young people as well.'

Violet smiled. 'Yes, don't worry, I'll be talking to people of all ages. As a matter of fact, I was hoping you'd give me an interview.'

Sophie grinned. 'I thought you'd never ask.'

'And if you have any suggestions as to who else I should speak to . . .'

'I'll have a word with a few mates, see if they're up for it,' Sophie said. 'Obviously, *I'm* happy to help. You're Mum's friend . . . I can hardly refuse, can I?'

'Well, you could, but your mum might give you some grief. But thanks, Sophie. I appreciate your support. How about I interview you in the café? That way, you'll get some free advertising for the place.'

'Sounds like a plan. Not that we need the publicity. The café's been absolutely rammed this week. It must be the good weather. The tourists are finally coming out of hibernation.'

'Maybe some of them will wander in the direction of *The Memory Box*,' Violet said. 'I'll head back there now and wait with bated breath.'

'I'm surprised you've got any time to take on new clients,' Sophie said. 'Haven't you got your hands full making this film?'

Violet smiled. 'Trust me, there's always time for paying customers. The more, the merrier as far as I'm concerned.'

* * *

Back at her desk, Violet compiled a work schedule for the next few weeks. She'd already lined up interviews with Sandra Feddingborough, Eric Nash, and two of the parish councillors: Judith Talbot and Colin Packer. The school had also agreed to get parental permission for her to interview a group of children about growing up in Merrywell in 2022. She still had to fix a time to visit the Derbyshire Records Office in Matlock to source old photographs of Merrywell, and she also needed to talk to Matthew Collis about the history of the village – assuming he was still speaking to her after their earlier conversation.

Frustratingly, as Violet glanced down her list of actions, she realised that all of them were scheduled for the following week. Today – right now – there wasn't a lot for her to be getting on with. The only outstanding task was typing up the transcript of Damian Rushcliffe's interview.

She made herself yet another mug of tea, sat down and opened a new Word document. Locating the correct digital file on her audio recorder, she flexed her fingers and began to type.

An hour later, she was listening to Damian's concluding words. *I have no regrets. Merrywell's a grand village, and I've had a good life here.* Violet could think of no better way of ending the interview. The old man's story had spotlighted Merrywell as a place of welcome and friendliness. Judith Talbot would rub her hands in glee when she watched the interview.

As she switched off the voice recorder, it struck her how much had changed in the last eighty years – not only in Merrywell, but in the world as a whole. In the twenty-first century, the speed of that change had accelerated at a startling rate – so much so, there were times when Violet was reluctant to keep up – not because she was incapable of change (she was far more adaptable than most people) – but rather that she disliked change for change's sake.

There was, of course, another factor at play in her aversion. The truth was, she had experienced far too many life-altering developments of her own recently. In the last two years alone, she'd gone through a separation and divorce, and been made redundant from her job. Admittedly, the stress of unemployment had been swiftly alleviated by the offer of an alternative, highly paid position at a London-based marketing agency (a job that had more perks than she could shake a stick at). She'd been very tempted – but despite years of pursuing promotion and career progression, Violet had quietly turned down the offer. She'd surprised everyone with that decision (including herself) – but, the truth was, she couldn't stomach another helping of the same-old-same-old. She longed for something more, something different – a sweeping, radical change. What she'd wanted, *needed*, was a whole new way of life – hence her arrival in Merrywell. She only hoped the move wouldn't turn out to be a case of *be careful what you wish for*.

As she sat at her desk, filtering through some of the memories of her old life with Paul, Violet toyed with the idea of ringing him, and calling in a favour.

It was probably a bad idea. She didn't even know if he'd talk to her, never mind help find Helen Slingsby. Over a period of twenty years, their relationship had gone from passionate and loving, to unexciting and indifferent. During their divorce, there had been times when it had verged on acrimonious – but ultimately (mainly for Amelia's sake) they had agreed to call a halt to hostilities.

Even so, the prospect of contacting Paul wasn't something to be relished. It was months since Violet had spoken to him, and reconnecting again after such a long time felt strange and awkward. On the other hand, what had she got to lose?

Picking up her phone, she opened her list of contacts, and made the call.

Chapter 8

Paul's phone rang three times before he answered.

'Violet.' His tone was cool, but polite. 'Is everything OK? Is Amelia all right?'

'Yes, don't panic,' she said. 'I'm not ringing because there's an emergency.'

It felt weird talking to him again. Uncomfortable. Almost stressful.

'So why *are* you calling?'

Typical Paul. Never any time for small talk.

'I need a favour,' she replied, deciding to follow his lead and go straight to the point.

'I'm at work, Violet.' He sounded annoyed now. 'I'd rather you rang me back this evening.'

'Actually, the favour is . . . sort of work-related.'

'Is it now?' He laughed drily. 'You've never had a good word to say about my job, and now you want a favour? That'd be funny if it wasn't so galling.'

Violet suppressed a sigh. 'It was never the job I objected to,' she said. 'It was what it did to you.'

'Yes . . . well. You knew what you were signing up for when you married me.'

Violet gripped her phone. *Here we go again*, she thought, dismayed at how quickly the conversation had gravitated towards the old grudges; the futile and yet familiar toing and froing.

'None of that matters now,' she said, determined to avoid another bickering session (there had already been enough of those to last a lifetime). 'I'm not looking for an argument.'

'Well, that's a relief,' Paul said. 'The rows are something I *don't* miss.'

Violet pulled in a deep breath. How was she meant to interpret that? Did he mean there were things he *did* miss? *Her*, for instance?

'You said you were after a favour,' Paul said, his voice snapping in her ear, derailing her sentimental train of thought. 'Fire away . . . what is it you want?'

Had he always been this impatient? This truculent? Or was she only now seeing his true nature?

'I need your advice,' she said.

Keeping her tone warm and friendly, she told him about Nigel Slingsby, and the search for Helen.

'I wondered whether the police . . . more specifically, *you* . . . would be able to look her up? Check the employment or passport records, maybe? I know the police have databases . . . ways of tracking people down.'

'We do,' Paul said. 'But I can't make an unauthorised search as a favour to you, Violet. Accessing data to help out a friend is strictly against the rules. I could lose my job.'

Is that what they were now? *Friends?* Violet blinked, glad that Paul couldn't see the tears that had sprung up in her eyes.

'Come on, Paul,' she cajoled. 'When have you ever stuck to the rules? It's not as if I'm asking for myself. The information is for someone else . . . someone with a genuine reason for wanting to know.'

Paul maintained a disapproving silence.

'I've checked every online source I can think of,' Violet

continued. 'And I've found a big fat nothing. Doesn't that strike you as odd?'

'Odd in what way?'

'Don't be obtuse. You know what I mean . . . something must have happened to her.'

'In all likelihood, it has,' Paul said. 'You say this woman left forty years ago?'

'Almost.'

'Then it's not beyond the realms of possibility that's she died, is it?'

'Then why is there no record of that?' Violet said. 'Helen Slingsby isn't mentioned at all online, either in the deaths register or anywhere else. She's dropped off the radar completely.'

Paul gave a soft, derisory snort – it was the noise he always made whenever he thought she was being melodramatic.

'Don't be dismissive,' she said. 'Something's wrong. I know it is.'

'*How* do you know? What evidence do you have?'

'None . . . it's just a feeling. Call it instinct.'

'Sorry,' Paul said. 'That's not good enough.'

'You've always trusted my instincts in the past.'

He sighed. 'What is it you're asking me to do?'

'I want you to trace Helen Millicent Slingsby, née Grogan. She was born on the eighth of July 1946.'

'And . . . what? You believe she's disappeared?'

'Yes.'

Another snort.

'For pity's sake, Paul. You could at least try to take this seriously.'

'Why should I?' he said. 'This is nothing to do with me. What is it you're hoping for, anyway? Are you expecting me to launch a missing persons inquiry?'

Bubbles of frustration were exploding in Violet's chest. This flippant, conversational point-scoring was one of the reasons their marriage had failed.

'I rang for your advice, not to receive a verbal drubbing,'

she said. 'I thought you might help, for old times' sake – but forget I asked. I'll make enquiries elsewhere.'

'It's not your place to be making enquiries,' Paul said, his voice tense and disapproving. 'If you're that worried, get this Nigel bloke to speak to the local police. If he reports the situation officially, they may be able to do something.'

'Yeah . . . if they can spare the time.'

Paul's snort changed to a huff.

'If *they* can't find the time, how do you expect me to? I'm a busy man, Violet. I have a massive caseload of my own to worry about. I'm not going out on a limb for some guy I've never met, and you shouldn't either. Let him sort his own problems out.'

'Fine,' Violet said, even though it wasn't fine at all. 'Seeing as you're so busy, I'd better let you get on.'

'OK . . . although . . . before you go, there is something I want to tell you. I've been meaning to call you, actually . . .'

What a bloomin' cheek! thought Violet. *He's too busy to discuss what I want to talk about, but I'm supposed to listen patiently while he imparts his nugget of news.*

Paul had gone quiet and, as the silence lengthened, she recalled her last conversation with Amelia. What was it she'd said? *Have you heard from Dad?* Had that been a red flag? Was something wrong?

Her stomach flipped.

'Go on then . . .' she said, readying herself for whatever it was Paul was about to say.

'It's . . . I'm . . .' He sounded flustered, uncharacteristically so. 'I'm seeing someone.'

He blurted out the last three words, and then paused before continuing.

'It's early days yet,' he said. 'But I thought you should know.'

Paul wasn't the kind of guy who would stay single for long, so this was hardly unexpected. But what Violet hadn't anticipated was that the announcement would squeeze all the air from her lungs, leaving her temporarily mute.

She steadied her breathing and tried to analyse her feelings. It wasn't the thought of Paul being with another woman that bothered her. On the contrary, she was pleased for him – because, despite everything, she wanted him to be happy.

So why did she feel so sad?

The only reason she could think of was because this truly was the end. The *very* end. There was no going back now – not that she would if she could – but the elimination of that option was an emotional sea change. Here, right now, a line was being drawn under her relationship with Paul. That was a *good* thing, but it was nevertheless a solemn occasion.

'Violet? Are you still there? Did you hear what I said?'

'I'm here,' she replied. 'I'm pleased for you, Paul. I want you to be happy – you do know that, don't you?'

'Thanks,' he said, sounding relieved. 'And the reverse applies.'

Another pause.

'I've been putting off telling you . . . I suppose I felt nervous about it.'

'You've no reason to be,' Violet said. 'We're divorced. You're free to see whomever you want.'

'Whomever?' Paul laughed. 'Good old Violet. Even at a pivotal moment like this, you can be relied upon to be grammatically correct.'

'*Is* this a pivotal moment?' she said.

'It feels like it,' Paul replied. 'It's the last step, isn't it? You and me . . . after all those years together . . . it really is over.'

'I thought the decree absolute was the end of the road,' Violet said. 'But you're right – this feels more final somehow.'

Paul murmured his agreement. 'What about you?' he asked. 'Are you seeing anyone?'

Violet wasn't ready to start a new relationship. She'd been married for the whole of her adult life, and what she needed now – more than anything – was a chance to be herself and enjoy her independence.

'I'm too busy to even think about dating,' she said.

'Sometimes these things creep up on you when you're not looking,' Paul told her. 'That's how it was with me and Janis.'

'That's her name, is it? Janis?'

'Yes. With an "s", as in Joplin.'

'Then I hope you and Janis-with-an-s will be very happy together – and I mean that, Paul. Life's short. If the chance to be happy presents itself, you should grab it with both hands.'

'Cheers, Vi,' he said. 'That means a lot. And make sure you practise what you preach. Grab some happiness for yourself, yeah?'

It was a good note on which to end their conversation. Making vague promises to keep in touch, they ended the call.

The breaking news about Janis-with-an-s had rather eclipsed Paul's refusal to help in the search for Helen Slingsby. Later, as Violet thought about his lack of co-operation, she felt a stab of disappointment.

As she drank a comforting cup of herbal tea, a welcome distraction landed in her inbox: an email from a woman in Youlgreave, who was interested in recording a series of family stories for her relatives in New Zealand. Brushing aside any thoughts of Paul or Helen Slingsby, Violet pulled her shoulders back and composed a friendly but business-like reply to the enquiry.

Right now, she needed to pour her energies into making *The Memory Box* a success. Her marriage had failed, and it looked as though her attempts to locate Helen Slingsby were going the same way. What she couldn't do was let her business suffer the same fate.

Chapter 9

The light was beginning to fade when Violet arrived home from work. As she let herself in through the gate, she waved to her neighbour, Toby, who was out in his garden, dead-heading something in his flower border.

'Been working late have you, Violet?' he said.

'I didn't intend to,' she replied. 'I rather lost track of time.'

As she walked up the path towards Greengage Cottage, she could see there was something on the front step. As she got closer, she realised it was a plant: a dense mass of tiny leaves sprawling over the edges of a small terracotta pot. As she bent down to pick it up, she discovered an envelope tucked behind it, addressed simply to 'Violet'.

Pushing her finger under the flap of the envelope, she tore it open. Inside was a reproduction Victorian postcard, illustrated with a variety of blooms (including a violet) and the words *The Language of Flowers and Plants*. Intrigued, Violet turned the card over to read what was written on the back, and was surprised to find it blank. Turning the pot in her hands, she examined it for clues, trying to determine who it was from.

Next door, her neighbour had finished his pruning and was about to head inside.

'Toby,' she shouted. 'I don't suppose you saw who left this?'
She held up the pot for him to see.

'No, sorry,' he said, as he ambled towards the stone wall that separated their properties. 'Isn't there a card, or a note?'

'There is,' Violet replied. 'But it's not signed. It's a charming little plant though.' She crossed the garden to show it to him.

Toby leaned in to get a better look.

'I wouldn't describe it as charming,' he said, frowning at the tumbling shoots that were hanging from the pot. 'I'm a massive fan of plants, as you know, but I wouldn't give that one house room.'

'That's a bit harsh,' Violet said, feeling unexpectedly protective towards the little plant. 'I think it's really sweet.'

'Oh, it looks nice enough, I'll give you that,' Toby said. 'And you're right . . . maybe I am being a tad unfair. The truth is, it will make a nice enough house plant, but whatever you do, don't plant it in the garden. You'll never get rid of it if you do. It'll run riot . . . spread everywhere . . . including into my garden, given half a chance.'

'I'll keep it in its pot then, in the kitchen,' Violet said. 'Do you know what it's called?'

'*Soleirolia soleirolii*,' Toby said, sounding very knowledgeable. 'That's its Latin name, of course. It's more commonly known as the mind-your-own-business plant. It's a strange choice of gift, if you don't mind me saying. I wouldn't give one of those to my worst enemy.'

Toby's blunt honesty left Violet feeling unsettled. As she carried the plant inside and placed it on her kitchen windowsill, she reread the short adage on the postcard.

The language of flowers and plants.

The floriography attached to this anonymous offering was impossible to misinterpret. The message was clear: *mind your own business*. Had someone taken umbrage at something she'd done, or said, or asked? Was this a friendly warning? A subtle way of telling her to butt out? Or was the message more menacing, meant to intimidate?

In the windowsill, the small, shiny leaves of the plant were creeping down the sides of the pot, emphasising just how much of a misnomer its common name was. Rather than minding its own business, this plant encroached where it wasn't wanted. It was invasive, and when allowed to spread, it was unwelcome, even harmful. Like gossip.

Violet shivered. She was tired, so maybe she was letting her imagination run away with her, but she couldn't shake the feeling that this plant had been left as a threat, rather than a gift. And if that was true, then someone somewhere was obviously unhappy about the questions she'd been asking.

Chapter 10

At nine-thirty the following morning, Violet pulled on an old T-shirt and a pair of faded jeans, and set off for the bakery to buy a brace of warm croissants for breakfast.

'Is this your Saturday morning treat?' Fiona said, as she handed over the pastries.

'It's more of a reward,' Violet replied. 'In advance of what I'm about to do.'

'Ooh . . .' Fiona pouted her lips. 'Do tell.'

Violet laughed. 'Don't get your knickers in a twist . . . it's nothing exciting. I'm going to spend the morning unpacking the boxes of books that are currently cluttering up my living room.'

The boxes in question were extremely heavy and had caused a succession of scowls and winces from the poor guys who'd had to carry them in from the removal van. The least Violet could do was unpack them.

'You do know Eric buys second-hand books?' Fiona said. 'They have to be things he can sell on, of course, but if you can't fit everything onto your shelves, do bear him in mind.'

'I will,' Violet said. 'Although I should be OK. I had a massive cull before I moved, even though I hate letting go of books.'

'Eric used to be like that,' Fiona said. 'When we lived in

Nottingham, there were books in every room in the house . . . even the bathroom. Thankfully, he indulges his passion through the bookshop these days . . . talking of which . . .' Fiona's lips twitched into a mischievous smile. 'Someone was in here a little while ago . . . asking after you.'

Violet raised an eyebrow. 'Who was that, then?'

'Matthew Collis,' Fiona said, nodding meaningfully. 'He wanted to know if you'd be working today.'

'And what did you tell him?'

'That I didn't know.' Fiona winked. 'But I told him you'd probably call in here at some point, on account of you being unable to resist my delicious baked goods. I offered to pass on a message . . . but he said it was OK, he'd speak to you himself.'

'I wonder what he wants?'

'Maybe he doesn't *want* anything,' Fiona said. 'Have you considered the possibility that he enjoys talking to you? He's single, you know. A widower. And you have to admit, he's good-looking.'

Violet smiled. 'He is,' she said. 'And from what I can tell, he's also friendly and funny and intelligent – but if you're trying to play Cupid, you can forget it. I'm not ready for another relationship.'

'Fair dos,' Fiona said, looking disappointed. 'I get it. All I'm saying is . . . if you change your mind . . . you could do a lot worse than Matthew Collis.'

'Thanks for that, but I suspect you're letting your imagination run away with you. I doubt Matthew's seeking me out for my scintillating company. He's promised to give me some background info on the history of the village . . . and he probably wants to fix a time.'

'Why don't you go and find him?' Fiona suggested.

'I'd rather not bother him on a Saturday. He'll be in his workshop and he's bound to be busy.'

'Matthew doesn't work on Saturdays,' Fiona said. 'His son, Rhys, runs the shop at weekends. Matthew's where he always is

73

at this time on a Saturday morning – browsing in the bookshop. He took a coffee in for Eric not five minutes ago, so he'll still be in there. I said I'd point you in his direction if you came in. Don't let me down.'

The bookshop side of *Books, Bakes and Cakes* was a delight. It consisted of a warren of book-lined aisles and booths on the ground floor, from where a twisting staircase led to a wide, book-lined balcony, and a comfortably furnished reading nook.

When he wasn't stocking shelves, Eric Nash was usually ensconced behind the large, wooden counter, which was centrally positioned, directly in front of the main shop door. There was also access at the side, directly into and out of the bakery and café. Violet used the latter to make her entrance.

Passing the merchandise section, which was stocked with literary-themed mugs, stationery and cards, Violet paused at an impressive display of newly released crime fiction – her favourite genre. The only problem was, her to-be-read pile was spiralling out of control, and she was beginning to experience overwhelm whenever she caught sight of the growing stack of books on her bedside table. Consequently, she'd pledged not to buy any more books until she'd made some inroads into the ones she already had. Even so, it was hard to resist the pull of the just-published titles from her favourite authors.

'The latest Ann Cleeves has arrived, Violet,' Eric said, addressing her from behind the counter. 'I can highly recommend it . . . only available in hardback at the moment . . . but there's a buy-one-get-one-half-price offer on all the books on that table.'

Violet's gaze lingered on the tempting display.

'I mustn't buy any more,' she said, forcing herself to step away. 'Not until I've read the backlog of books waiting for me at home. Actually, I'm looking for Matthew Collis. Fiona said he might be here.'

Eric smiled warmly, despite the non-sale. 'You'll find him down there . . .' He nodded towards the back of the shop. 'In the history section.'

She wandered down one of the aisles, past shelves of cookery books and arts and crafts titles. Up ahead, in the darkest end of the shop, she could see the tall figure of Matthew, his head bent over the heavy tome he held in his hands.

As she got closer, she leaned in to see what he was reading, but the title was obscured by Matthew's fingers. She could make out the word *Saxon*, but that was all. It was obviously interesting, because he was fully absorbed in its contents.

'Is it good?' Violet said.

Matthew jumped at the sound of her voice. 'Blimey, Violet. You startled me. Do you make a habit of sneaking up on people?'

'I wasn't sneaking. It's not my fault you were too engrossed in your book to notice me.'

'I guess that answers your question then. It must be a good book, mustn't it, if I didn't hear you coming?'

He had closed the pages, and the title was now visible: *The Anglo-Saxon World*. Violet didn't think it sounded the least bit interesting – but each to their own.

'I've just come from the bakery,' she said, staring up into Matthew's dark brown eyes. 'Fiona said you were looking for me.'

'Did she?' He looked embarrassed. 'I wouldn't say I was looking for you exactly . . . I just wondered if you were working today. I thought we could agree a time to talk about the history of the village. We could have a chat now, if you're free.'

'I've got plans for today.' She swept her hands down the front of her body, indicating her scruffy clothes. 'As you can see, I'm all set to get my hands dirty.'

He looked at her tatty jeans and smiled. 'Very fetching. What is it you're doing? DIY?'

'No, thankfully not. Greengage Cottage was totally reno-vated last year, so I don't need to do any major improvements. What I do need to do is unpack the last of the boxes from my move. I'll be spending the next few hours putting books onto shelves. It's an easy enough job, but potentially dusty, and very time-consuming – especially when you've got as many books as I have.'

'How will you be shelving them?' Matthew said. 'Alphabetically by author would be my guess.'

Violet lifted an eyebrow, prompting him to guess again.

'By subject?'

She shook her head.

'Please tell me you're not arranging them by colour?' he said, shooting her a look of mock horror.

She laughed at his expression. 'I'll be stacking them in the order they come out of the boxes,' she said. 'I'll put the large volumes together on the bottom shelves . . . other than that, it'll be completely random.'

'You've shocked me,' he said, sticking out his bottom lip. 'I had you down as the ultra-organised type.'

'Books are for enjoying,' she said. 'Not marshalling into place.'

Smiling, Matthew lifted the Anglo-Saxon tome. 'Talking of books, I need to go and pay for this one.'

'Can we arrange to meet sometime next week?' Violet suggested, as she followed him back down the aisle. 'I'd love to get an overview of the history of the village . . . I can use it as an introduction to the film.'

'I'm free on Monday morning, if you want to meet up then,' Matthew replied, speaking over his shoulder.

'OK. Where shall we do the interview?'

'Interview?'

Violet bumped into him as he stopped dead in his tracks.

'I thought I was giving you background information,' Matthew said, turning to face her.

'An interview would be better,' she replied. 'You'll only appear briefly . . . but I can put together some footage of the village and use whatever you tell me as a voice-over. All I need from you is a short narration . . . a minute or two at the most. A potted history of Merrywell, if you like.'

He stepped past her and backtracked along the aisle, stopping at a shelf labelled *Local History*. He reached to the top shelf and selected a book.

'If it's a proper potted history and an interview you're after, then you'd be better off talking to the author of this.'

He handed her a slim volume: *A Short History of Merrywell* by Brian Collis.

'Collis? Is he a relative of yours?'

'He is.' Matthew smiled. 'Brian Collis is my dad. I'll have a word with him . . . see if he'll do an interview. He enjoys all that stuff, so I don't think he'll mind. Any information I can give you will have been gleaned from him anyway, so you may as well get it straight from the horse's mouth.'

'That sounds great,' Violet said. 'Assuming your dad's all right with that.'

'He will be, don't worry.'

She held up Brian Collis's book. 'I promised not to buy anything today, but I'll make an exception for this. I'll read it over the weekend.'

'I'll check with Dad, see if he's free sometime next week,' said Matthew. 'If you let me have your phone number, I'll send you his address.'

Violet reeled off the number, and Matthew saved it directly to his phone before composing a message.

'I'm sending you a text,' he said. 'I'll speak to Dad later . . . Am I OK to give him your number?'

'Yeah, that's fine,' she said, hearing her phone ping in her pocket.

It was only after she and Matthew had gone their separate ways that she read the text. As well as Brian Collis's address, Matthew had added something else to his message.

P.S. Don't forget you owe me a coffee ☺

Chapter 11

Violet returned to Greengage Cottage and spent the rest of the morning stacking books onto the shelves in her living room. With that task completed, she changed into a pair of slightly less scruffy jeans, and swapped her old T-shirt for an emerald-green sweatshirt. Then, grabbing her copy of Brian Collis's *A Short History of Merrywell*, she went outside to sit in a sunny part of the garden. Turning to the first page of the book, she began to read.

The pretty village of MERRYWELL, in Derbyshire's Peak District, is located just off the A6, approximately 6 miles from Matlock. Although small (population 5231), the village has benefited historically from being situated on the confluence of the rivers Wye and Derwent, where a 17th-century mill once prospered.

A settlement was first established at this site on the river by the Anglo-Saxons, and is mentioned in the Domesday Survey as an outlier of the Royal Manor of Bakewell. There are several theories as to how the village got its name, but the most likely explanation is that it is derived from the Old English 'Myrige' meaning pleasant or attractive and 'Wiell' meaning spring or well. These days the village well (which is located next to the church) is no longer in use, but it continues to be decorated each year as part of an annual well-dressing festival.

The village boasts several interesting buildings, including an ancient bridge over the river Derwent (originally a packhorse bridge); the 19th-century St Luke's Church; and the White Hart Inn, which was erected in 1652 as a manor house, and later converted to a coaching inn when the grander Merrywell Manor was built nearby.

The railway arrived in Merrywell in 1849, initially as part of the Manchester, Buxton, Matlock and Midland Junction Railway (which ran as a branch line from the Midland Railway at Ambergate, calling at Merrywell en route to Buxton). Later, it became part of the Midland Railway's main line between London and Manchester.

Merrywell railway station was located half a mile north of the village, and was historically a stop for tourists on excursions to the Peak District. The line was also used to transport milk and other agricultural goods produced by the communities it served. The line and the station closed in 1967.

Merrywell Manor was built in 1794 and was the home of local landowner Sir Francis Tufnell. By 1921, the Tufnell family had died out and the manor house was in decline. After the Second World War, it stood empty for many years. Thankfully, the property was rescued in the late 1990s when a local developer converted it into a boutique hotel and wedding venue. The associated stables, barns and other outbuildings were later transformed into a small shopping village, housing a bookshop and bakery, a café, antiques and craft shops, and artisan workshops. Merrywell Shopping Village is open all year round and is a popular attraction for tourists and locals alike.

In the following chapters, we will take a more detailed look at the history of the village and its many wonderful buildings.

[1] As at the 2011 census

Violet flicked through the rest of the profusely illustrated pages, thrilled to spot an old black-and-white photograph of Greengage Cottage, taken in 1900. It looked almost exactly the same as it did now.

Towards the back of the booklet were a collection of photographs taken in the second half of the twentieth century, including one capturing a group of haymakers in the 1960s. The photograph featured an ancient tractor attached to a fully loaded hay wagon. A middle-aged couple were standing at the front of the tractor, holding long forks, and a man was standing on top of the haystack wiping his forehead with his arm. In the foreground, directly in front of the wagon, were six young people – four boys and two girls – most of them teenagers. Violet squinted at the young man on the far right of the line-up. His arm was draped around a dark-haired girl, who was smiling up into his eyes.

Fascinated, she peered more closely at the faces of the radiant couple, who looked happy and carefree, and utterly in love. The caption underneath simply said: *Making hay while the sun shines.*

Although the people in the photograph weren't named, there was no question in Violet's mind that the young pair were Nigel and Helen.

What went wrong? she wondered. *How had they gone from the loved-up couple in the photograph, to Helen walking out . . . never to be seen again?*

'What *is* your story?' she said, speaking out loud. 'What happened to you, Helen?'

Violet knew she wouldn't rest easy until she found out.

At nine a.m. the following morning, she received a follow-up text from Matthew.

Have spoken to Dad and he's happy to do the interview and appear in the film (think he was quite chuffed TBH). He's away until Monday, but could do Tuesday morning at 10.30 a.m. if that's any good for you?

Violet messaged back to say that Tuesday morning would be perfect, and Matthew responded by sending his dad's phone number. Inexplicably, Violet was disappointed there was no further mention of coffee, and she deliberated about saying something herself. In the end, she decided against it – responding instead with a thumbs-up emoji and a smiley face.

Half an hour later, there was another brief text from Matthew.

Forgot to mention . . . if you need any old photographs of Merrywell for the film, Lionel Pilkington is your man. He has a huge collection dating back to the early days of photography, several of which are in Dad's book.

Grateful for the heads-up, Violet replied instantly.

Sounds great. How do I get in touch with him?

It was another half an hour before Matthew responded.

I don't have Lionel's number saved, so can't ask him to contact you. He's on the parish council though, so you may already have his email address. If not, Dad will be able to put you in touch. His house is that enormous place by the river, the one with the fancy lawn. (Lionel's house, that is, not my parents'. Their cottage is a lot less grand!)

As it was another bright, sunny morning, Violet decided to take a stroll to the shop to buy a Sunday paper. Ordinarily, she kept track of the latest news online, but having spent a large chunk of her working week staring at a computer or phone screen, she fancied getting her hands on a good old-fashioned printed newspaper. She would save the supplements until later, and read them in a lavender-scented bubble bath.

She went the long way round to the shop, telling herself it was to get some exercise – but the real reason was so that she could stroll past the Pilkington residence and have a 'nosy'.

The *enormous place by the river* Matthew had mentioned was the house Violet had admired a few days earlier – the sprawling, stone-built one with the weeping willow. When she reached its ornate double gates, she examined the house sign affixed to the gatepost. The property was called *Fern Lodge*.

She thought about marching down the long driveway, knocking on the front door, and introducing herself. Lionel Pilkington had been on the parish council interview panel, so it wasn't as if they'd never met. If she stopped by unannounced, he'd know who she was and would probably be able to guess her reason for calling. But was it socially acceptable to drop in on someone at ten-fifteen on a Sunday morning? What if Lionel Pilkington and his wife were having a lie-in?

She stifled a giggle as a sudden vision of one or other of them answering the door in their pyjamas flashed before her eyes. Perhaps paying them a visit wasn't such a good idea after all. Lionel Pilkington in his PJs was not a sight she would be able to un-see.

Having made up her mind to walk on, she heard a voice, calling to her.

'Hello, dear. Are you lost?'

Standing at the side of Fern Lodge was a tall, waif-like woman. She had salt-and-pepper hair and a pale complexion and was beckoning Violet towards her.

With tentative steps, Violet walked through the main gate and onto the long, curving driveway. 'I was just admiring your garden, and your lovely lawn,' she said, as she approached the woman. 'I assume you're Mrs Pilkington? I'm Violet Brewster. Your husband may have mentioned me? I'm making the community film for the parish council.'

'I'm Irene,' Mrs Pilkington said. 'Would you care to come inside?'

Without waiting for an answer, she turned and went through a small gate, into a rear garden that was even vaster and more luxuriant than the one at the front of the house. Violet followed her across an enormous sandstone patio, and they entered the house through a pair of French doors.

'Is Lionel at home?' Violet asked. 'As I'm here, I may as well ask him about his photographs of Merrywell. I'm told he has an impressive collection.'

'The photography collection was originally my father's,' Irene said, as she lowered herself into an armchair. 'My husband has taken it over and added to it. He's out at the moment . . . at work. He won't be back until five o'clock at the earliest.'

Violet was surprised. She'd assumed that Lionel Pilkington was retired. What work could he be doing on a Sunday? Was he a volunteer of some sort?

'If I leave you my number, would you be kind enough to ask him to call me?' she said.

Frowning anxiously, Irene searched the cluttered side table next to her chair. A look of relief flooded her face as she retrieved a notepad and pen.

'You'll have to write the message down, otherwise I'll forget,' she said, pointing to the notepad. 'What did you say your name was again?'

'Violet. Violet Brewster. Lionel will know who I am.'

As she scribbled down her phone number and a quick note to Lionel, Irene scrutinised her closely. The intensity of her gaze was unsettling.

'You'll have to watch him, you know,' Irene said, her voice a mixture of humour and warning. 'My husband can be quite a charmer with the ladies.'

Pressing the note into Irene's hands, Violet smiled nervously. She had assumed the woman was joking – but it was clear from her expression that she was deadly serious.

'Or perhaps I'm the one who needs to keep watch,' Irene added.

Violet shifted uncomfortably, overcome by a sudden urge to leave. 'You've nothing to worry about.'

Behind them, a door flew open, and Lionel Pilkington strode into the room. Thankfully, there was no sign of any pyjamas – on the contrary, he was wearing a smart blue shirt and chinos (a look that was somewhat ruined by the tartan carpet slippers he wore on his feet).

'Mrs Brewster!' Lionel's tone was not in the least bit welcoming. 'What are you doing here? I didn't hear the doorbell.'

He stood in the centre of the room, as shocked to see her as she was to see him.

'Hello, Mr Pilkington ... Lionel,' Violet said, feeling unaccountably guilt-ridden, as though she'd been caught doing something she shouldn't. Perhaps it was the councillor's sphinx-like expression that was making her feel that way.

'I didn't ring the bell,' she explained. 'Your wife spotted me on the lane and invited me in. We came round the back. Sorry ... I thought you were at work.'

She looked to Mrs Pilkington for backup, but Irene had got up and wandered over to the French doors.

'I'm glad I've run into you though,' Violet said. 'I hoped you'd be here. I want to talk to you about your photographs of old Merrywell.'

Lionel smiled at last. 'I thought you might enquire about them. In fact, if you hadn't sought me out, I would have contacted you. I believe a selection of photographs, used as stills in the film, would add a certain *je ne sais quoi.*'

'So, you'd be happy for me to use images from the collection?'

'Certainly. I've digitised most of them, so they can be viewed online . . . but perhaps we could talk about this some other time? I have other things I need to do today.'

His dismissal made Violet feel like the worst kind of interloper.

'Of course,' she said. 'I'm sorry to have intruded.'

'Your presence was more of a surprise than an intrusion,' Lionel replied. 'And most surprising of all is that you're working on a Sunday.'

'I'm not really working,' Violet admitted. 'Not officially. I was on my way to buy a paper and paused to admire your garden. I did think about calling in on you, but decided against it . . . and then your wife spotted me and invited me in.'

Irene made no effort to join in the conversation. Instead, she gazed into the garden absent-mindedly, her arms hanging limply by her sides.

'Goodbye, Irene.' Violet waved to attract her attention. 'It was lovely to meet you.'

Although she turned and smiled, Mrs Pilkington didn't reply.

'I'll call in again another time,' Violet told her. 'We can have a longer chat . . . get to know each other properly.'

Lionel swung his hand to the right, indicating that Violet should exit through the front of the house. There was nothing overtly unfriendly in the gesture, but even so, she felt like an unwanted guest being escorted off the premises.

Once they were in the hallway, he pulled the door to behind him and brushed past her.

'I apologise for being brusque in there.' He reached the front door and rested his hand on the latch. 'The thing is, other than an occasional duty call from our son, we're not used to visitors. We don't socialise anymore: people don't come here, and we don't go out. My wife isn't well, you see. You may have noticed. She gets distracted . . . forgets things. The doctor tells me it's the beginning signs of dementia.'

'I'm sorry to hear that,' Violet said, reassessing the things Irene had said before Lionel showed up. 'I hadn't realised.'

'There's no reason why you would. To most people, Irene seems perfectly lucid – but I'm afraid appearances can be deceptive. A moment ago, you said you thought I was at work. Did my wife tell you that?'

'Yes,' Violet said. 'She said you wouldn't be back until after five.'

Lionel sighed. 'Other than my parish council duties, I haven't worked for well over a decade. I've been at home all morning.

I must have been upstairs when you arrived. Irene gets confused. Lately, she's been talking as though I'm still employed. Last week, for instance, I found her standing by the front window, waiting for me to come home. Even when I stood next to her and explained that I'd retired years ago, she didn't believe me. It's distressing when she's like that.'

'Does that sort of thing happen often?'

'With increasing frequency,' Lionel said. 'She still has good days, but those are becoming few and far between. To be honest, I'm struggling to cope with it. Seeing someone you love drift away . . . slowly disappear . . . it's not an easy thing to watch.'

'I wish someone had warned me,' Violet said. 'If I'd known, I would never have come barging into your home uninvited.'

'Other than the doctor and my son and daughter-in-law, no one is aware of my wife's condition. I haven't confided in anyone in the village, so there's no way you could have known.'

Violet was beginning to understand why Lionel had given her such a lukewarm reception.

'You can rest assured I won't say anything,' she told him.

Lionel gave a feeble smile. 'Things have reached the stage where it wouldn't matter if you did. I've been keeping quiet, hoping the problem will go away . . . but lately, I've come to realise what a fool I've been. Things are only going to get worse. I need to start making people aware of the situation.'

'From what I've seen, the people of Merrywell are a supportive bunch,' Violet said. 'I'm sure they'll give you and Irene whatever help they can.'

'You're absolutely right. This is a close-knit community,' Lionel said, as he opened the door. 'We know how to rally round our own.'

'Well . . . I'd better go and buy a paper, before they sell out,' Violet said, as she stepped outside.

'Yes, of course. Irene and I are going to do a spot of gardening later. We bought some bedding plants at the garden centre the other day, and she wants to get them planted. In my opinion it's too early . . . I fear there may be a few more overnight frosts yet to come.'

'I do hope not,' Violet said. 'Anyway, I'll leave you to get on. Have a good day. Apologies again for disturbing your morning.'

'Don't be sorry,' Lionel replied. 'No harm done, and I'm pleased you've asked about the photographs. I have the digital images stored on "the cloud". I'll send you a link so that you can browse through them at your leisure. Let me know which ones you decide to use, and I'll send you the high-res versions.'

Violet waved to him as she walked up the driveway. When she got to the road and looked back at the house, she was surprised to see he was still there, standing in the doorway. Watching her.

Chapter 12

She bought the last copy of *The Observer* from the shop, together with a punnet of early strawberries and a carton of cream.

As she scurried home, she pulled out her phone to check for messages – and that's how she ended up colliding with minute-taking Molly, who was being pulled along the pavement by an overexcited Jack Russell.

'Sorry.' Violet stuffed her mobile into her pocket and offered up an apologetic smile. 'I used to tell my daughter off for staring at her phone and not looking where she was going, but I'm as bad myself these days.'

'It wasn't entirely your fault,' Molly said. 'When I'm with Alfie here, I have no control over where I'm going. He takes *me* for a walk, rather than the other way around.'

When Violet bent down to scratch the dog under his chin, he jumped up and put his front paws on her knee.

'Get *down*, Alfie,' Molly said. 'Sorry, we've been across the fields and his feet are muddy.'

'Don't worry,' Violet said, laughing as she examined the set of wet paws prints on her jeans. 'It'll dust off.'

'How are things?' Molly asked. 'Are you settling into village life?'

'I am indeed. Merrywell already feels like home.'

'Did I spot you going into Fern Lodge earlier?' Molly said. 'I live up the road from the Pilkingtons . . . I saw you going down their driveway as I set off on Alfie's walk.'

Violet sighed inwardly. She was rapidly coming to conclusion that it was impossible to do *anything* in Merrywell without being observed.

'I called in briefly,' she replied. 'There was something I wanted to discuss with Lionel.'

'You should be honoured they let you over the threshold,' Molly said. 'The Pilkingtons tend to discourage callers. They're a nice enough couple, but extremely wrapped up in each other. They keep themselves to themselves, if you know what I mean. I've heard Irene isn't well.'

Clearly, Molly was fishing for gossip, but Violet wasn't going to bite.

'Lionel's going to let me use some of his old photographs for the film,' she said, changing the subject. 'I did the first interviews this week. It's all coming together nicely.'

At the mention of the film, Molly's eyes lit up. Despite the dog pulling on his lead, she told Violet how desperate she was to be interviewed, almost begging to be included.

In the face of such enthusiasm and willingness, Violet didn't have the heart to turn her down. Subject to the weather being dry, she agreed to interview Molly in the park on Monday afternoon.

Chapter 13

That was how she found herself waiting on a bench in Merrywell Park at two o'clock the following day. The sky was overcast, but the rain was holding off. Violet had arrived early to set up, and the camera was in position, ready to interview Molly when she arrived.

Merrywell Park was small, but meticulously maintained by a group of local volunteers. Close to the entrance was a play area, consisting of a set of swings and a climbing frame. From there, a gravelled pathway wove through a series of low-lying flower beds to an ornate Victorian bandstand at the far end of the park. Violet had chosen to sit halfway along the path, next to a dazzling display of tulips that were the colour of freshly squeezed orange juice.

When she saw Molly clomping along the path in a pair of high heels, she suppressed a smile. The young woman had obviously dressed up for her interview. She was wearing black Capri pants with a white, frilly, off-the-shoulder blouse. As she got closer, Violet realised that Molly's face was also heavily made-up. Smoky eyes. Mascara. Shell-pink lipstick. The works. It was a look that wouldn't have been out of place in a nightclub, but it was somewhat OTT for a Monday afternoon stroll in Merrywell Park.

'Ey up,' Molly said, waving excitedly. 'This is *so* exciting. Can you believe it? *Me*, in a film.'

It was hardly a Hollywood blockbuster, but Violet refrained from saying so, not wanting to dampen Molly's enthusiasm. Instead, she invited her to take a seat at the other end of the park bench, and positioned the camera at an angle that best hid the dark line of foundation along Molly's jawline.

Violet began by making small talk, to help Molly relax. Then, slowly, she segued into the real interview – so slowly, in fact, that Molly didn't seem to notice she was answering important questions about her life in the village.

Beneath the superficial layer of make-up was an erudite and articulate young woman. When Molly explained how hard it was for young people to get onto the property ladder, Violet felt a pang of guilt. She was, after all, part of the exodus from London that was pushing up house prices in places like the Peak District.

When the interview was over and the camera had been switched off, Molly leaned back and continued to chat. She said she was a single mother, worked part-time, and had a non-existent social life.

'This film is about the most exciting thing that's happened for yonks,' Molly said. 'It's so boring around here. There's nothing for people like me, who are on our own. The council's happy enough to fund a youth club, and stuff for the older folks, but there's absolutely nothing for people my age. We get overlooked.'

'Have you thought about starting a social group yourself?' Violet said, realising that Molly was probably lonely. 'Or perhaps you could do some studying. An evening class, maybe?'

'I'd love to, if I could get a regular babysitter,' Molly said. 'My parents run the White Hart . . . Mum helps out with childcare whenever she can, but it's a bit hit and miss as to when she's going to be available. If there's something on at the pub or it's a busy night, I've got no chance.'

'What about an Open University course?' Violet suggested. 'That way, you could study at home when your son's gone to bed.'

'Maybe I will . . . one day. But I'm guessing the fees for that kind of course would be expensive, yeah? That pretty much rules it out at the moment. I can hardly make ends meet as it is.'

'You should talk to the parish council,' Violet said. 'They might pay for you to study online as part of your professional development . . . a minute-taking or facilitation course, maybe . . . something that will help you do your job and give you some more qualifications.'

'I can't see Judith Talbot agreeing to that,' Molly said.

'You don't know if you don't ask. It's worth a try, surely?'

'I suppose so. And come to think of it . . . Judith isn't as bad as I'm painting her. She can be stuck-up at times – but underneath that snooty exterior, she's all right really.'

Their conversation continued as Violet packed away her equipment. When Molly mentioned her grandmother, Sandra, Violet realised she was referring to Sandra Feddingborough.

'Sandra's your grandma?'

'Yes,' Molly said. 'She says you've been helping Nigel find his wife.'

'I've tried,' said Violet. 'But I've not had much luck. There's nothing online. It's all very puzzling.'

'My mum reckons Helen Slingsby's whereabouts are better off staying a mystery,' Molly said. 'She says she wasn't a very nice person.'

'I have heard that Helen could be difficult,' Violet said. 'I get the impression she wasn't very popular.'

'Is it any wonder, after what she did?'

'Leaving Nigel, you mean?'

'Well, yeah . . . that as well,' Molly said. 'But actually . . . I meant stealing that baby.'

Violet was bending down, fastening her camera case. 'Baby?' she said, lifting her head and wondering if she'd misheard. 'Are you serious? What baby? No one said anything to me about that. When was this?'

'Oh, years ago,' Molly said. 'Ages before she left the village.'

Despite all the negative reports about Helen, Violet found this latest bombshell hard to believe. Was it true, or just idle gossip?

'So, what happened?' she said.

'I don't know much about it,' Molly replied, nonchalantly wafting a hand. 'By the time I was born, Helen Slingsby was long gone. All I know is, the whole thing was covered up . . . swept under the carpet. I'm surprised Gran's not mentioned it to you.'

'If it's only a rumour, perhaps she thought better of it,' Violet said, keeping her tone light.

'It definitely wasn't a rumour, although nobody seems to know the full story, except for Nigel, of course. Gran's tried to wheedle it out of him, but he refuses to talk about it. And if *she* can't charm him into spilling the beans, no one can.'

Violet made a mental note to broach the subject with Nigel the next time she saw him. Given that he was desperate to find Helen, why hadn't he mentioned this? What's to say it wasn't the reason she disappeared?

'Was this baby-stealing incident why Helen left the village?' Violet asked.

Molly shrugged. 'I don't think so, but you're asking the wrong person. Helen left in the Eighties, and I wasn't born until 1997. I only know what Mum and Gran have let slip. The baby snatching was a long, long time ago. Mum must still have been a baby, because I remember Gran saying it could just as easily have been her that Helen took.'

Violet contemplated this latest revelation as she zipped up her camera bag. With each interview she'd conducted, she had inadvertently uncovered another facet to Helen's personality – and so far, none of them were good.

The rest of the afternoon passed uneventfully. Violet returned to *The Memory Box* and ploughed on with edits for the film, pleased to be making good progress.

But when she broke off to make a cup of tea, she found herself brooding once more on the Helen Slingsby conundrum. *What is wrong with me?* she wondered. *Why can't I let it go . . . disengage from the whole thing?*

For the most part, she blamed her own burning curiosity – but that wasn't the only factor at play here. Today, for instance, she'd had no intention of talking to Molly about Helen. Why would she? As far as Molly was concerned, Helen Slingsby was ancient history.

And yet – unprompted – their post-interview chat had generated an unexpected and startling piece of information. Even when Violet *did* set out to avoid it, there was no escaping the subject of Helen.

This was a small village, and people were connected in multiple ways. Violet recalled something Fiona had told her about the village network.

'Try to avoid talking about the locals, because there will always be someone earwigging,' Fiona had said. 'And I can guarantee they will know – or worse, be related – to whoever it is you're slagging off.'

Violet had no intention of 'slagging off' anyone, but it would be prudent to heed Fiona's warning and follow her advice. In villages like Merrywell, people had long memories. They held grudges and, when necessary, the community was more than capable of closing ranks.

Chapter 14

At eight o'clock that evening, Amelia texted to confirm the dates of her planned visit.

Violet tapped out a reply.

Thanks, love. That's fine with me. Like I said, you're welcome any time. xx

Amelia's reply arrived less than a minute later.

Great. I'll be coming up on the train, so I'll need you to pick me up from the station. I'll probably buy a ticket to Chesterfield. xx

Violet sent another quick text.

Not a problem. Just let me know what time and I'll be there. xx

Assuming that would be the end of their exchange, she switched on the television. As she settled down to watch the first part of a new crime drama, another text popped onto her phone.

BTW, Dad said you called him. He seems to think you're on a mission to solve a mystery. Is he right?

Rather than writing a long explanatory text, Violet set the television programme to record and called her daughter's number.

'I wouldn't exactly call it a mission,' she said, when Amelia answered.

Stretching out on the sofa, she settled down for a long chat, filling Amelia in on what she had discovered about the elusive Helen Slingsby.

'It does all sound a bit weird,' said Amelia, when Violet had finished telling her what she knew about Helen. 'But what's even weirder is why *you're* involved in all this. I thought you moved to Merrywell for some peace and quiet. What happened to your plan to embrace a more laid-back lifestyle?'

'I am more laid-back,' Violet said, sounding overly defensive even to her own ears. 'But just because I've moved to a village doesn't mean I've got to slide into an apathetic torpor. I'll always take an interest in what's happening around me, no matter where I live.'

'Dad reckons you're playing with fire. He's worried your inquisitiveness will get you into trouble with the locals.'

'He could be right there. Some disgruntled resident has already left a mind-your-own-business plant on my doorstep.'

Amelia burst into a fit of giggles. 'Mind-your-own-business plant? What the heck's one of those?'

'It's a funny-looking thing,' Violet said. 'Like a plant pot with a bad haircut.'

Amelia gave a belly laugh. 'Whatever it is,' she said, 'it's wasted on you. There's no chance of you keeping your curiosity in check.'

'Cheers, love.'

'Seriously though, Mum,' Amelia said, once she'd finished laughing. 'Don't take any notice of Dad, or anyone else for that matter. You should roll with whatever feels right. Do be careful, though. Don't think twice about stepping away from something if it feels off.'

Violet smiled. 'You do realise you're beginning to sound like me?' she said.

'I know. Who'd have thought I'd end up dishing out advice to my own mother. It's not exactly cool, is it?'

'Probably not,' said Violet. 'But it does show you care. And don't you worry, I'll watch my step.'

After the call with Amelia, Violet tuned in to the TV drama, but lost patience with it after twenty minutes and switched off. She put another hunk of wood into the log burner and went into the kitchen to get herself a glass of wine. Beyond the kitchen window it was dark, and the wind was getting up. She thought of her little car, nestled in the small parking space at the side of the cottage. Somewhere in the boot was the shoebox that Nigel had forced on her. Maybe it was time to have a look inside it.

Retrieving her car keys from her handbag, she went outside and rounded the corner of the house. The car winked at her through the gloom as she pressed the remote key, and a blast of wind buffeted her as she opened the boot and grabbed the box. Balancing it in the crook of her arm, she relocked the car and hurried back inside.

Armed with the box and her glass of wine, she headed into the living room and settled onto the sofa. When she lifted the box lid, she was surprised to see it was only half full. Lying on top of the pile of contents were a couple of photographs. One showed Helen on a beach somewhere, the wind tugging at the headscarf she was wearing. Another showed her leaning in to smell a rose that was growing around an unknown door. Disappointingly, there were no photos of Helen and Nigel together, and none of Helen pictured with friends or relatives – although it was possible she could have taken those with her when she left.

The photos were lying on top of a white handkerchief, which

had a butterfly embroidered in one corner. It was made from poor quality cotton, so Violet assumed Helen must have hung on to it for sentimental reasons – although, clearly, she hadn't been too attached to it, otherwise she would have taken it with her.

Beneath the handkerchief were two dog-eared pieces of paper: a receipt from a furniture shop in Matlock, dated 8 November 1979, relating to the purchase of a dining table; and an estimate from a landscaping company for installing a garden pond and water feature. There were also three postcards. One from Skegness, another from Portmeirion in Wales, and one from the Costa Brava. The handwriting was identical on each of them and they were all signed *Aunt Agnes*. Violet wondered if this was the great-aunt in Baslow that Nigel had mentioned. The brief messages on each of the cards offered reports about the weather, the food, and the hotel accommodation.

Violet sighed. These ordinary, random pieces of ephemera revealed absolutely nothing about Helen.

It was the item at the bottom of the box that made Violet's heart race. She picked it up, turning it over in her hands: a hardbacked notebook, covered in brown faux leather. Was this Helen's journal?

With impatient fingers, she flipped through the pages, but rather than the lined paper she'd been anticipating, the book contained the plain pages of a sketchpad, and every one of them was filled with drawings. Written on the inside front cover were the words: *This book belongs to Helen Slingsby*. She must have been an amateur artist, or perhaps a frustrated fashion designer – because most of the pages were filled with sketches of elegant dresses and coats. There was even a pair of high-heeled shoes.

A few of the pages were crammed with more naturalistic subjects: butterflies, trees, flowers and animals, and a couple of sketches of the local landscape.

Halfway through the sketchbook, Violet came across a pencil portrait of a much younger Nigel. Frantically, she flicked through the rest of the book, wondering if Helen had also sketched the face of her lover – but she'd obviously not been keen on drawing people, because there were no other faces on any of the pages.

It was the series of drawings towards the end of the book that captured Violet's attention. The pencil sketches covered six pages in total, and were all a variation on a similar design, which featured the sinuous, whiplash curves reminiscent of the art nouveau style. Was it a pattern for bespoke wallpaper? Or something that Helen intended to embroider? The first couple of pages showed early versions of the design, which were developed in ever greater detail with each rendering. Eventually, Helen appeared to have settled on a design she was happy with.

The final drawing filled the whole of the last page. By this point, it was clear this was a piece of jewellery, because the scrolled framework was now inset with precious stones. Rather than a rough sketch, this design was carefully crafted, and each of the stones was labelled. A sapphire in the centre; diamonds either side; a tear-shaped ruby drop hanging from the bottom.

Why did the design seem so familiar? Violet stared at it, searching her memory, trying to recall where she'd seen it before.

The answer came to her in a flash. It was in the framed photograph of Damian Rushcliffe's wife, Zelda. That was it. This looked like the necklace she'd been wearing.

In fact, scrub that, Violet thought. *It isn't* like *the necklace Zelda Rushcliffe was wearing. It's the exact same one.*

Chapter 15

By the following morning, the weather had taken a turn for the worse. Violet was inside *The Memory Box*, peering out through the front window, craning her neck to assess the patch of sky above the courtyard. A fine drizzle was falling from dreary clouds that showed no sign of retreating. Her ten-thirty interview with Brian Collis would have to be filmed indoors.

Violet wandered back to her desk, feeling preoccupied. Since the previous evening, one thing had been dominating her thoughts: Zelda Rushcliffe's necklace.

She had conjured up a couple of explanations as to why there was a drawing of it in Helen's sketchbook. The first was that Helen had seen Zelda wearing the pendant at some point and admired it. Later, she could have made rough sketches as she'd tried to recall what it looked like, drawing from memory until she got it right.

The second possibility was that Helen had designed the necklace for Zelda – but that seemed a lot less likely. Helen was a school secretary, not a jewellery designer.

Violet tapped her fingers on the desk. There were two ways to discover the history of the stunning piece of jewellery. She could speak to Damian Rushcliffe and ask him outright about the pendant his wife was wearing in the framed photograph, or she could talk to Nigel and find out what he knew about the sketches. Violet decided to start with the latter.

'Hi, Nigel, it's Violet,' she said, when he answered her call. 'I'm just ringing to let you know that I had a look through the shoebox last night.'

'You did?' he said. 'Find anything interesting?'

'Not especially, but there's a drawing in Helen's sketchbook I'd like to ask you about.'

Nigel huffed out a laugh. 'She was always drawing in that thing . . . scribbling away with her pencil. I once bought her a set of watercolours for Christmas, thinking she might like to paint some landscapes, but she wasn't interested. It was sketching she liked, and she was quite good at it too.'

'She definitely had an artistic bent,' Violet said. 'There's a very striking drawing at the end of the book . . . it seems to be a design for a piece of jewellery. Do you know anything about it?'

He hummed and hawed for a moment before answering. 'I do vaguely recall seeing the drawing, and I know Helen was planning to create a piece of jewellery. She had a great-aunt . . . Agnes . . . who she was very close to. When Agnes died, she left a couple of pieces of jewellery to Helen . . . a brooch and a ruby ring. Neither were to Helen's taste, so she decided to get the stones set into a pendant. She was going to design it herself and commission a jeweller to make it, in memory of her aunt.'

'Do you know if she got round to doing that?'

'Not that I know of, but it's possible she went ahead without telling me . . . we weren't really talking much towards the end. All I know is, after she left, there was no sign of the brooch or the ring. Then again, they were quality pieces . . . worth a fair bit, I'd imagine. She was hardly going to leave them behind for me, was she?'

'I guess not,' Violet said.

'Why are you asking, anyway? What's so special about this drawing?'

'I thought it looked familiar,' Violet said, deciding not to say any more until she'd had a chance to speak to Damian Rushcliffe. 'But maybe that's because I've seen a lot of art-nouveau-style pendants in my time.'

'Did anything else strike a chord?' Nigel said. 'From in the shoebox?'

'No. To be honest, Nigel, there's wasn't a lot in there. I've put everything back and I'll make sure I return it to you when I'm next passing.'

'Whenever's convenient,' Nigel said. 'There's no rush. You will let me know though, won't you? If you remember any more about the pendant?'

'Yes, of course,' Violet replied, feeling guilty that she hadn't been completely honest with him. 'I'll keep you posted.'

The first thing Violet did when she'd ended the call with Nigel was check her watch. There were still twenty minutes before her interview with Brian Collis. Just enough time to make another call – this time to Damian Rushcliffe.

The number rang several times before he answered. Violet imagined him shuffling into the hallway, where the landline was located, and lowering himself onto his 1970s telephone table seat as he picked up the receiver.

'Hello,' he said, before reciting his number.

'Damian, it's Violet. Violet Brewster.'

'Hello, Violet. What can I do for you?'

She took a deep breath and launched straight in with her question.

'This may seem like an odd thing to ask,' she said. 'But in the photograph of your wife . . . the one on your sideboard . . . she's wearing a very distinctive necklace. I wondered where she'd got it from.'

'I gave it to her. It was a present, to mark our silver wedding anniversary.'

Violet tried to recall the year Damian said he'd got married.

1958? If she was right, that would mean their twenty-fifth anniversary would have been in 1983. The year after Helen left.

'It looked like a very unusual design. Was it something you had specially made?'

'No, I bought it locally, at a jeweller's shop in Bakewell. I was lucky to get it, actually. I went in about another pendant . . . one that was in the window . . . but I ended up buying something totally different.'

'Do you mind telling me how that came about?'

'No, I don't mind. Not at all. Obviously, with it being our silver wedding, I wanted to give Zelda something silver . . . but I also wanted it to be special . . . a quality piece, you know? The first necklace I looked at seemed lightweight and bit tacky, and when I mentioned that to the jeweller, he went in the back and came out with this other pendant, the one I ended up buying. At first, I assumed what he was showing me was silver, but he said it was platinum, and that the gemstones were a good size and clarity. Consequently, it was a lot more than I wanted to pay, but the jeweller gave me a very good deal. It still cost a pretty penny, mind . . . but my Zelda was worth it.'

'Can you remember the name of the shop?'

She heard Damian chuckle. 'As a matter of fact, I can,' he said. 'It was River Jewels, which, at the time, I thought was a very clever name. You see, the shop was near the bridge, close to the river, and the proprietor's name was Rivers. Very apt.'

'One more question, and then I'll let you go,' Violet said. 'Do you know if the shop is still there?'

'That I couldn't tell you,' Damian replied. 'It's a while since I was in Bakewell, so I wouldn't know.'

'Don't worry,' said Violet. 'That's something I can easily find out.'

'Why are you asking about this?' Damian said.

'I'm trying to get to the bottom of something,' said Violet. 'But I can't really say what.'

'A secret, eh? It all sounds very cloak and dagger to me.'

'I hope not,' Violet said. 'I'd much rather it turned out to be something and nothing.'

'Well, if and when this veil of secrecy can be lifted, I'd love to know what my wife's necklace has to do with whatever it is you're looking into.'

'You and me both,' said Violet.

Chapter 16

The address Matthew had given for his parents was *Well View Cottage*, which Violet had worked out was directly opposite the church, less than a minute's walk from the shopping village.

At twenty-five past ten, she pulled on a lightweight raincoat, grabbed an old telescopic umbrella, and hoisted her camera bag onto her shoulder.

Postponing any further speculating on the necklace, she crossed the courtyard, fumbling with the brolly and chuntering under her breath as she grappled with its handle.

'Violet!' Matthew was sheltering in the doorway of his shop. 'Are you off to my parents' house?'

'Yes,' she replied, as she finally secured the umbrella and lifted it over her head. 'I'm looking forward to meeting them.'

'Do you want me to walk over there with you? Do the introductions?'

Tempting though the offer was, it would mean Matthew having to close up, if only for a short while.

'You're all right,' she said. 'I'm more than capable of introducing myself.'

He laughed. 'I don't doubt it. Just make sure you let Dad know who's in charge, yeah? Don't let him give you any waffle.'

'Don't worry. I'm well prepared. I read his book over the weekend, so I'm genned up to ask the right questions.'

'Things are going well, are they? On the film?'

'Yes, it's coming together. There's still a lot to do, but – so far – everything's going to plan.'

Matthew smiled. 'That's good to know. I'm glad you haven't allowed yourself to get sidetracked by the Helen Slingsby thing.'

Violet bristled. Was he implying she'd been in danger of letting the project slide?

'There was never any chance of that,' she said. 'I wouldn't do anything to jeopardise the film, but that doesn't mean I've given up on Nigel entirely.'

Matthew sighed. 'You're not going to let it go, are you?' he said. 'You're tenacious, I'll give you that. Like a dog with a bone.'

Violet shrugged.

'You know, even dogs give up chewing eventually,' Matthew added. 'If the bone has no meat on it.'

'Not if there's a chance they can get to the marrow,' Violet said. 'That's the thing, you see. Just when you think you've reached a dead end, you find something new . . . something that puts a whole new spin on things.'

'I take it you're referring to yourself now, rather than making a general observation about dogs and bones?'

'I am,' Violet said. 'Let's just say I've uncovered a few interesting facts.'

'Facts?' Matthew frowned. 'Really? I don't know what you've been told, but be aware, when it comes to village gossip, it can be hard to decipher fact from fiction.'

Violet adjusted the strap of her shoulder bag.

'Are you going to tell me what you've heard?' Matthew said.

'Some other time,' she said, glancing at her watch. 'I don't want to be late for my appointment with your dad.'

'Don't worry about that. If you're late, you can blame it on me.' He folded his arms. 'Before you go to my parents' house,

I'd like to know what you've heard about Helen Slingsby. Please, it's important.'

Violet could tell from his pinched expression that he was annoyed. What was it with this man? She seemed to have a knack for winding him up.

Rain was dripping off the back of her umbrella and running down her neck. She pulled the handle closer and adjusted the angle of the canopy.

'I interviewed Molly Gee yesterday,' she said. 'She told me Helen Slingsby stole a baby, and that the whole thing was hushed up. I don't know how true it is, or if it's connected in any way to her leaving . . . but I intend to ask Nigel about it. There's something decidedly odd about this whole Helen business . . . and when odd things happen, I get suspicious.'

Matthew leaned against the doorjamb. 'Just leave it, Violet,' he said. 'Trust me . . . some things are kept quiet for a reason. The good folks of Merrywell have long memories, but certain things are best forgotten.'

His eyes were glistening, hard and flinty.

'Matthew Collis, what is it you're not telling me?'

He pressed his lips together and shook his head.

'Can you at least tell me whether there's any truth in what Molly said?' she asked, frustrated at his unwillingness to communicate. 'Did Helen Slingsby steal a baby?'

'Yes.' He nodded once. 'She did.'

'And the whole thing was covered up?'

'It was.'

'You're absolutely sure about this?'

'I'm certain,' Matthew said. 'And the reason I'm able to speak with such authority is because the baby Helen stole . . . was me.'

Chapter 17

Matthew's declaration had rendered Violet temporarily speechless. She cringed inwardly and reeled her head back, retreating under the umbrella like a tortoise disappearing into its shell. Why hadn't it occurred to her that the stolen baby might be Matthew? The clues had all been there: Matthew's reluctance to talk about Helen Slingsby; his scornful expression whenever her name was mentioned. Why, oh why hadn't she worked this out for herself?

She shuffled anxiously, mortified as she recalled the glib, blundering way she'd raised the subject, utterly impervious to Matthew's feelings. If she'd known the truth, she would never have behaved so insensitively. The last thing she wanted was to hurt him by opening up old wounds.

'Perhaps now you can see why I don't want you tittle-tattling to my parents about Helen Slingsby,' Matthew said. 'She's persona non grata in our house. You'll get short shrift if you ramble on about her to my mother.'

'I'll admit to indulging in an occasional bit of tittle-tattling,' Violet said, as she struggled to recover her composure. 'But I never ramble.'

Matthew stared at her, unsmiling. He was furious with her – that much was obvious.

'I'm really sorry, Matthew. I had no idea you were the baby who was taken. Had I known, I wouldn't have been so flippant. Now that I know the truth, I can well understand your family's antipathy towards Helen. And for what it's worth, her name probably wouldn't have cropped up in my conversation with your parents anyway.'

Matthew spun away, his hands dropping to his sides. Clearly, he didn't believe her.

'And it goes without saying, now that I'm aware of what Helen did, I'll avoid mentioning her in your mum and dad's presence,' she added.

'Thank you.'

'I'll understand if you don't want to,' she said, 'but are you willing to tell me what happened? Or say why the incident was hushed up?'

Matthew threw back his head and laughed unconvincingly. 'You really are something, Violet. There's doggedly determined . . . and then there's you.'

'That's the second time you've compared me to a dog,' she said, determined to inject some humour into their conversation before it descended into a full-blown argument. 'It's a good job I'm not easily offended.'

'I'll add *thick-skinned* to the descriptive mix as well then.'

Violet resisted the temptation to pull a face.

'As I'm sure you'll appreciate, the incident was deeply disturbing for my parents,' Matthew told her. 'Their way of handling it was to put the whole thing behind them, and not talk about it.'

'And you don't want to either?' said Violet. 'That's fair enough, and a perfectly natural reaction. But, for Nigel's sake, I'm curious to learn how this all fits in with Helen's disappearance.'

With an irritated sigh, Matthew stepped into the courtyard and locked the door of his shop.

'I'll walk with you to Mum and Dad's,' he said. 'You have the time it takes to get there to ask your questions.'

Violet grinned. 'Can we walk slowly?'

She was relieved when he returned her smile, even if it was begrudgingly. She'd pushed him as far as she dared, and it was to his credit that he'd managed to cling on to his sense of humour.

'Tell you what,' Matthew said. 'Rather than you peppering me with questions, why don't I give you the bare facts?'

'OK,' she said, moving the umbrella across to bring him under its shelter. 'I'll settle for the basics . . . but feel free to elaborate, if you feel so inclined.'

Giving her a look that said *don't push it*, he launched into his story as they exited the courtyard.

'I was two months old,' he said. 'Mum took me to the village shop . . . pushed me there in my pram. Back then, pushchairs and prams were great big, cumbersome things – far too clunky to take inside a shop. Instead, they were parked outside, usually with the baby still tucked up inside.

'I was fast asleep, so Mum left me in the pram at the front of the shop. She was only gone a couple of minutes. When she came out, she bent down to put her shopping in the basket under the pram . . . and that's when she realised . . . I wasn't there.'

Violet put a hand over her mouth. 'It's every mother's worst nightmare,' she said, muttering between her fingers. 'What did she do when she saw the pram was empty?'

'Screamed blue murder, apparently,' said Matthew. 'The shop-keeper came running out, someone else went to the phone box to call the police, and a couple of passing youths were roped in to scour the village. Understandably, my mum was beside herself . . . totally distraught.'

'How do you know all this?' Violet asked. 'I thought you said your parents refused to talk about it.'

'I heard rumours about it, when I started secondary school. I kept pestering my parents for information, and they finally sat me down and told me the whole story. It's the one and only time we've discussed it.'

Violet knew she would never have been able to suppress something so shocking. Her way of dealing with trauma was to talk it out . . . reliving whatever was bothering her until it no longer had the power to worry her. But that was *her* way of coping. Thankfully Violet had never faced anything as stressful as having her child stolen. Perhaps if she had, she would have chosen to do exactly what Mr and Mrs Collis had done – bury the memory deep, to avoid having to think about it.

'Mayhem broke out at the shop,' Matthew continued. 'And then Helen Slingsby walked around the corner with me in her arms. Believe it or not, I was still fast asleep. I must only have been gone for three or four minutes.'

'And did Helen admit that she'd taken you?'

Matthew shook his head. 'Not at first. It wasn't until the police questioned her that she finally broke down and told the truth. She said she snatched me out of my pram in a moment of madness. Then, a few minutes later, she came to her senses and brought me back.'

Violet raked a hand through her hair, holding it away from her face. 'Why would anyone do that? Even the most evil of people would think twice about walking away with someone's child.'

'Helen was having some kind of breakdown,' Matthew said. 'Taking me was an aberration, an ill-considered and imprudent moment in time. She was ill . . . an emotional mess . . . That's why the whole thing was hushed up.'

'Your mum must have been overjoyed when she realised you were safe.'

'She told me she almost collapsed with relief – but then, gradually, that relief turned to anger. Initially, she and Dad were all for pressing charges.'

'Why didn't they?' Violet said.

'Nigel intervened. He spoke to them and told them why Helen had done it. He said they'd been seeking medical advice after trying for a baby for years. A few weeks before she snatched me,

Helen had been told that she and Nigel would never have children, and she didn't take the news well. She became depressed. Nigel said it was the loss of hope that got to her the most. She wasn't thinking straight.'

'That's something of an understatement,' Violet said. 'I mean . . . I sympathise with Helen's situation, but it's impossible to condone what she did. Taking someone's baby? That's indefensible.'

'Nigel promised he'd take Helen to see a doctor, and he begged my parents not to pursue criminal charges.'

'Was Helen working at the school back then?'

'She was, yes.'

'So, if she'd been arrested, she would have lost her job,' Violet said.

'For sure,' Matthew said. 'She would definitely have been sacked. Mind you, considering how she treated the pupils, that might have been no bad thing.'

'Maybe she was different back then . . . nicer,' Violet said. 'Perhaps it was finding out that she couldn't have children of her own that triggered her resentment towards the kids at school.'

Matthew shrugged. 'Possibly. I don't suppose it could have been easy for her . . . working somewhere where she was surrounded by young children. It would have been a constant reminder of what she was missing.'

'Did Helen ever apologise to your parents, or show any remorse?'

'Not immediately, she was in no fit state. She was admitted to hospital for a while, and took some time off work. It was only later, after she'd recovered, that she paid my parents a visit to ask for their forgiveness.'

'And they gave it to her?' Violet said.

'They did.'

She released a huff of air. 'I'm not sure I would have been that magnanimous. Your mum and dad must be good, kind people.'

'They are,' Matthew said. 'But although they forgave Helen,

they never forgot. They understood *why* she behaved as she did – they even sympathised – but Mum never trusted Helen after that, or had anything more to do with her.'

'I can't say I blame her.'

'It was Nigel they felt most sorry for. Mum and Dad had always got on well with him, but . . . afterwards, things became awkward and it was easier to cut ties with him.'

'If the truth had come out, I suppose Helen would have become the village pariah,' Violet said.

'Exactly . . . and given the circumstances, that's not something Mum and Dad wanted to let happen. No one was ever told the full story.'

'And yet, only yesterday, I was told that Helen had stolen a baby. People may not know the whole truth, but the rumours have obviously persisted over the years.'

Matthew smiled. 'This is Merrywell,' he said. 'There are always rumours. On the day I was snatched, the news roared around the village like a bushfire, but Helen's role in things was always played down. She was described as the person who found and returned me. I suspect the shopkeeper guessed the truth, and he may well have speculated with his customers about what really happened, but the gossip died down eventually. The only legacy from the incident was that Mum became extremely overprotective of me, which was a real drag when I was a teenager. She was constantly wanting to know where I was going, where I'd been, who I'd been with. It was a nightmare.'

'Actually,' Violet said, 'I did my share of that when my daughter was in her teens. I was always keeping tabs on her . . . She used to say I kept her under surveillance.'

Matthew laughed. 'I did the opposite with my son. Having had someone constantly on my back as I grew up, I was determined not to subject Rhys to the same treatment. Thankfully, he's a good lad . . . always has been . . . so he's not caused me too many sleepless nights.'

Violet wondered how old Rhys had been when his mum had died. It must have been tough on Matthew, raising a teenager alone. Ordinarily, she would have asked him about it, but she'd done more than enough prying for one day. Matthew was a nice guy, but even he must have his limits.

Besides, they had arrived at *Well View Cottage*. In the front garden, a tall, white-haired man – an older version of Matthew – was standing in the drizzle, picking hellebores. He held up an arm to greet them as they walked up the path.

'Violet, this is my dad, Brian.'

'Pleased to meet you,' Violet said, shaking his hand. 'And thanks for agreeing to an interview.'

Brian smiled. 'My pleasure. I'm pleased you asked.'

'Why are you picking flowers in the rain?' Matthew asked.

'Because your mum asked me to,' Brian said, holding up the hellebores. 'Come into the house, Violet, and I'll introduce you to her. Are you stopping, son?'

'Nah, I'll get back to work,' Matthew said. 'I'll speak to you later. Remember what I told you, Violet.'

The look he gave her was loaded with meaning. *Not a word*, it said. *Don't even think about it.*

Chapter 18

The information Matthew had divulged left Violet feeling uneasy about her meeting with Mr and Mrs Collis. They knew next to nothing about her, but she was now privy to one of their deepest, darkest secrets. That knowledge put her at an advantage, and made her uncomfortable.

As it turned out, she needn't have worried. The couple were relaxed and sociable, and very down-to-earth. Brian kissed Joyce on the cheek as he presented her with the bunch of hellebores. Evidently, the Collises thought the world of one another.

Their cosy kitchen had an AGA, sage-green painted units and a large scrubbed pine table – on which Joyce placed a chintz-patterned vase containing the hellebores. Fuelled by a cup of tea and a slice of Joyce's lemon drizzle cake, Violet set the camera rolling, sat back, and listened as Brian explained how the village had evolved over time. He was articulate and erudite, managing to deliver a concise history of Merrywell in just one take.

'That was a flawless interview,' Violet told him, when it was over. 'I wish everyone was as good as you.'

'When you know your subject inside out, talking about it is easy,' Brian said. 'If there's ever anything you want to know about Merrywell, all you have to do is ask. I'll help if I can.'

* * *

Violet walked back to work feeling ashamed. Mr and Mrs Collis were warm, trusting people who had welcomed her into their home. Would they have been so hospitable if they'd known she'd been poking around, trying to locate the seemingly notorious Helen Slingsby?

Brian and Joyce were her near neighbours, people she'd be living alongside for many years to come. Getting to know them had left her with a pleasing glow of contentment, but the warmth of that feeling had been tainted by a chilling sense of guilt. Matthew shouldn't have needed to tell her not to discuss Helen Slingsby – that should have been a given. When visiting the Collises' home, she should have been focused on one thing, and one thing only: the film. All the other stuff . . . her curiosity about Helen's whereabouts, her latent suspicions that something must have happened, the necklace . . . none of that was relevant to the community project. Quite the opposite.

What she needed to do was reset her thinking and pull herself back into line before she made an irreversible error of judgement. She was living in a village now, and she needed to proceed with caution. London had offered a certain degree of anonymity: her actions had gone largely unnoticed, mainly because no one cared what she did. That wasn't the case here in Merrywell. She could no longer say or do exactly what she liked – not unless she was willing to face the consequences. The anonymously donated plant proved that she had already drawn attention to herself. If she wanted to gain people's trust and – more importantly – avoid hurting anyone, she had to stop raking up the past and learn to 'mind her own business'.

The rain had petered out by the time she re-entered the shopping village, and patches of blue sky were peeking through the retreating clouds. As she let herself into *The Memory Box*, Violet resolved to rein in her curiosity before it was too late. The last thing she wanted was to get a reputation as a nosy parker.

She needed to put aside her questions about Helen, and concentrate instead on finishing the film – making it the best it could possibly be.

Despite her newly adjusted mindset, it wasn't long before Violet's resolve was being well and truly tested. She'd turned her phone off during the interview with Brian but, when she sat down at her desk and switched it on again, a number of alerts popped onto the screen. They were an unwelcome distraction – one that threatened to lure her back into the web of intrigue surrounding Helen Slingsby.

There was a missed call and voicemail from Martha Andrews' number; and a text message from Paul. She opened the text first.

Against my better judgement, I searched the PNC for that name you gave me. Other than the birth details you already had, I found nothing. There's no death record, and no employment record after 1982. I even checked for a change of name or gender. Nothing there either. I agree it's odd. I suggest you get your guy, Nigel, to speak to the police in your neck of the woods.

Violet leaned forward and reread the message, astonished that despite his initial refusal, Paul had come up with the goods. Apart from herself, he was the stubbornest person she knew. He rarely backed down on anything, and the irony of him choosing to do that now wasn't lost on Violet. Twenty-four hours ago, she would have been delighted that he'd done the search. Now, having pledged to extract herself from this whole messy business, she felt conflicted. She was obliged to pass on this information to Nigel – but if she did, she ran the risk of getting drawn back into his search.

Violet dialled her voicemail service next, waiting as a male voice told her, in a clipped, almost robotic tone, that she had *one new message, received today at 11.17 hours.* Then she listened to Martha say: '*Violet, I've been thinking about our conversation the other day. You asked if I knew where Helen might have gone . . . I'm afraid I still don't have a clue about that, but I have remembered something . . . or rather, someone. He worked at the school and left at the same time as Helen. It's possible he might know something. It even crossed my mind that he and Helen could have been . . . you know . . . involved in some way. I've started to make some enquiries, so I should have more information for you soon. Anyway . . . sorry for babbling on . . . I've got to go. There's someone at the door. Call me back when you get this message, or drop in to see me if you're passing.*'

Violet had half a mind to ignore the message – delete it altogether – but that wasn't her style. Snubbing Martha would be both rude and unnecessary. If Violet was going to disentangle herself from the Helen Slingsby mystery, it had to be in a way that was honourable but unequivocal. She would talk to Martha and be honest with her.

Taking a deep breath and telling herself to be firm, she dialled Martha's number. Disappointingly, the call went straight to voicemail. She would have preferred to speak to Martha in person, but if she had to leave a message, then so be it.

'*Hi, Martha,*' she said. '*I got your message. Thanks for the information. I'm sure Nigel will be interested in whatever it is you've remembered. I'm busy with the film at the moment, and I need to concentrate on that . . . so it's probably best if you ring Nigel directly. Hopefully you've got his number, but – if not – let me know and I'll ask him to get in touch with you. Bye for now.*'

With a renewed determination to immerse herself in her work, Violet spent the afternoon editing the day's rushes. The film was shaping up nicely, and a few themes were emerging – mostly around community and a sense of belonging.

If everything went according to schedule, all of the interviews would be in the can by the end of the following week. A few days after that, at the next parish council meeting, Violet planned to show the first draft of the film to the committee. Providing they didn't request too many major changes, the finished film would be completed by the end of the month.

She had also received a couple of email enquiries from other potential customers, including one from a youth charity in Chesterfield.

Violet sat in her tiny workspace, experiencing a warm feeling of contentment. At last, things were beginning to happen. *The Memory Box* was up and running, and her new life was slowly taking shape.

She lifted her head briefly when she heard the faint wail of a siren on the other side of the village, assuming it must be an ambulance. Fleetingly, she wondered who was in need of medical assistance, but in the spirit of minding her own business, she batted the thought aside and pressed on with her work.

Chapter 19

Violet was thinking about paint colours as she walked home. The feature wall in her bedroom was currently rose pink (her least favourite colour), and she was torn between repainting the whole room in white, or changing the feature wall to teal blue (possibly too cold) or pale apricot (warmer, but perhaps a bit twee). By the time she drew level with the White Hart, she had come to the conclusion that wallpaper might be a better option.

As she weighed up the merits of a traditional William Morris design versus a more modern, abstract pattern, Molly Gee came charging out from under the smoking shelter at the side of the pub.

'Have you heard?' she said. 'They've found a body.'

Abandoning all thoughts of wallpaper, Violet sucked in a shocked breath and stood stock-still. 'Body?' she said, her heart thumping beneath her ribcage. 'Whose body?'

Molly stretched out her hands and shrugged. 'All I know is, the police have cordoned off the road down by the school. Someone's posted on Facebook that it's because a body's been found.'

Violet felt a flicker of doubt. Perhaps this was all a mistake, a miscommunication.

'You can't always believe everything you read on social media,' she said.

'I don't,' Molly replied, 'but the person who's posted is my best mate's cousin, and she's really nice. She wouldn't say something like that if it wasn't legit.'

Violet squeezed her fingers together to stop her hands from trembling. If the Facebook claim was true, could the body be that of Helen Slingsby? Had someone finally discovered her remains?

'There's definitely been *some* kind of major incident, because there are four police cars down there,' Molly said. 'Maybe you could go and find out what's happening.'

'Me?' Violet said. 'There's nothing I can do. If the police have blocked off the road, we'll just have to be patient and wait until they release the details.'

'You could go and talk to them,' Molly said. 'Tell them you're the press.'

'But I'm not.'

Molly smiled. 'They won't know that, will they?'

Violet screwed up her nose. 'The police aren't stupid. The whole area will be cordoned off and there'll be an officer on guard. I'd have to show them a press pass, which I haven't got – and even if I had, they wouldn't tell me anything. Their first priority will be to protect the crime scene – if it *is* a crime scene – and get a forensic team in to look for evidence.'

'How do you know all this stuff?' Molly said.

'My ex-husband was . . . is a copper. And I'll tell you something for nothing – he wouldn't let a rubber-necking member of the public within a mile of one of *his* crime scenes.'

Molly rubbed her upper arms. 'I can't believe something like this is happening in Merrywell,' she said. 'The worst thing that's ever happened around here was when a gang of youths set fire to some dustbins.'

Violet's skin prickled and a heaviness settled in her stomach. This certainly wasn't what she'd been expecting from village life.

A young lad waved as he rode past on a bike, and Molly flagged him down to share the unfolding news. Leaving the two of them talking, Violet staggered away on shaking legs, keen to get home.

The first thing she did after letting herself into Greengage Cottage was put the kettle on to make a hot drink. Dinner could wait. The only thing she was hungry for now was the truth.

As she made a pot of Earl Grey, she wondered who to call. Matthew, perhaps? He seemed like the kind of guy who would know what was happening. Then again, he might think she was being ghoulish. He already thought she was inquisitive – there was nothing she could do about that – but she didn't want him tagging her as someone with a morbid fascination for death.

As she nursed her teacup, another idea formed in Violet's mind. Martha Andrews didn't live too far from the school. She might know what had happened.

She called her number and waited. This time, it didn't kick straight in to voicemail. It was answered on the fourth ring – but not by Martha.

'Who is this?' said a male voice.

'Violet Brewster,' she replied. 'Can I have a word with Martha if she's there, please?'

'I'm sorry, that won't be possible. My name's DS Charlie Winterton and I'm at Ms Andrews' house, investigating a crime. Is she a relation of yours?'

Violet experienced a queasy feeling in the pit of her stomach. She hoped nothing had happened to Martha.

'No, she and I aren't related,' she replied, wanting to say that Martha was a friend, but feeling that was too presumptuous. 'I live in the village. She left me a voicemail this morning and I returned her call a couple of hours ago. She didn't answer, so I left a message. As she hasn't rung me back, I thought I'd try again.'

She wasn't going to tell DS Winterton the real reason for calling – to get the lowdown from Martha on whatever it was the police were investigating. Besides, that seemed inappropriate now – if the incident had taken place at Martha's house.

'Whereabouts in the village do you live?' DS Winterton asked.

'On Church Road . . . at Greengage Cottage. It's the one with the green door.'

'And are you at home at the moment?'

'Yes,' Violet said. 'I've just got in from work.'

'Then please stay where you are. I'll send one of my officers round to talk to you.'

In the end, it was DS Winterton himself who knocked on her door. He was tall and out of shape, and in desperate need of a haircut. His face was kind, but considerably older and flabbier than the photo displayed on his warrant card.

Violet invited him to sit down at her kitchen table and poured him a cup of tea. He winced when he drank it.

'What the hell is *that*?' he said.

'Earl Grey. Are you not a fan?'

'I can't say that I am. I'd rather have a proper cup of tea, if you don't mind. Summat like Tetley's or Ringtons or PG Tips.'

'Is Martha OK?' Violet asked, as she poured boiling water over a Ringtons teabag. 'You said you were at her house investigating a crime.'

'I'm afraid Ms Andrews is far from OK,' DS Winterton replied. 'Her body was discovered earlier this afternoon.'

Violet's insides turned to ice.

'Oh, my God,' she said, placing a hand on her chest to quell a sudden wave of nausea.

She put the kettle down and passed the mug of tea to the detective with shaking hands.

'I can't believe it,' she said, as she sat down. 'What happened? I only saw her the other day. I interviewed her for a film I'm making for the community. She was full of life . . . planning her next trip abroad.'

'Sadly, that's a trip she won't be making,' DS Winterton said, as he added a splash of milk to his tea, and stirred in three spoonfuls of sugar.

'How did she die?' Violet asked. 'I'm assuming from the police presence it wasn't natural causes.'

'I'm afraid I can't discuss the details of an ongoing case,' DS Winterton said. 'But what I will say is this . . . we're treating her death as suspicious. We believe Ms Andrews may have disturbed an intruder – but, as I'm sure you'll understand, I'm not at liberty to disclose any further information at this stage in the investigation.'

Violet nodded. 'My ex-husband is a detective with the Met, so I'm familiar with the protocol. I assume you're here because you'd like to listen to the message Martha left on my phone?'

'That's one of the reasons for my visit, yes. I'd also like to know what your connection was to the deceased.'

Violet blinked. 'I wouldn't describe us as connected,' she said. 'As I mentioned a few moments ago, I've been commissioned by the local council to make a community film for the village. Martha was one of the first people I interviewed. But that was the first and only time I met her.'

'But you must have known *of* her. Everybody knows everybody in a place like this, don't they?'

'I only moved to the village three weeks ago,' Violet said. 'Martha and I haven't had time to establish a friendship – although I like to think that would have happened, had we been given the time to get to know one another properly. She was an interesting lady.'

'Interesting how?'

'She'd travelled the world, and she had lots more trips lined up. She told me she'd booked to go to Morocco in a few months. Martha was still very young at heart. I guess she'd had what you'd call a colourful life.'

DS Winterton looked less than impressed. Violet wasn't sure whether it was her description he was unhappy with, or the thought of Martha Andrews living it up.

'May I listen to the message she left for you?' he said.

Violet picked up her phone, turned the volume to maximum, and called her voicemail, playing Martha's message on loudspeaker.

She studied DS Winterton's expression as he listened, but apart from a brief twitch of the lips, his face was inscrutable.

'Thank you,' he said, when the voicemail had finished playing. 'We now know that Ms Andrews was alive at 11.17 a.m. when she left this message. Who is this Helen she refers to?'

Violet took a deep breath and gave him a condensed version of who Helen was, and why she and Martha had talked about her.

'And when did this Helen Slingsby leave the village?' DS Winterton asked.

'In 1982.'

The detective lifted the corner of his top lip. Violet wasn't sure whether he was sneering contemptuously, or doing an Elvis impression. On balance, she thought the latter was unlikely.

'Forty years ago?' DS Winterton gave a huff. 'Nothing to do with what happened to Ms Andrews earlier today, then?'

'Probably not,' Violet said. 'Then again, at this stage, I suppose you can't afford to rule anything out.'

The detective lifted his chin and held out his hand. 'May I?' he said, waiting for Violet to hand over her phone.

She watched him use it to enter a number and send a text.

'I've forwarded a copy of the voicemail audio file to my phone,' he said. 'I'm also going to save my number to your contacts list, just in case you remember anything else that might help the investigation. Please call me if you do.'

'Would you like me to send you a copy of the interview I did with Martha?' Violet said.

'Yes please,' he replied. 'I'll add my email address to your contacts.'

'Do you want the edited version,' Violet said. 'Or the full interview?'

'Send me the whole thing. I'll get one of my officers to view it, see if it contains anything relevant to the case.'

'It was mostly her talking about her younger days,' Violet said. 'I'm not sure how useful it will be in terms of your investigation. The voicemail, on the other hand . . . well, I suppose there are a few things there you'll want to follow up.'

'I hope you're not trying to tell me how to do my job, Ms Brewster.'

Violet gave him her most disarming smile. 'Not at all. And, please, call me Violet.'

DS Winterton cracked a reluctant and slightly crooked smile. 'That's an unusual name for someone your age,' he said. 'I associate it with old ladies. My wife had a great-aunt Violet. She'd be about a hundred and twenty now, if she was still alive.'

Violet laughed. 'It is an old-fashioned name – but violets are my mother's favourite flower. That's why she chose it.'

'I suppose you have to be grateful she isn't a fan of tulips.'

Violet grinned. 'Or chrysanthemums,' she said. 'Imagine that . . . Chrysanthemum Brewster.'

DS Winterton gave a wry smile. 'That would present a challenge for me,' he said, as he handed back her phone. 'Seeing as I'm not the best speller in the world. However, what I am good at, is my job.'

He gave her a hard stare.

'I don't doubt it,' said Violet.

'And yet, here you are, bursting at the seams to make a suggestion.'

Violet widened her eyes in an attempt to look innocent. 'Am I?'

'I expect you think I should follow up on the enquiries Ms Andrews had made about the fella . . . the one who worked at the school?'

'I agree that would be a good idea,' Violet said. 'You must admit it's strange that I can't find any trace of Helen? What if Martha asked questions of the wrong person? Maybe she got them rattled.'

'If you're suggesting her death might be connected in some way to this Helen Slingsby, I think that's extremely unlikely. However, I will get someone to follow up on what Martha Andrews said at the end of her message. *I've got to go. There's someone at the door.* We need to find out who that was.'

'Do you think it could have been her killer?' said Violet.

'Yes,' DS Winterton replied. 'I believe there's a very strong chance it was.'

Chapter 20

By five past nine the following morning, a small crowd had gathered inside the café at the BBC.

'Is there some kind of meeting going on?' said Violet, who was observing the growing throng from the bakery counter.

'Nothing official,' Fiona replied. 'It's more of an informal council of war . . . with Judith Talbot playing the role of general.'

The council leader was standing at the front of the café addressing the people sitting around her. Violet was surprised to see Matthew among them. Molly Gee and Colin Packer were also in attendance and, slightly removed from proceedings, were Nigel and Sandra. Next to them was a young woman called Emily, who Violet knew lived on the same street as Martha.

Sophie was behind the café counter, preparing drinks, although it was obvious from the way she was leaning away from the hiss of the coffee machine that she was listening in to the unfolding conversation.

'Everyone's in shock,' Fiona said, as she handed over Violet's takeaway coffee.

'I know, poor Martha. It's hard to believe something like this has happened in Merrywell. When I moved here, I thought I was coming to a safe, quiet place.'

'You've heard what they're saying then?' said Fiona. 'That Martha's been murdered? The police haven't confirmed anything officially, but that's the rumour.'

Violet shuddered. 'I suspect the rumour mill has got it right this time. One of the detectives came round to my house last night . . . DS Winterton. He wouldn't tell me very much, but he did confirm they're treating Martha's death as suspicious.'

A vertical line appeared between Fiona's eyebrows. 'Why was he talking to you? I hope you're not a suspect.'

Violet shook her head. 'Thankfully not . . . at least, I don't think I am. He came round because Martha called me yesterday and left a voicemail message. The detective wanted to listen to it.'

'What did this message say?'

Violet pulled out her phone and played the voicemail on loudspeaker, keeping the volume low, to make sure it wasn't audible in the café. As she listened, Fiona's eyes filled with tears.

'It's weird, listening to her voice, knowing what's happened,' she said. 'Why was she ringing you about Helen Slingsby? I didn't realise you'd spoken to Martha about her.'

'I only mentioned her in passing, and I had no idea she was going to follow up on what I said. You don't suppose . . .' Violet hesitated, reluctant to put into words the thought that had been niggling at her ever since she heard about Martha's death.

'What?' said Fiona.

'In her message, Martha says she's made some enquiries. What if she asked questions of the wrong person . . . and put herself in danger?'

'You're not seriously suggesting her death could be connected to whatever's happened to Helen Slingsby?'

'Anything's possible,' Violet replied. 'Although, I sincerely hope not, because that would make me responsible for Martha's death.'

'How do you make that one out?' Fiona said, with a shake of her head.

'I've been digging up the past, haven't I? And possibly reigniting old resentments in the process. What if the questions I've been asking have triggered a reaction from someone . . . someone who prefers to let sleeping dogs lie?'

'I think you're jumping to conclusions, Violet.' Fiona frowned sympathetically. 'But even if you're right, whatever's happened to Martha is not your fault. And for pity's sake, don't go saying you feel responsible in front of that detective. He might take it as a confession. Before you know it, he'll be reading you your rights and slapping you in handcuffs.'

Violet mustered a smile. 'This isn't some American TV cop show,' she said. 'That's not how things work in the real world. The police can't go around arresting people unless they've got evidence.'

Fiona scoffed cynically. 'All I'm saying is, be careful what you say. To the police *and* to that lot in there.'

She tilted her head towards the café, where the bevy of residents were now sipping warm beverages and helping themselves from a plate piled high with Danish pastries. Scanning their faces, Violet wondered whether one of them had been responsible for leaving the mind-your-own-business plant.

'Do you think I should go in there? Tell them what I know?'

Fiona rested her chin in her right hand. 'It'll look odd if you *don't* join them, but if I were you, I'd say nothing.'

'Why? It's not like DS Winterton has sworn me to secrecy or anything.'

'I just don't think it's wise to give too much away,' Fiona said. 'And you *definitely* shouldn't tell anyone what Martha said in her voicemail.'

Violet smiled. 'I've already played it to you.'

'Yeah, but you can trust me. Can you honestly say the same about the people in the café?'

'I trust some of them,' Violet said. 'But not all of them. I guess you're right. I'd be wise to tread carefully. Who knows, someone in there might be a killer.'

Chapter 21

The group in the café had decided to drag some of the tables closer together. When Violet walked in, the sound of table legs scraping on the tiled floor set her teeth on edge. Judith was observing from a seated position at the head of the moving bank of tables, watching as more and more residents huddled around her, their faces pale and worried. Violet stood behind a spare chair that was directly opposite Matthew.

'Is it OK if I join you?' she asked, as she sipped the takeaway cappuccino she'd brought with her from the bakery. 'I take it you're meeting to discuss yesterday's incident?'

'Yes, take a seat,' Judith Talbot replied, with an impatient wave of her hand. 'This isn't a formal meeting, merely a gathering of concerned citizens. You've obviously heard the terrible news, about poor Martha?'

Violet nodded. 'What have the police said?'

'Very little,' Judith replied. 'I've spoken to the officer on duty at the scene, and I've let him know I'm happy to be the village spokesperson, should the need arise. I'm concerned the press and television people will descend at some point today. We need to handle the situation carefully, to avoid any adverse publicity.'

'If Martha *has* been murdered, I can guarantee the media will

130

turn up,' said Matthew. 'A situation like this is bound to attract the press. We can't avoid it.'

'Quite so,' Judith said. 'But it needs to be dealt with appropriately so that our reputation as a village doesn't sustain any long-term damage.'

'If there's a murderer on the loose, I'd say that's the least of our worries,' said Colin Packer.

'I agree,' said Matthew. 'And if we are going to nominate someone as a spokesperson for the village, I think Violet would be the ideal person for that role. She has experience of these things, and knows how to handle negative publicity.'

Violet felt a warm, inner glow, flattered that Matthew had nominated her.

Judith, on the other hand, looked less than impressed. 'No disrespect,' she said, puffing out her chest, 'but Violet is a newcomer to Merrywell, and she isn't accustomed to how things work around here. I am a long-standing resident and . . . whilst I don't have Violet's professional experience . . . I believe I know what's best for the village.'

'I agree,' Violet said, eager to pacify Judith and stave off any rivalry. 'I'm more than happy to lend a hand if you want to put together a PR crisis management plan, but Judith should be the voice and face of Merrywell during what is likely to be a testing few days.'

'Do we need to arrange an emergency council meeting?' Colin said. 'Agree on a course of action?'

'That's an excellent idea,' said Judith.

'Perhaps we should hold fire for now,' Matthew said. 'We don't even know whether Martha *was* murdered. What if she died from natural causes?'

Violet bit her lip. She should say *something*, but how could she contribute to the discussion without giving away the details of her conversation with DS Winterton?

'In the case of a sudden death, the situation is usually assessed by the first police officer on the scene,' she said, hoping a general comment about investigative procedures might lead them to the obvious conclusion. 'If there's any possibility the death is suspicious, an investigation team is called in, along with forensic CSIs.'

'That's what I saw yesterday afternoon,' said Emily, speaking from the periphery of the group, her voice barely audible. 'I live directly opposite Martha, so I was able to see everything from my front window.'

Judith rolled her eyes. 'For goodness' sake, Emily. Why didn't you say so earlier?'

'I wasn't sure I should,' Emily replied.

'In the absence of any details from the police, you could be our only source of information,' Judith said. 'Tell us everything you know. Stand up, and please speak up. We want to hear what you have to say.'

Emily got to her feet reluctantly, clearing her throat before describing what she had seen the previous afternoon.

'A police car and an ambulance arrived first . . . that's how I knew something was up. I was in the kitchen at the back when I heard the sirens. I went into the front room to find out what was going on and saw the police car and the paramedics, and then a forensic unit turned up. It was awful, like something you see on the telly. Three people went into the house wearing those white hooded overall thingamajigs, and plastic covers on their feet. I couldn't believe what I was seeing.'

'It does sound as though they're treating Martha's death as suspicious,' Violet said. 'I expect there'll be a post-mortem, and I would imagine the police will conduct door-to-door inquiries today.'

'They've already spoken to me,' Emily said. 'Not that I could tell them anything. I didn't see nothing.'

Violet cringed at the double negative, but what bothered her more than Emily's grammar was that the young woman hadn't spotted anything out of the ordinary.

'You must have seen something,' Judith said, staring at Emily over the top of her glasses.

'No, I didn't,' Emily replied. 'I was in the back garden first thing, then I was in the kitchen, baking. I only went to the front of the house when I heard the sirens.'

'And you didn't see anyone entering Martha's house, other than the emergency services?' said Violet. 'Or anyone hanging around on the lane?'

Emily gave an apologetic shake of the head. 'No, sorry. It's like I told the police. I didn't see nothing.'

'What about CCTV?' said Violet. 'Do you know if any of the houses on your street have security cameras?'

Emily shrugged. 'No, the police asked me that un' all. As far as I know, there's no cameras round where I live. I haven't got one . . . I didn't think I needed one. Mind you, I'll be keeping my doors locked and bolted from now on. Until the police tell us otherwise, I'm going to assume there's a crazed killer on the loose.'

Judith tutted. 'There's no need to overdramatise the situation, Emily. We still don't know the facts, so it's a little premature to be making assumptions. That said, the question of CCTV is an interesting one. It's a subject the parish councillors have been debating for months. We've shied away from installing cameras in the village because of the cost, but this horrific incident proves just how essential they are.'

'Cost isn't the only factor,' said Colin Packer. 'Some of us have concerns about how CCTV would impact on people's privacy. Not everyone wants to have their every movement monitored.'

'Considering what's happened, Colin, I would have thought even you could see the importance of a security system.' Judith's voice was verging on a shriek. 'Surely the safety of residents is more important than their privacy?'

'I'd say both are equally important,' Colin said, tapping his fingers on the table top.

Matthew held up a conciliatory hand. 'Now is not the time to get into this,' he said. 'We can debate the pros and cons of CCTV at the next council meeting. Add it as an item on the next agenda, would you, Molly?'

Molly looked to the head of the table for approval, and Judith nodded her assent.

'The best thing we can do now is go home, or go back to work,' Matthew added. 'If the police *are* conducting door-to-door inquiries, we need to be where they can find us. It's our duty to help in any way we can, but we also need to exercise patience and allow the police to get on with the investigation as they see fit.'

'Matthew's right,' said Judith. 'Let's finish our coffees and go home. And for heaven's sake, if anyone remembers seeing any dodgy-looking characters hanging around, or if you can think of any reason why someone might have wanted to harm Martha, please tell the police. We need them to catch whoever's responsible.'

Violet listened to the clattering of spoons and coffee cups, as one by one, the residents finished their drinks and got up to leave. Nigel and Sandra were among the last to depart.

As they walked out of the café door, Violet made a spur-of-the-moment decision.

'Nigel! Sandra! Can I have a word?'

As she followed the pair into the courtyard, they exchanged a wily look.

'What can I do for you, Violet?' Nigel said.

'I need to talk to you,' she said. 'Let's go over to *The Memory Box*, shall we? It's more private there.'

Nigel and Sandra followed her across the cobbled courtyard, waiting silently while she unlocked the door.

'Have a seat,' Violet said, once they were inside. 'It's cramped in here, but at least there's no one listening in to our conversation.'

Fearing she might come to regret it, she sat at her desk and told them about Martha's voicemail and the visit she'd had from DS Winterton.

'You don't seriously think the attack on Martha has anything to do with me looking for Helen?' Nigel said, the expression on his face wavering between hostility and alarm.

'That's exactly what I'm starting to think,' Violet said. 'And I hinted as much to DS Winterton. I thought I'd better let you know that, because it's possible the police will be in touch to ask some questions. I wanted you to be prepared.'

A deep frown had gathered in the lines on Nigel's forehead and his cheeks had gone red and blotchy. 'What the hell have you done, Violet? It sounds like you've dropped me right in it.'

'Not necessarily,' she said. 'But if I have, I'm sorry.'

'I should think so too. When I asked for your help, I didn't expect you to go blabbing to the police. I don't want them involved.'

Violet folded her arms, pressing them against the guilty ache that had lodged itself in her stomach. 'The last thing I want is to cause you hassle, Nigel, but I had no choice. The voicemail Martha left for me was probably one of the last things she did. It may or may not be significant, but I couldn't *not* tell the police about it.'

'I'm sure Nigel understands that, right enough,' Sandra said. 'But that doesn't mean he has to be happy about it.'

'The thing is Violet, lass, you and I are still getting to know one another,' Nigel said, shuffling forward in his seat. 'And for that reason, perhaps you can be forgiven for not understanding that I like to keep myself to myself. The last thing I want is for all and sundry to be delving into my past. I've decided it's best to give up the search for Helen. It's ancient history, and I'd rather it stays that way.'

Violet had been planning to talk to him again about the necklace and quiz him about the day Helen took Matthew, but now obviously wasn't the right time. Nigel was annoyed, and he was getting agitated.

Sandra placed a soothing hand on his forearm. 'You have to admit, Nigel, there was summat peculiar about the way Helen took off like she did,' she said. 'If Martha's death *does* turn out to be connected, then maybe the police will uncover a lot more than they bargained for.'

'Just leave it, Sandra,' Nigel snapped. 'If the police decide to ask questions, I'll have no choice but to co-operate – and if that happens, I'll answer as honestly and as fully as I can. What I'm not going to do is volunteer information to them. All that stuff that Violet's been talking about . . . it's pure speculation.'

'Is it?' Sandra said. 'I wouldn't be so sure, love. We don't know where Helen is, do we? Violet's right – anything could have happened to her.'

Nigel scowled. 'If Violet wants to feed the police a load of unsubstantiated theories, there's nothing I can do about it,' he said. 'Just don't expect me to back her up.'

'I'm sorry,' Violet said. 'I've obviously upset you.'

'I'm not upset,' he replied. 'I'm annoyed.'

'I hope you understand that I *had* to speak to the police. And who knows, maybe this person Martha had remembered can tell us something. Do you know who she was talking about when she said someone at the school left at the same time as Helen?'

As Nigel opened his mouth to respond, the door flew open, and Judith Talbot flounced into *The Memory Box* (although the lack of space did, thankfully, keep the flouncing to a minimum).

'Violet,' Judith said, 'may I have a word?'

'Of course,' she replied. 'How about if I come over and meet you in the café in five minutes?'

'I'm afraid this is something that can't wait,' Judith said, standing her ground like a soldier on guard, her right hand gripping the strap of her shoulder bag.

Seizing the chance to escape, Nigel stood up and nudged Sandra, prompting her to do the same.

'We were leaving anyway,' he said. 'There you go, Judith. You can have my seat . . . I've even warmed it up for you.'

Pressing her lips together, Judith lowered herself onto the vacated chair.

'Hang on a sec, Nigel . . .' Violet said, exasperated by Judith's rude interruption.

'Sorry, Violet. We'll have to continue our conversation another time,' he said. 'In the meantime, I'll let you know if I hear anything.'

He opened the door, and Sandra followed him out. Judith looked on, her face twitching with unrestrained impatience.

When Nigel and Sandra had gone, Violet leaned back and turned to the councillor.

'I'm running a business here, Judith,' she said, struggling to stay calm. 'I don't appreciate you barging in when I'm in the middle of talking to people. What's so important that it couldn't have waited?'

'Please don't treat me like a fool,' Judith retorted. 'I know what you were talking to Nigel Slingsby about, and it wasn't business.'

Given that Judith's guesswork was spot on, Violet thought it best not to retaliate.

'It's been brought to my attention that you've been making certain enquiries around the village,' Judith continued, glowering like a nineteenth-century schoolmistress. 'When the council commissioned you to make our community film, we did not expect you to go around prying into unrelated matters. You are *supposed* to be asking people about their experiences of living in Merrywell, getting positive news stories from them – not dragging up gossip about Nigel Slingsby's estranged wife.'

Violet opened her mouth to object, but Judith was in full flow.

'Let me finish, Mrs Brewster. You'll get your turn to speak in a minute. I want to make it abundantly clear that . . . going forward . . . I, and the rest of the parish council, will expect you to focus on the job in hand. You need to quash gossip and irrelevant trivia and concentrate on *making the film*. And please bear in mind that if you're unable to complete the project within the agreed timescale, we will consider that a breach of contract and will seek to enforce the penalty clause.'

'Penalty clause?'

'Yes, I'm assuming you've read the contract? If not, I suggest you rectify that as soon as possible. If you don't deliver the film on time, we reserve the right to apply a discount to the agreed fee . . . and the later you are, the bigger that discount will become.'

This was news to Violet. She hadn't spotted anything about a penalty clause when she'd skim-read the small print, and she hadn't had time since to read the contract thoroughly. But it didn't matter, because she had absolutely no intention of missing the project deadline.

'The film will be delivered on time,' she said, her voice polite but firm. 'Everything's on schedule, Judith, so there's nothing for you to worry about. I *always* meet my deadlines. You're right about Nigel asking for my help, but that is a completely separate matter. The questions I've been asking about Helen Slingsby are nothing to do with the film.'

'And yet I hear you've been tagging them on to the end of your interviews,' Judith said. 'You appear to be using the contacts you're making for the film as an "in" . . . to pry into something that is none of your business.'

'That isn't true,' Violet said. 'Most of the information I've gleaned about Helen has been offered voluntarily, without any prompting from me.'

Judith held up a hand. 'This film is supposed to engender a sense of pride and good will within the community,' she said. 'Your questions about Mrs Slingsby are having the opposite effect.'

'Has someone complained about me?' Violet asked, wondering if it was the same person who'd left the plant on her doorstep. 'If they have, I believe I have the right to know who it was.'

'There hasn't been a formal complaint,' Judith said. 'The matter has been drawn to my attention by a concerned individual whose motives are pure and well intentioned. They're worried you're creating the wrong impression among your neighbours. Quite frankly, Mrs Brewster, you're gaining a reputation as a busybody.'

It takes one to know one, thought Violet.

'Are you going to tell me who this "concerned individual" is?'

'No, I'm not,' Judith said. 'They spoke to me in confidence . . . and anyway, their identity is irrelevant. What *is* important here is that you understand the need to focus on your job. Make the film, Violet, and make us proud.'

Having said her piece, Judith stood up, hoicked her bag onto her shoulder, and made her exit. Violet watched her go, fuming inside. She also felt saddened – because it was obvious that someone in the village had snitched to Judith. And apart from Nigel, there were really only two people who knew about her pursuit of Helen Slingsby.

Fiona, and Matthew.

And the thought of either of them betraying her hurt more than she cared to admit.

Chapter 22

Feeling irked after the dressing-down from Judith, Violet switched on her Mac and set to work on the latest batch of edits. She truly didn't need or appreciate Judith Talbot's advice on how to run her life, or her business. What peeved her the most about the councillor's verbal attack was that it had been both unpleasant and unnecessary. She'd already decided to give up her pursuit of Helen Slingsby, having come to the conclusion, independently, that she needed to focus her efforts on the film. Now, thanks to Judith, she was having a change of heart.

The truth was, Violet didn't like domineering people. Whenever someone insisted she do something, she immediately developed a contrary urge to do the opposite. Judith's ban on asking questions about Helen was compelling Violet to do exactly that.

Still boiling with fury, she pressed on with placing the Brian Collis interview into the opening section of the film.

At eleven o'clock, a text arrived from Fiona.

Sounds like the police are making door-to-door inquiries. Several customers have said they've been questioned, although no one seems to know anything. I wonder how the investigation is going? Any chance you could have a word with your detective to find out? xx

Violet rattled off a reply.

He's not MY detective, and I'd rather not get involved.

Fiona's response pinged back thirty seconds later.

I may be way off beam here, but am I right in thinking you're in a grumpy mood? What's up? xx

Had the question come from anyone else, Violet would have ignored it, or responded with a few choice words. But Fiona deserved an honest answer.

Judith Talbot came round earlier to give me a bollocking.

Fiona's short reply arrived within seconds.

What?!? Why!? 😠

The excessive use of question marks and exclamation points in Fiona's message, as well as the angry-face emoticon, suggested outrage on her part – and confirmed the conclusion Violet had already come to: that Fiona wasn't the one who'd complained to Judith.

It would have been a lot easier if she could have rung her friend, instead of exchanging a string of text messages – but Violet knew that Fiona had a strict rule about not taking personal calls while she was working in the bakery.

Someone's told her I've been spending too much time asking questions about Helen Slingsby. She's worried I'm not concentrating on the community film.

It was a couple of minutes before the next, short message came through.

Who told her that?

Violet tapped out a reply.

She wouldn't say, but I suspect it was Matthew Collis. Will tell you more when I see you.

Fiona replied immediately.

Nah! Matthew wouldn't do that. He's one of the good guys.

Fiona had known Matthew for years, so admittedly she was in a better position to make a judgement. But if it wasn't Matthew who'd ratted on her, who was it?

I'm not sure who else it could be. Speak later. I'm coming over at 3 p.m. to interview Sophie in the café.

Fiona's next text put paid to any plans for a catch-up.

Hope the interview with Soph goes well. I won't be around this afternoon. I have a dental appointment. Wish me luck.

Despite immersing herself in her work, Violet couldn't get the confrontation with Judith Talbot out of her mind. She found herself replaying it over and over in her head, furious that she'd been made to feel like a naughty child. Surely, if there was even the remotest chance of a link between the fates of Helen and Martha, Helen's whereabouts was something well worth pursuing.

She flipped the door latch, put the 'closed' sign in the window, and slipped into the back room. After retrieving a pack of Post-it Notes from a drawer, she cleared a space on the wall and, with a mug of tea in one hand and a pen in the other, wrote down a series of questions.

Q1:   Was Martha murdered? When will the police confirm?

Q2:   Is Martha's death connected to Helen Slingsby's disappear-
       ance?

Q3:   Who is the man Martha mentioned in her voicemail? Was
       it a coincidence that he left the school at the same time as
       Helen, or were the two of them in a relationship?

Q4:   Who killed Martha?

Q5:   Did someone kill Helen, or is she still alive?

Q6:   If Helen is dead, was she murdered? If yes, did the same
       person kill Martha?

Violet fixed the yellow sticky notes in a line along the wall and
then stood back, reading through each of the questions again. To
build the next part of her 'murder board', she was going to assume
that the answer to both parts of Q6 was 'yes'. If she was wrong,
and the women's deaths were unrelated, she knew she had little
hope of solving either crime.

Selecting another set of Post-it Notes – blue ones this time
– Violet began to create a list of suspects, although it wasn't
something she was entirely comfortable with. The names she was
about to write down were people she knew, or was starting to get
to know. Could she, in all conscience, list them as suspects and
still look them in the eye?

Tapping her pen against her teeth, she thought about Nigel
Slingsby. In many ways, he was the most unlikely suspect, but
also the most obvious. Violet wrote down his name.

Suspect 1:   Nigel Slingsby

Paul had told her countless times that the majority of murders were committed by someone known to the victim – and spouses were always top of the suspect list. Had Nigel's request for help been a clever ruse? Was his so-called search for his wife a subterfuge? If he was desperate to marry Sandra, the only way he could do that was to divorce Helen or prove she was no longer alive. Perhaps he already knew she was dead, but couldn't say so without incriminating himself.

Violet shivered. Her initial impression of Nigel had been of a thoroughly decent chap. A gentleman. But what if her instincts were wrong? What if Nigel was hiding something?

Violet peeled off another Post-it and wrote down another name.

Suspect 2:   *Sandra Feddingborough*

If it was betting odds she was compiling, rather than a list of suspects, Sandra would be a 100/1 outsider. OK, there was a *slim* chance she could have been involved in Martha Andrews' death – but Helen's? That sounded highly improbable. In 1982, Sandra had been a new mother, living in Merrywell – presumably with her first husband.

Had Sandra and Helen been friends back then? Had Sandra's *husband* known Helen?

Violet realised her imagination was starting to run wild. It would be so easy to jump to the wrong conclusion. After all, what she was playing here was, in effect, an elaborate guessing game.

Common sense told her to screw up the Post-it and throw it away, but in the end, she decided to add a question mark under Sandra's name before placing it on the wall.

She wrote down the next two names reluctantly.

Suspect 3:   *Joyce Collis*

Suspect 4:   *Brian Collis*

The prospect of placing these two names on the wall filled her with shame. Mr and Mrs Collis were kind, gentle people. How would they feel if they knew they were on her suspect list? What would Matthew think?

Even though her gut was telling her it was wrong, Violet fixed Joyce and Brian's names to the wall and stood back. There was no denying they had a motive. Despite expressing forgiveness for what Helen had done, their ongoing reluctance to talk about the incident suggested they still bore a grudge. From what Matthew had told her, the enmity between the Collises and Helen Slingsby had endured long after the event that had caused it in the first place. But whilst Violet couldn't rule out their involvement in Helen's disappearance, she point-blank refused to believe they would harm Martha.

She groaned with frustration. There were so many unanswered questions, so many permutations. *If* Helen Slingsby had come to harm all those years ago (and that was still a big if), any number of people could have been responsible – some of whom were no longer around. According to Brian Collis's book, of the five hundred people who now lived in Merrywell, over two hundred were long-standing residents who had lived in the village for forty years or more.

Lionel Pilkington had been the head teacher at the school and may have worked there at the same time as Helen. And what about Damian Rushcliffe? He was old and frail now, but forty years ago he would have been in his prime. Who was to say he wasn't the mystery man in Helen's life? It would certainly explain how he'd come into possession of the distinctive jewelled pendant – that was a puzzle that definitely merited further investigation.

Violet added their names to the wall.

Suspect 5:   *Lionel Pilkington*

Suspect 6:   *Damian Rushcliffe*

The sheer number of possibilities was overwhelming. Perhaps she'd be better off tearing down the sticky notes, throwing them in the bin, and letting the police crack on with their investigation. If DS Winterton had taken her claims a little more seriously, there would be no need for her to compile a list of suspects at all.

Admittedly, the detective hadn't completely ruled out a connection between Helen's disappearance and Martha's death, but Violet didn't hold out much hope of him vigorously pursuing that line of inquiry.

She fanned through the pad of unused sticky notes before peeling one off.

Suspect 7:   ?_ _ _ _ _ _ _ _ _ _?

Her final suspect was the unnamed man Martha had mentioned in her voicemail. How could Violet glean the information she needed to fill in the blanks? The man had left the school at the same time as Helen, but had he left the village? And if he was still around, had he silenced Martha to keep his secret safe?

And what about that pendant? Why had there been a drawing of a necklace owned by Zelda Rushcliffe in Helen's sketchbook? Violet pulled out her phone and searched for *River Jewels Bakewell* – the shop where Damian claimed he'd bought the unusual piece of jewellery. After forty years, she didn't hold out much hope of the place still existing. Shops came and went and changed hands frequently.

Which is why, when she read the top search result, she punched the air, unable to believe her luck. There it was. *River Jewels*, jewellery store in Bakewell. Not only did it still exist, but it was also open today until five p.m., and the online listing included a telephone number and an address. The location of the shop was even conveniently marked on a map.

Violet glanced at her watch. Never mind what Judith Talbot might say . . . it was time to jump in the car and take a trip to Bakewell.

Chapter 23

Even though the tourist season wasn't yet in full swing, crowds of people were milling around the quaint market town of Bakewell, and a steady flow of traffic was weaving through its main street.

Violet found a space in the car park by the river, and from there walked the short distance to *River Jewels*; it was located on Bridge Street, on the ground floor of an imposing Georgian building. A buzzer sounded as she entered the shop, which was fitted out luxuriously: dark blue carpet, a series of glass-fronted presentation cabinets, and a chandelier hanging from the ceiling. Inside the cabinets, an array of rings, watches, earrings, bracelets and necklaces were displayed under subtle lighting to show them at their sparkling best.

A tall, slightly bored-looking man in his late thirties smiled from behind the counter.

'Can I help you with anything?' he said, as Violet examined a necklace draped artistically on a sprawl of velvet inside one of the cabinets.

She looked up and returned his smile. 'I'd like to speak to Mr Rivers, if that's possible.'

'I'm Martin Rivers,' he said, warily. 'What can I do for you?'

Violet narrowed her eyes. 'You're too young to be the Mr Rivers

I'm looking for,' she said. 'The person I was hoping to speak to would have been working here forty years ago.'

'Ah . . . that would be my father,' Martin Rivers replied. 'He's in the back . . . Can I ask what it is you want to talk to him about? If you're a rep, then it's me you need to speak to. Dad doesn't deal with that side of the business anymore.'

'I'm not here to sell you anything,' said Violet. 'What I'm after is information about a piece of jewellery bought from this shop back in the Eighties.'

She expected him to grill her further, but surprisingly, Martin Rivers swivelled away immediately. Opening a door to a room at the back, he leaned inside.

'Dad, there's someone here to speak to you,' he said.

Seconds later, a grey-haired man emerged. He was slim and wiry, and a full head shorter than his son.

'Hello,' he said, peering over the half-moon spectacles that were perched on the end of his nose. 'I'm Ged Rivers. How can I help?'

'You worked here in the early 1980s?'

'That's right.'

'In that case . . .' Violet smiled at him. 'I was hoping you could tell me something about this.'

Pulling out her phone, she located the photograph she'd taken of Helen's drawing and held it up so that Ged Rivers could see it. His eyes widened as he stared at the screen.

'One of my neighbours bought a necklace like this from you back in 1983,' she said. 'I'm hoping you can tell me about it.'

Ged Rivers rocked his head ambiguously.

'I've sold thousands of items of jewellery over the years,' he said. 'You can't expect me to remember them all.'

'Take a closer look,' Violet said, holding her phone out to him. 'It's a very distinctive design, and it would have been something you made yourself.'

Instead of inspecting the image again, Ged Rivers took a step back and folded his arms.

'I used to make a lot of bespoke pieces, but there's not much call for that sort of stuff now.'

'We're more of a jewellery retailer these days,' Martin Rivers chipped in. 'Although we do still offer a repair service, don't we, Dad?'

His father nodded uneasily.

'The piece of jewellery I'm talking about was stunning,' Violet said, hoping to flatter its creator into an admission. 'Almost a work of art. I'd certainly remember if it was something I'd made.'

'Sorry.' He unfolded his arms. 'I can't help you.'

Violet was certain he'd recognised the pendant, so why wasn't he being honest with her? What was he hiding?

She put her phone away and decided on a less confrontational approach. 'Look, I'm not here to complain or cause trouble. All I'm after is information. I'm trying to find someone who left Derbyshire a long time ago, and it's possible this necklace could help me work out what became of her.'

Ged Rivers remained close-lipped.

'Please,' Violet added. 'I don't like bothering you, but this is important. If you do know anything . . . anything at all . . . I'd really appreciate you sharing it with me.'

He stared at her, silent and contemplative. Then, finally, he nodded.

'OK,' he said, grudgingly. 'But you'd better come into the back. Someone could wander in at any moment . . . This is not a conversation I want to have in front of customers.'

Intrigued, Violet followed him into the room behind the counter, which was obviously used as a workshop. It was windowless, but two spotlights illuminated a desk in the corner, where a selection of tools and a jeweller's loop awaited Ged Rivers' return.

'I'd rather Martin didn't hear what I'm about to tell you either,' he said, as he closed the door on his son.

Violet felt a flutter of expectation. Was she about to solve the Helen Slingsby mystery?

'I am familiar with the design you showed me,' Ged Rivers said. 'A woman brought it to me many years ago, not long after I took over the shop.'

'Do you recall her name?'

'Yes.' He sighed. 'Ordinarily, I wouldn't remember a customer from forty years ago, but this transaction was unusual, which is why her name is etched into my memory banks. She was called Helen Slingsby.'

Violet's heart was racing. 'In what way was the transaction with Helen unusual?'

The jeweller held up a hand. 'Before I say any more, perhaps you'd care to tell me who you are, and why you're asking me these questions.'

'I'm a friend . . . of Helen Slingsby's husband. He's trying to track her down and he asked me to help. That's all there is to it. I'm not here to catch you out. I'm simply gathering any information that could point to where she went to. So, please, tell me why the transaction with Helen was so unusual.'

He stared for a moment, as if weighing up how much to say. 'It's probably best if I give you the full story,' he said, eventually. 'Then all will become clear.'

He sat down before continuing. 'It started when she came into my shop with a drawing, and a couple of pieces of jewellery she'd inherited from an aunt: a sapphire and diamond cluster brooch, and a large Victorian-style ruby ring – both set in platinum. They were good pieces with quality gemstones, but Helen Slingsby thought they were old-fashioned. She said she wanted a pendant instead.'

'So, she sold you the brooch and the ring?'

'No, she wanted me to use the stones and the platinum to create something more aesthetically pleasing, made to her own design. When she said that, I assumed she was going to present me with a drawing of something contemporary – maybe even quirky – but what she gave me . . . *that* drawing . . .' He paused and pointed towards the phone in Violet's pocket. 'It was like something straight from the art nouveau period. Lots of flowing lines and curves.'

'And you agreed to make it for her?'

'Of course. My business was struggling at the time. I was willing to take on any job, large or small. Normally, when someone commissioned a piece of bespoke jewellery, I would ask for a fairly substantial deposit in case they didn't turn up to collect it. However, in Mrs Slingsby's case, I didn't ask for a down payment.'

'Why not?'

'I didn't think it was necessary. She was leaving the two pieces of jewellery with me as collateral, and they would also provide the materials needed to make the new pendant, so I didn't have to buy in any stones or metal. We agreed on a fee for my work, and she said she'd collect the finished pendant four weeks later.'

'But she never came back?'

'Oh, she came back all right. The problem was, she turned up a week early, and the pendant wasn't ready. She was really annoyed . . . quite irate, in fact . . . wanted to know what the hell I was playing at, and what was taking me so long.'

'That was rather unfair if she'd arrived a week too soon,' said Violet. 'Did she give any reason for turning up early?'

'Apparently, she was going away. Leaving the area. In the end, she demanded that I post the pendant on to her, when it was finished. To be frank, I wasn't too enamoured with the idea. Sending jewellery through the Royal Mail is fraught with difficulty.'

Violet felt a frisson of excitement. 'Did she leave a forwarding address with you?'

Ged Rivers pulled a face. 'No, she wasn't certain where she was going. She said she'd be in touch once she'd found somewhere to live. Surprisingly, she even paid my fee up front, in cash, so she was obviously desperate to get her hands on the pendant. I think it must have meant something to her . . . sentimental value, you know?'

'So, what happened next?'

'Nothing.' He shrugged. 'I finished the pendant the following week, and put it in the safe until I heard from her. A few weeks rolled by, then a few months . . . but she didn't contact me.'

'Did you make any attempt to get in touch with her?' Violet asked.

'Yes, although I probably didn't try as hard as I should have done. When she commissioned the piece, she left a telephone number, and I rang it as soon as the pendant was ready to collect. Turns out it was the number for Merrywell School. I was told that Helen Slingsby didn't work there anymore and the school didn't have a forwarding address for her. As I had no other way of getting hold of her, I left the pendant in the safe and waited for her to contact me.'

'But she never did?'

'No.'

'Didn't you think that was odd?' Violet said. 'The pendant was hers . . . a valuable piece of jewellery that she'd paid for in full. More importantly, it sounds as if it had sentimental value. It was a keepsake, a reminder of her aunt. You must have thought it strange that she didn't get back in touch.'

His jaw tightened. 'I didn't know what to think,' he said, shifting his position on the stool. 'Though I'll admit I was surprised. It was an unusual situation, but one I could do nothing about. There were no mobile phones back then . . . no email. I had no way of contacting her.'

'So, what happened to the pendant?'

Ged Rivers lowered his eyelids. 'I sold it,' he said. 'Not straight away. I kept it for in the safe for a year, half expecting her to turn up and claim it – but by 1983, things weren't going well for me. The country was in an economic slump, and buying jewellery was low on most people's agendas. I was a young man at the time, not long married with a kid on the way, and I'd put everything I had into buying this shop. I was barely keeping my head above water, and there were bills that were overdue. One day, I got a final reminder to pay the annual business rates. It was a case of pay up, or go out of business. I couldn't afford to leave something as valuable as the pendant sitting in my safe. I had no option but to sell it.'

'I understand,' Violet said, smiling sympathetically. 'I would probably have made the same decision.'

Ged Rivers puffed up his cheeks and gave a relieved sigh.

'Tell me about the person who bought the pendant,' Violet said.

'He was a nice chap. He came in looking for a twenty-fifth wedding anniversary present for his wife, but he didn't like any of the silver jewellery I showed him. He said he wanted something a bit more expensive . . . better quality. So I showed him the pendant. It was platinum, of course, not silver, but it was silver-coloured with beautiful stones. He baulked a bit at the price, but I could tell straight away that he liked it, and he said his wife was worth it.'

It was reassuring to hear that the jeweller's version of events tallied with what Damian Rushcliffe had told her.

'Did you reveal anything about the history of the pendant when you sold it?' Violet said.

'Not likely. I was just glad to get it off my hands and put some money in the till. If I'd said anything, it might have jeopardised the sale.'

'And that was the end of it?' Violet asked. 'There's not an unexpected twist to this story, is there?'

'No, there's nothing else to tell. I sold the pendant, used the money to pay my rates, and somehow managed to cling on by my fingernails until business picked up again. I'll admit I was on edge for a while, wondering if Helen Slingsby would suddenly get in touch, asking for her pendant – but as the months rolled by, I worried less and less. Eventually, I put the whole thing out of my mind. I'd pretty much forgotten about it until you showed up with that drawing. Seeing it gave me quite a turn.'

'I'm sorry about that,' Violet said. 'That wasn't my intention. Like I said, all I wanted was to find out what had happened. I appreciate you taking the time to talk to me.'

'I'm not sure if anything I've said will help you, but if you do manage to track down Helen Slingsby, please tell her I'd have sent the pendant on if I'd known where she was.'

'If I do find her, I'll be sure to let her know.'

Violet spoke confidently, reassuringly, but now, more than ever, she was convinced that the chances of finding Helen Slingsby alive were almost non-existent.

Chapter 24

The next morning, she began to review the footage from her interview with Sophie Nash, which had been filmed shortly after the thought-provoking visit to *River Jewels*. As she worked, Violet replayed the conversation with Ged Rivers in her head. It had confirmed what she already believed to be true: that something untoward had happened to Helen – either before she left Merrywell, or immediately after.

Helen's failure to return for the pendant, or arrange for it to be sent on, strongly suggested she had fallen prey to tragedy or disaster. The necklace would have been of enormous value to Helen, both financially and sentimentally. Surely, she would have done everything within her power to claim something that precious.

At ten o'clock, Violet's deliberations were interrupted by an email from Lionel Pilkington. In it was a link that provided access to his digital archive of photographs.

She scanned the online folders, which were extremely well organised, labelled according to subject, with the images within each folder saved in date order.

She opened up a folder called *Merrywell School*, and perused the numerous thumbnail images it contained. She clicked on an image file called *SchoolExterior1921.jpg*, and zoomed in to study the architectural features of the school, which had been built in the Victorian era. Its large classroom windows were typical of the period, designed to let in plenty of light, but positioned high up enough to stop pupils staring out of the window instead of concentrating on their lessons.

Violet opened another file. This one was an interior black-and-white shot taken during the early days of the school. Rows of unsmiling children sat on long, narrow benches, wooden-framed slates on the desks in front of them. The girls wore white aprons and the boys had short trousers.

She examined a batch of photographs from the 1940s, trying (unsuccessfully) to pick out Damian Rushcliffe among a sea of faces. One photo showed the children wearing their gas masks – presumably during some kind of drill – and there were a few shots of the air raid shelter that Damian had mentioned.

Violet moved on to the images from the 1980s. Surprisingly, there were fewer from this era, but one staff photo did catch her eye. She recognised Lionel Pilkington, sitting centre front, and behind him was a younger Martha Andrews. On the far right of the shot was an unsmiling brunette who could only be Helen Slingsby.

Violet scrutinised the male faces in the photograph. Apart from Lionel, there were only three other men: an older guy, with thinning hair and a trimmed beard; another younger man who was standing to one side with his hands in his pockets; and a middle-aged man on the back row. Could one of these be the person Martha had referred to?

The thumbnail image was low resolution, but good enough to allow Violet to take a screenshot and save it to her desktop.

Next, she reopened Lionel Pilkington's email, which had a sign-off that included his phone number.

He answered almost immediately.

'Lionel, it's Violet. I got your email and the link to the photo files, thank you. I've not had the chance to study them all properly, but the few I have browsed through look great. I really appreciate you giving me access to the collection.'

'You're very welcome,' Lionel said. 'I'll arrange download links to the high-resolution images once you've decided which ones to use.'

Violet paused, unsure how to steer the conversation in the direction she wanted it to go.

'I take it you've heard about Martha Andrews?' Lionel said, giving Violet the opening she needed. 'Terrible business. Terrible.'

'Yes, it's come as a shock to a lot of people. I only met Martha once, but she was a very interesting person, and so full of energy. You must have known her well . . . with her being a teacher at the school.'

Lionel hemmed a little. 'Yes, she was what you might call a "personality". Martha had strong views, and she knew how to make them known. But you're right, she was an interesting woman . . . and very well travelled.'

'She mentioned there was someone at the school who left in 1982, around the same time that Helen Slingsby resigned.'

There was a slight pause before he answered. 'Why on earth would she tell you that?'

Violet squirmed, aware that, as a parish councillor, Lionel was in regular contact with Judith.

'I told her that Nigel Slingsby was trying to track down his wife,' she said. 'Martha remembered there was a guy at the school . . . and she wondered whether his departure in 1982 might have had something to do with Helen leaving. Martha didn't tell me his name, and I wondered if you might remember.'

Lionel gave a loud huff. 'I'm sorry, my dear, but you're asking me to cast my mind back to something that happened four decades ago. Obviously, I remember Helen leaving, mainly because it was all so sudden . . . The damned woman only gave a few days' notice. As for anyone else leaving at the same time . . . I really can't recall, but we did have quite a turnover of staff back then. It was hard keeping track of everyone.'

'That's a shame,' Violet said, disappointed that Lionel was unable to supply the name she was after.

'Since I retired, I've forgotten most of my old colleagues,' Lionel explained. 'When you're working with people day in, day out, they're a part of your life . . . but once you leave that life behind, their names become less important and they slowly fade from your memory.'

'What year did you retire?' Violet asked.

'In 2008,' Lionel replied. 'I was only sixty but, by then, I'd had enough. The teaching profession had changed beyond all recognition compared to the early days of my career. As for being a head teacher – and note my use of the word head teacher, rather than head*master*, which I gather is no longer considered PC – well . . . the role had become that of a business manager. I went into teaching to make a difference . . . to help shape young lives. I certainly didn't expect to end my career as a glorified accountant.'

'My daughter considered becoming a maths teacher,' Violet said. 'She even did a short placement at a school, but in the end she decided it wasn't for her. *Too much hassle* was how she put it. She's now working for a financial services company and loving every minute of it.'

'Good for her,' Lionel said. 'Now, if you'll excuse me, I need to go and check on Irene.'

It was only after he'd ended the call that Violet remembered the staff photograph she'd found in the *Merrywell School* folder. Seeing the faces of his old team might jog Lionel's memory. She sent the image to her phone, ready to send it on to Lionel – but as she composed a text, she had second thoughts. Lionel was a councillor: she couldn't run the risk of him saying something to Judith Talbot.

She remained totally committed to learning the name of the mystery man, but after the telling-off she'd received from Judith, she would have to be more circumspect about how she uncovered that information.

* * *

158

She was due to meet the current head teacher of Merrywell Primary School at two-fifteen that afternoon.

Rebecca Meads greeted Violet with a warm, firm handshake and a wide smile. Despite holding the top job at the school, Rebecca's office was tiny, but it was bright and cheerful, and remarkably tidy.

Rebecca was in her late thirties. She was bubbly and energetic, and exuded positive vibes. Violet thought the school was lucky to have her.

'Please, call me Becky,' she said. 'I've heard all about this film you're making, and it sounds fab.'

'Thank you,' Violet replied. 'It's shaping up nicely, but if I can include the views of some of your pupils, that would make it extra special.'

'That's good to know,' Becky said. 'In a project like this, age diversity is important.'

'I agree,' Violet said. 'In twenty years' time, the children you teach here will be Merrywell's adults. Their views are important.'

'Absolutely. Which is why I'm pleased to report that the parents are on board,' Becky said. 'I sent a message out a couple of days ago to explain the project, and I've already had loads of signed permission slips back. The response has been phenomenal . . . getting parents to return forms is usually like pulling teeth.'

'I have to confess, I was hopeless at returning stuff like that when my daughter was at school,' Violet said. 'Amelia had this habit of stuffing things into her backpack and forgetting about them, and then she'd present something to me at the last minute.'

Becky laughed. 'Thankfully, permission slips are sent electronically these days. For your project, the replies have come back really quickly. Both the children and their parents are keen as mustard to get involved.'

'Shall you and I look at our diaries then?' Violet said. 'That way we can agree a day for filming, and I'll talk you through what I'll need.'

After fixing a date, they discussed where to do the filming, and how best to engage with the children. Providing the weather was good, Violet would capture some general footage outside in the playground, and Becky promised to set up a quiet area in the assembly hall, where the children could be interviewed in small groups.

With the details agreed, Violet stood up and shook Becky's hand once more. As she turned to leave, she decided to chance her arm.

'This is a long shot,' she said. 'But I'm trying to discover the name of someone who worked here forty years ago. He left in 1982, around the same time as another member of staff . . . one of the teachers – Helen Slingsby.'

'We do keep records, but unfortunately, they don't go back that far,' Becky said. 'Even if they did, I'm not sure I'd be able to give you any information . . . data protection, and all that.'

Violet held up her hands. 'I understand. Like I say, it was a long shot.'

'You could speak to Mr Pilkington. He would have been the head back then, and he still lives in the village. He might recall whoever it is you're looking for.'

'I've already spoken to Lionel,' Violet said. 'Unfortunately, he couldn't remember.'

Becky shrugged. 'I don't know what else to suggest. Sorry.'

'Don't be,' Violet said. 'You've been more than helpful. I look forward to visiting next week and talking to some of your pupils.'

There was a dearth of goodies in the bakery when Violet called in at three-thirty.

'Please tell me you have some muffins left.'

''Fraid not,' Fiona replied. 'I sold the last one half an hour ago, but there'll be a fresh batch waiting in the morning . . . and I'll be trying out a new flavour: raspberry and white chocolate.'

'Sounds divine, but I can't wait until then. I skipped lunch, so I need something now.'

'I could make you a sandwich, or there are some Chelsea buns and flapjack slices left. Or I've got one last piece of millionaire's shortbread, if you fancy that?'

'Go on, then,' Violet said. 'It'll be nice to feel like a millionaire for a few minutes. And can I have a cappuccino to go with it, please?'

'Have you heard any more about the police investigation?' Fiona asked, as she made the coffee.

'No, but I was over at the school this afternoon, which meant going past the end of Martha's road. I couldn't see an officer on duty at the house, so the police must have handed back the scene.'

'Does that mean the investigation's over?'

'I doubt it,' Violet said. 'I'm going to watch the local news tonight. Hopefully, there'll be some kind of update or even a press conference. It's about time they told us something.'

'What were you doing at the school?' Fiona said, as she pressed a lid onto the coffee.

'Arranging a day for filming. I'm keen to get some of the kids involved with the project, and the head teacher was really helpful.'

'Becky's lovely,' Fiona agreed. 'She lives in Derby, so she's not local, but we can't hold that against her.'

Violet laughed. 'I thought she might be able to help me with a touch of sleuthing, but it wasn't to be.'

Fiona narrowed her eyes. 'What are you trying to find out this time?'

'The name of the man who worked at the school . . . you know, the one Martha mentioned in her voicemail. I've asked Lionel Pilkington, but he couldn't remember.'

'Have you spoken to Lesley Gilman?' said Fiona.

'No. Who's she?'

'The widow of George Gilman. He used to be the village doctor.'

'And does she live in Merrywell?'

'She does. Her house is that big old place out beyond the church . . . the one with the wrought-iron gates . . . set back from the road?'

'I know it,' Violet said.

'Lesley's got a memory like an elephant. She remembers everyone. I'd say she's the person to ask about your mystery man.'

162

Chapter 25

After she'd polished off her millionaire's shortbread, and before she'd had time to talk herself out of it, Violet set off to visit Lesley Gilman.

Her house was about a hundred and fifty yards from the church, the last property on the lane that led out towards the local farm and open fields. It was a secluded kind of place, set in an acre or so of land, behind a tall hedge and double-wide gates.

The woman who answered the door was wearing a prim buttoned-up cardigan and a tweedy calf-length skirt, and she had a beautiful blue Persian cat draped over her shoulder.

'Come in,' Lesley said, when Violet had introduced herself. 'I was in the middle of grooming Misty, but that can wait.'

She placed the cat on the floor and it shot off, looking relieved to have made its escape.

'She hates being combed,' Lesley said. 'I tell her it's for her own good, but I don't think she believes me.'

They followed the same route the cat had taken, into a small parlour at the rear of the house. It had a beamed ceiling and tiny windows that let in very little light – but the room was cosily furnished and, even though the fire wasn't lit, a pleasant hint of wood smoke lingered in the air.

Violet sat down and explained the reason for her visit. She also pulled out her phone and showed Lesley the school staff photograph, in case it helped to jog her memory.

'It was this chappy here that left shortly after Helen did,' Lesley said, pointing to the young man standing at the side of the group, his hands in his pockets. 'He was the school caretaker for a while. A Scottish man. Now . . . what was his name? Give me a minute.'

She placed her hands either side of her temples and stared down at the carpet. Violet crossed her fingers, hoping the woman's elephantine memory wouldn't let her down.

'Duncan.' Lesley lifted her head and clicked her fingers. 'Duncan Kirkwood. He didn't stick around for long . . . got himself a job on the oil rigs, and cleared off pretty sharpish. He'd worked on the rigs before I think, and he was keen to get back.'

'What made him come to Merrywell in the first place?'

'I believe there was a woman involved. She lived in Matlock, and Duncan had met her on holiday in Blackpool, or some such place. From what I heard, the romance fizzled out fairly quickly, and Duncan decided to go back to Scotland. He only worked at the school for a few months . . . four or five at the most.'

'Would he have worked closely with Helen Slingsby?'

'I'd imagine they would have spoken on a daily basis, so they must have known each other reasonably well. In those days, the caretaker was a jack-of-all-trades, expected to turn his hand to almost anything. Duncan would have been responsible for all sorts: buildings maintenance, security, window cleaning, the upkeep of the playing fields. Back then, the job came with a little cottage next to the school. I shouldn't imagine the pay was very good but, if nothing else, it meant he had somewhere to live . . . which was a blessing, seeing as his relationship with the Matlock woman didn't work out.'

'This may sound like an odd question,' Violet said, 'but is it possible Duncan Kirkwood could have been in a relationship with Helen Slingsby?'

'Relationship? Oh goodness me, no.' Lesley wafted the idea away with her right hand. 'The man was rude and unfriendly, and rather uncouth. In stark contrast, Helen tried to come across as refined and sophisticated. She was always looking for ways to improve herself. Duncan Kirkwood was an odd bod. It wouldn't have been him she was having an affair with.'

'Are you sure?' said Violet. 'They do say opposites attract.'

'Trust me, Helen would *not* have been attracted to Duncan, and vice versa. And, he was about ten years younger than her. Not Helen's sort at all.'

'And yet, just now, you said *it wouldn't have been* him *she was having an affair with*. Forgive me if I'm wrong, but that sounds as if you think she *was* having an affair with someone.'

Lesley hesitated, appearing to be in two minds about how to respond. When the cat reappeared, tail in the air, she played for time by scooping it up and putting it on her knee.

'I'm certain Helen was seeing someone,' she said, as she stroked the space between the cat's ears.

'Do you know who it was?'

'No, but even if I did, I'm not sure I'd tell you. The fact is . . . I shouldn't be speaking about this at all.'

'Why not?' said Violet.

'Because the only reason I know Helen was having an affair is because my husband mentioned something . . . in confidence.'

'Are you willing to tell me what that was?' Violet asked, hoping that Lesley wouldn't retreat into silence.

The cat sat down, purring loudly as it kneaded Lesley's skirt.

'I don't think I should. My husband . . . George . . . he shouldn't even have told *me* about it. I assume you've heard of doctor-patient confidentiality?'

Violet nodded.

'George and I were married for forty-five years – so it goes without saying, he trusted me implicitly, but even so . . . he rarely talked about his patients. Occasionally he'd let something slip inadvertently, which is how I got to know about Helen Slingsby. Afterwards, he swore me to secrecy, and I'm reluctant to break that promise.'

'I understand,' Violet said, smiling reassuringly. 'It's unfair of me to ask. If your husband were still alive, I expect he'd be honour-bound to keep Helen's medical records confidential, even though forty years have passed.'

'He would,' Lesley said. 'But forty years is a long time, and if – as you suspect – Martha's death *could* be linked to Helen's disappearance, there's a lot more at stake here than my husband's professional reputation.'

'I have to be totally honest with you,' said Violet. 'I have no conclusive evidence to back up my suspicions. All I have is supposition and a gut feeling.'

'Then I would say you have good instincts. And given your lack of evidence, I feel it's my duty to tell you what I know. What harm can it do after all this time? Who knows, it might even give you the proof you've been looking for, albeit circumstantial.'

Violet leaned forward, listening intently as Lesley drew in a long breath and began to talk.

'I was astonished at how suddenly Helen left the village,' she began. 'I thought it rude of her not to say goodbye to anyone, and I said as much to George. He told me he was anything *but* surprised.'

'What did he mean by that?' Violet asked.

'He wouldn't tell me at first, but when I pressed him, he said that Helen had been to see him the week before she left Merrywell. She was pregnant.'

Violet sat up straight. 'Pregnant?' she said, recalling what Matthew had said about Helen and Nigel being unable to conceive. 'Someone told me that Helen couldn't have children. How could she be pregnant?'

'I asked the same question,' Lesley said. 'Years before she left the village, Helen had done something awful . . . and that incident led me to the same assumption that you've made – that Helen was unable to have children.'

'You're referring to when she stole a baby?'

Lesley looked surprised. 'You know about that?'

'Someone in the village mentioned it,' Violet said, deciding not to reveal that she knew the identity of the baby. 'There were rumours at the time, apparently.'

'Poor Helen,' Lesley said, her voice soft and sympathetic. 'She was very depressed when it happened. She'd found out that she and Nigel would never have children. I presumed it was *her* that was unable to conceive. It was only later, after Helen became pregnant, that George explained that Nigel was the one who was infertile.'

'So, when Helen came to your husband to confirm her pregnancy, George would have known that Nigel couldn't possibly have been the father.'

Lesley nodded. 'When Helen left Merrywell, George assumed she'd run off with whoever was the father of her child. Or gone away to have the baby on her own.'

'Did Nigel know she was pregnant?'

'I've no idea,' Lesley said. 'I doubt it. Neither George nor I ever spoke to him about it. But . . . if Helen did tell him, I'd imagine Nigel would have been deeply hurt and utterly crushed.'

Or angry, Violet thought. Angry enough to lash out? To kill?

'There's something else that struck me as odd after Helen left,' Lesley said. 'Usually, when someone moves away from the area, they register with a different surgery and their new GP arranges the transfer of the patient's health record. I believe it's all done electronically these days, but back then, those kind of requests were received either by telephone or in writing – but George said that no one ever got in touch to ask for Helen's medical notes. I thought that was strange, especially as she was pregnant. You'd think she would have made registering with a new doctor a priority.'

167

'You would indeed,' Violet agreed.

These further snippets of information were vital pieces in the puzzle. On their own, they meant nothing, but when you put them alongside other indicators – such as Helen failing to claim her pendant – a picture was forming . . . or, at least, part of one. As yet, there was no irrefutable evidence, but everything Violet had learned so far pointed to one obvious conclusion: that Helen had vanished into thin air.

Chapter 26

That evening, after dinner, Violet stretched out on her powder-blue sofa and admired her new living room. A vast rug covered the pale flagstone floor, and several large paintings hung on the white walls. It was a comfortable, traditional room, with a modern twist. The décor was bright and light and uplifting, and there was a cosy fire flickering in the log burner.

Smiling happily, she plumped up a cushion and slid it into the small of her back. Pulling her MacBook onto her knee, she began to search online for Duncan Kirkwood.

There were dozens of people with that name on social media, but she didn't think any of them were the Duncan Kirkwood she was looking for. Based on what Lesley had said, he would have been around twenty-five in 1982, so next she looked on the births, deaths and marriages records for someone born in 1957 +/- three years. That produced a whole rash of results, but by then, Violet's energy and enthusiasm were beginning to flag. If Lesley's theory was correct, and Duncan was *not* Helen's lover, there seemed little point in continuing to search for him.

But if Duncan Kirkwood was out of the picture, then who *was* Helen having an affair with? Her pregnancy was proof positive that she had been in a relationship with someone, even if only casually.

The more Violet cogitated on the information Lesley had disclosed, the more convinced she was that Nigel Slingsby's name should go to the top of her list of suspects. If Nigel had found out about Helen's betrayal, he could have been jealous or angry. Would he also have wanted revenge?

At half past six, she turned on the television and listened to the news. Ten minutes into the programme there was a short report about Martha Andrews.

'Derbyshire Police's serious crimes unit is investigating the death of an eighty-three-year-old woman in Merrywell. The body of Martha Andrews was discovered on Tuesday afternoon by a courier who was making a delivery to the property. Police are appealing to anyone who was in the vicinity of School Lane that day between the hours of eleven a.m. and four p.m. If you noticed anything suspicious or have any information that could help the investigation, please get in touch with the police on 101 or through Derbyshire police force's social media channels.'

As far as Violet was concerned, the brief news item had only provided one new piece of information: that it was a delivery driver who had discovered Martha's body. That in itself was surprising. If there was no answer, deliveries were usually rescheduled. Had the courier spotted something through the glass panel in Martha's front door? Had she been lying in the hallway when the police found her body?

Violet was desperately hoping the news appeal would be successful. Surely someone would come forward with information? It was virtually impossible to go anywhere unnoticed in Merrywell, although admittedly School Lane was in a quiet part of the village. There was little passing traffic along there, except in the mornings and late afternoons, when children were dropped off or picked up from school.

Violet thought back to what she'd been doing between eleven a.m. and four p.m. on the day that Martha died. She'd been at the Collises' until eleven-forty-five, and hadn't noticed anything suspicious as she'd walked back to the shopping village. She'd spent the rest of the afternoon cooped up in *The Memory Box*, working at her desk. It had been around five-thirty when she'd set off for home, by which time, Martha's body had already been discovered. There was nothing she could contribute to the ongoing murder investigation in the way of eyewitness testimony.

What she could do, was keep banging the Helen Slingsby drum. She would tell DS Winterton what she had learned from Ged Rivers and Lesley Gilman. If the detective was seriously considering a link between the recent murder and Helen Slingsby's disappearance, the information should be of interest to him. But what were the chances? Charlie Winterton was more likely to harrumph loudly, or tell her not to waste police time. Even so, Violet felt duty-bound to let him know what she had uncovered.

It was almost seven o'clock, and although she didn't like ringing so late, she assumed that DS Winterton and his team would be sitting by their phones, awaiting calls following the televised appeal.

Violet was keen to pass on the information about Helen Slingsby's pregnancy and her failure to send for her pendant. She would also give DS Winterton Duncan Kirkwood's name. With any luck, he would agree to do a proper search for the ex-caretaker, using his national insurance number or whatever methods the police used to find people these days.

'Hello, it's Violet Brewster,' she said, when the detective answered the call. 'I realise it's late. I hope I'm not disturbing you.'

'No, I'm still at work, and will be for a good while yet,' DS Winterton said. 'Normally at this time of day, I'd be at home, having dinner with my lovely wife. As it is, my missus will have to clingfilm my shepherd's pie, so I can heat it up at whatever ungodly hour I get home.'

Violet knew all about the working life of a detective. The long, unsociable hours had been an aggravating factor in her divorce from Paul, but as DS Winterton appeared to be happily married, she decided not to mention that. Instead, she told him what she'd learned since their last conversation, praying he wouldn't dismiss the information out of hand.

'Thank you for letting me know,' he said. 'Although I'm not sure how any of this helps with the case I'm working on at the moment. I realise *you're* convinced of a link between the fate of Helen Slingsby and Martha Andrews' death, but I'm not sold on the idea. I just can't see the connection.'

Violet suppressed a sigh. DS Winterton was proving to be a tough nut to crack.

'Is Martha's death being treated as a murder investigation?' she asked.

'It's a suspicious death,' DS Winterton said. 'Until we get the results of the post-mortem, we don't know for certain what we're dealing with. Our guess is that Ms Andrews struggled with an intruder who entered the property to commit burglary.'

'Was anything stolen from her house?'

'Mrs Brewster . . . I really can't discuss—'

'Because if it wasn't, how do you know this so-called intruder was a thief? What if they entered Martha's cottage with the sole intention of killing her?'

'When disturbed, it's not unusual for a burglar to flee the scene empty-handed, especially if they've inflicted violence on the homeowner.'

'Were there any signs of forced entry?' Violet asked.

'I'm not at liberty to tell you that.'

'I'm guessing there weren't,' she retorted. 'I'd say Martha let her killer into the house because it was someone she knew. It could well have been the person who came to the door while she was leaving a message for me. Have you found out who that was?'

'Not yet. Unfortunately, there's no CCTV in the area, so we've been unable to establish the identity of her visitor. We're hopeful the person will come forward, or another eyewitness might be able to tell us something. If we're really lucky, someone with a dash cam may have been driving down the lane at the time. We put out an appeal for information on tonight's news.'

'I saw it,' Violet said. 'Has it generated many calls?'

'Not as yet, but it's early days. The appeal only went out half an hour ago.'

'Someone's bound to have seen something,' Violet said. 'I've not lived in Merrywell long, but I'm learning that there's not much that passes under the radar around here.'

'There has been a spate of incidents in the wider area recently,' said DS Winterton. 'We've had reports of people posing as door-to-door salespeople, or bogus tradesmen. Unfortunately, that's how a lot of criminals operate these days. They worm their way into people's homes under false pretences in order to steal from the occupant.'

'Martha Andrews was an intelligent woman,' Violet said. 'She wouldn't have fallen for a trick like that.'

'It's not just the gullible that fall for these doorstep fraudsters,' said DS Winterton. 'They can be surprisingly convincing. It's easy to be taken in by them.'

'Martha had travelled the world,' said Violet. 'She must have encountered all manner of cons and rip-offs in her time. There's no way she would have been taken in by doorstop fraud.'

'All right then, maybe she realised what they were up to, and challenged them. That could have led to a confrontation that became physical.'

'Do you really believe they'd kill her to shut her up?' Violet said. 'Wouldn't the scammer have been more likely to scarper before Martha rang for the police?'

At the other end of the line, DS Winterton sighed. 'Please, Mrs Brewster . . . Violet,' he said. 'I know you mean well, but I'd appreciate you leaving the investigation to me and my team. We're already pursuing several lines of inquiry, and we haven't got time to waste on irrelevancies.'

'Will you at least ask one of your officers to track down Duncan Kirkwood? Ask him if he knows where Helen might be. And can you talk to Nigel Slingsby . . . to find out if he knew about his wife's pregnancy?'

The detective coughed. 'I can't make any promises, I'm afraid,' he said, the firm tone of his voice brooking no argument. 'Right now, we have far more pressing priorities. Every member of my team is busy pursuing other lines of inquiry. Feel free to come back to me if you can find unequivocal proof of a link between Helen Slingsby and the case I'm working on . . . maybe then I'll be willing to listen. In the meantime, you need to let me get on and do my job.'

Chapter 27

Strong winds battered the cottage overnight. Out in the back garden, the branches of the old beech tree creaked and rustled, and the sound kept Violet awake. She lay, staring at the uneven ceiling, feeling frustrated and furious that DS Winterton had blatantly disregarded the information she'd given him. It was his prerogative, of course, but his close-minded attitude was disappointing.

Despite her restless night, she arrived at *The Memory Box* early on Friday morning, determined to throw herself back into work to take her mind off the turmoil of the last few days.

At ten o'clock, she received a text from Matthew.

I'm in need of caffeine. Are you going to buy me that coffee you owe me?

She deleted the message, slid her phone to the edge of her desk and carried on working.

Ten minutes later, the door opened and Matthew wandered in, a quizzical expression on his face.

'So, you *are* here,' he said. 'Didn't you get my message?'

'I got it,' Violet said, staring hard at the screen of her Mac. 'But I'm busy.'

'You should have said. I'll make a flagon of coffee instead, and bring a cup over for you.'

Violet hardened her heart against the kindness in his voice.

'No thanks. I'm fine.'

Out of the corner of her eye, she saw him fold his arms and move his feet apart.

'I'm getting bad vibes here, Violet. Is everything all right?'

She sighed, realising he wasn't going to take the hint and clear off.

'Have I done something to upset you?' he persisted.

She didn't want a confrontation, but he wasn't leaving her much choice.

'You tell me,' she said, her chair squeaking as she spun around to face him.

He wrinkled his nose. 'Sorry? I'm not following you.'

'I had a visit the other day, from Judith Talbot,' Violet said. 'Someone has complained that I've become preoccupied with finding Helen Slingsby.'

Matthew pulled back his shoulders and pushed his hands into his pockets. 'What, and you think it was me?'

'Was it?' she said. 'I must confess, I hadn't got you down as a snitch, Matthew, but I've racked my brains and there's no one else it could have been.'

He shook his head defiantly. 'I can assure you, if I had a problem with your work, I'd speak to *you* about it. I wouldn't tell tales to someone else.'

'Well, someone has. If not you, then who?'

He gave an almost imperceptible shrug. 'I haven't the foggiest. Why don't you ask Judith?'

'I already have. She wouldn't tell me.'

'So what? You automatically assumed it was me?'

Violet was hit by a sudden wave of uncertainty. She'd been convinced of Matthew's guilt, but the hurt in his eyes suggested she had spoken out of turn. He seemed like a straightforward

176

kind of guy. If he'd blabbed to Judith, he would have admitted it, been up-front about it.

'I'm sorry,' she said, feeling like a complete heel. 'I obviously came to the wrong conclusion, and I apologise. It's kind of you to offer to make me a drink . . . I honestly wasn't making excuses when I said I was busy. So . . . if the offer's still open, then I'd love a cup of your excellent coffee.'

'You know what,' Matthew said, turning towards the door. 'I'll probably just get a takeaway from the bakery instead. See you later, Violet.'

She noticed he hadn't offered to get one for her while he was there – but who could blame him?

After he'd gone, Violet buried her head in her hands and let out a wail of frustration. When would she learn to keep her big mouth shut?

Chapter 28

Violet spent the rest of the day feeling guilt-ridden and remorseful. She knew from personal experience what it was like to be wrongly accused. What must Matthew think of her?

When she'd moved to Merrywell, the plan had been to befriend the locals and fit into village life, but over the last few days things had gone spectacularly awry. The downturn had started the moment she'd stepped in to help Nigel Slingsby. She had set out with good intentions, but in searching for Helen, she'd inadvertently entered forbidden territory and gotten herself into trouble. As a newcomer, she should be treading carefully, not making a name for herself as a meddler.

And if it wasn't Matthew who'd stitched her up, who had? Evidently there was someone out there who didn't like the way she was conducting herself. Was whoever complained to Judith the same person who'd left the mind-your-own-business plant?

Could it be Nigel who was behind all this? It seemed unlikely, given that he was the one who'd solicited Violet's help in the first place, but maybe this was his back-door way of putting a stop to her enquiries.

The dull pain of a stress headache was tightening across her forehead, so Violet decided to take a break. Pulling on her jacket, she set off across the courtyard, dogged by a cloying sense of disquiet. Perhaps some fresh air would revive her spirits.

She glanced over at *Collis Fine Furniture*, wondering whether to call in to apologise again for her earlier bolshiness – but the 'closed' sign was on the door, and there was no sign of Matthew.

Pushing her hands into her pockets and bending her head into the wind, Violet exited the shopping village and set off with no real direction in mind. The aim of her walk was to clear her mind and give her eyes a rest from constantly staring at a screen.

Merrywell was small and compact, and it was possible to cover the whole territory on foot in about twenty minutes. She turned left, passing the church and the well and Brian and Joyce's house, and when she reached the public footpath, she set off across the fields. Clumps of cowslips were blooming at the sides of the path, and in the meadow, buttercup flowers were beginning to open their golden heads.

When she reached the corner of the first field, Violet climbed a stile, glad that she was wearing a pair of sensible pumps. At the edge of the next field, the footpath rejoined the road, and she found herself wandering down onto School Lane.

When she reached Martha's house, she paused at the gate. The hyacinths in the front garden were beginning to wither now, but their heady scent still lingered.

As Violet stared at the house, she became aware that someone had come to stand next to her.

'I still can't believe she's gone.'

It was Emily, from the house opposite. She was rubbing her upper arms and looked as if she might cry.

Violet nodded in agreement. 'I interviewed her just over a week ago,' she said. 'She was so full of life, so energetic.'

'I keep expecting to see her,' Emily said. 'Martha was a nice woman. She didn't deserve to have her life snatched away like that.'

'I don't think anyone does,' Violet said. 'Have you heard any more from the police?'

'Not a thing,' Emily said. 'I reckon the coppers are stumped. Let's just hope someone comes forward who saw something on the day. Otherwise, Martha's killer might never be caught.'

'Do you know what's happened to Martha's cat?' Violet asked, remembering the little tortoiseshell that had been curled up on an armchair in the dining room. 'Is it being looked after?'

'Someone took her to the Cats Protection over in Ashbourne,' Emily said. 'Poor Rusty. She's a lovely cat . . . ever so friendly. I'd have had her myself, but my partner's allergic.'

When Emily had returned to her own house, Violet walked back along the lane. At the junction with the main street, she veered off, towards Nigel Slingsby's house. It was time she had another word with him.

'How are you, Nigel?' she asked, when he answered the door.

'Oh, you know,' he replied. 'Fair to middling.'

'Is it all right if I come in? I need to ask you something.'

'Shall I put the kettle on?' he said, as he led her into the kitchen.

'Not for me, thanks,' Violet said. 'I won't keep you long. Is Sandra not in?'

'She's out the back, having a crafty ciggy.'

He nodded towards the window. Sandra was at the bottom of the garden, standing with her back to the house, a cigarette between her fingers. The Labrador dog was out there too, lying at his mistress's feet.

'What was it you wanted to talk to me about?'

Violet offered up her broadest smile, but Nigel stared back at her warily.

'I wondered if you'd spoken to Judith Talbot recently?' she said.

'Judith? No, I haven't had a proper conversation with her for a couple of weeks. Why do you ask?'

'Someone's complained to her . . . about me helping you in your search for Helen.'

'What business is that of Judith's?' he said, his jowls quivering.

'She's worried it'll interfere with my work on the film.'

Nigel scowled. 'That woman doesn't half talk rubbish,' he said. 'How did she find out you were helping me, anyway?'

'I thought you might have told her.'

'Then you thought wrong,' he said, holding up a hand to fend off the accusation. 'You wouldn't catch me telling Judith Talbot my business.'

Violet smiled. 'She gave me quite a telling-off.'

'It's never a good idea to get on the wrong side of her,' he said, wincing apologetically. 'I'm sorry if I've got you into trouble.'

'Don't worry, I've dealt with fiercer adversaries than Judith in my time.'

'I doubt she'll give you any more grief,' Nigel said. 'Especially now . . . now that I've asked you to stop looking for Helen.'

'Ah,' Violet said, steeling herself for her next announcement. 'I know that's what you said when we last spoke, but I've recently found out some new information.'

She began by telling him what she'd discovered about the pendant.

'That's worrying,' Nigel said. 'Helen was very fond of her great-aunty . . . the two of them were really close . . . and, not to put too fine a point on it, my wife was also extremely parsimonious. There's no way she would have willingly abandoned something as valuable as that. I mean, she would have needed the money, wouldn't she? For her new life.'

'Talking of which . . .' said Violet, 'did Helen ever mention a colleague of hers at the school . . . a Duncan Kirkwood?'

Nigel huffed. 'That's a name I've not heard for long time,' he said. 'He was the school caretaker. Helen used to moan like hell about him. According to her, he was a lazy so-and-so.'

'So they didn't get on?'

'She couldn't stand the bloke.'

'You told me there were rumours in the village that Helen had been having an affair,' Violet continued, cringing inwardly. 'You don't think that could have been with Duncan?'

Nigel gave a wry laugh. 'No chance. She wouldn't have touched him with the proverbial bargepole. As for the rumours . . . well, that's all they were. Nothing more than idle gossip.'

'I don't think so, Nigel,' Violet said.

She closed her eyes and rubbed the middle of her forehead, wishing that Lesley Gilman had never told her about Helen's pregnancy. Knowing about it felt wrong . . . especially as Nigel seemed blissfully unaware. Being privy to Helen's 'big' secret felt like a burden, one that presented Violet with an impossible dilemma.

How could she break the news to Nigel without hurting him? Was it better to tell the truth, or say nothing to save his feelings? Honesty was usually the best policy, but Violet also knew that being honest could have unforeseen consequences.

Feeling torn and uncertain, she paused. 'I discovered something else yesterday,' she said, after a beat.

'About Helen?'

'Yes, but I'm not sure I should tell you about it. I don't want to hurt you, Nigel.'

'Don't you worry about that. I'm tougher than I look. Now come on . . .' He tapped the table top with his knuckles. 'Spill the beans. Whatever it is, I want to hear it.'

'In that case, I think you'd better sit down. What I'm about to tell you might come as a shock.'

'You're making me nervous now,' Nigel said, as he pulled a chair from under the table. 'Tell me, then. Out with it.'

'OK, but only if you're sure. I want you to know it's not my intention to be cruel or insensitive . . . I'm telling you this because you've asked me to.' She took a shuddering breath. 'Did you know that Helen was pregnant when she left?'

Nigel's jaw dropped open and his mouth formed an 'O' shape, like a silent scream.

'What?' He gripped the edge of the table with his hands. 'Pregnant? No, no, no. That can't be right. Whoever told you that is talking nonsense.'

'I have it from a reliable source.'

'Source?' He jerked his head and scowled. 'What source? Who the hell's been spreading that sort of talk?'

'No one's been spreading anything,' she said, in a bid to reassure him. 'I was told, in confidence, by Lesley Gilman. Her husband let it slip years ago. And before you say anything, she only told me in case Helen's disappearance turns out to be connected to Martha's murder.'

Nigel threw up his hands, holding them either side of his head. 'Don't start with that again,' he said, sounding horribly distressed. 'This is all a load of claptrap, Violet. I wish you'd leave well alone.'

'I'm sorry, Nigel. The last thing I want to do is upset you. I'm assuming from your reaction that you didn't know about Helen's pregnancy?'

'Of course I didn't know,' he snapped. 'Helen and I . . . we couldn't have kids.'

'And yet Dr Gilman confirmed her pregnancy only a week before she left you.'

Nigel ran a trembling hand through his thinning hair, looking ill at ease. 'Our lack of children . . . that wasn't her fault . . . it was me. It was hard for her to come to terms with that. It caused problems . . .'

'I know she had a breakdown,' Violet said. 'And I know about her snatching a baby. Matthew Collis told me everything.'

Nigel rubbed his hands up and down his face, as if to erase the pain that was etched there.

'It was a stupid thing to do . . . unforgivable,' he said. 'But Helen was ill. When she was told we couldn't have kids, she was inconsolable. I tried my best to support her, but nothing I said made any difference. In fact, it only made things worse. Helen began to resent me. She fell into a deep depression, and she wasn't thinking straight. The Collises could have kicked up a real stink, but in the end, they were very good about it.'

'And they've kept quiet ever since,' Violet said.

'Aye, they made a promise,' Nigel said. 'But obviously their lad has no qualms about telling people.'

'Please don't think badly of Matthew. It was someone from the village who mentioned it to me,' Violet said, being careful not to let on that the informer had been Sandra's granddaughter. 'When I heard the rumour, I asked Matthew about it. He ended up telling me the whole story, but only after I pressed him.'

Nigel sighed. 'After it happened, things were never the same between Helen and me,' he said. 'It was the beginning of the end for our marriage. All Helen had ever wanted was a kiddie, and I couldn't give her one. I'm surprised she stuck around as long as she did.'

'I can see that the news of Helen's pregnancy has come as a shock to you, Nigel. I'm sorry I had to be the one to tell you. Unfortunately, I've also mentioned it to the police.'

Nigel placed a hand on the back of his head and closed his eyes.

'Why in heaven's name did you do that?' he said. 'What's it got to do with them?'

'I didn't think I had a choice,' Violet said, feeling the need to justify her actions. 'Look . . . I know you don't agree, but I think the questions I've been asking about Helen have stirred things up. I'm convinced something happened to her all those years ago.'

'Like what?'

'You and I can find no trace of her,' Violet said, in an attempt to explain her thinking. 'I've even asked my ex-husband, who's a policeman, to try and track her down – but there's no record of Helen at all. The conclusion I've drawn from everything I've learned is that she never left the village.'

'Never left? What are you talking about? Where the hell is she, then?'

'That's a very good question,' Violet said. 'And, at the moment, it's one I can't answer.'

Nigel glared, slowly shaking his head. 'When I asked for your help, this isn't what I meant.' His voice was wavering – either with

184

sadness or anger, she wasn't sure which. 'I didn't think you'd go poking around . . . muck-raking. I should never have got you involved, Violet. And now, I'd like you to stop. I'd also like you to please leave, before Sandra finishes her ciggy and comes back in.'

After wrongly accusing Matthew, Violet had thought her day couldn't get any worse. She was wrong. Nigel's termination of their conversation (and potentially their friendship) had taken things to a new low.

To restore her reputation in the village, she would have to toe the line and get through the next few weeks without creating any more waves – although that might be easier said than done. Whether she liked it or not, she was now thoroughly ensnared in the tangle of intrigue surrounding Helen Slingsby.

Before things deteriorated any further – was that even possible? – she decided to call it a day and go home. The weather was turning colder and gloomy clouds were gathering. Violet pulled the zip of her jacket up to her chin to keep her neck warm, and marched on. All she wanted to do was hunker down at home. She would light the wood burner in the kitchen and cook herself something delicious for dinner. She might even open a bottle of red.

She re-entered Merrywell's main street, which curved past an abundance of pretty houses, flanked by dry-stone walls and green verges. There was invariably some kind of activity on the street – someone walking their dog, or going to the shop, or tending their garden – but today, everything was eerily quiet and empty. Were people staying inside, behind locked doors, afraid that Martha Andrews' killer might come back?

Violet wondered how much longer it would take DS Winterton to make an arrest. Until that happened, she didn't believe anyone in Merrywell would feel completely safe.

When she reached Greengage Cottage, she let herself in through the front gate, pausing to admire her charming home. It was sturdily built from local limestone, with coped gritstone gables and mullioned windows. Etched into the stone lintel above the door was the date: 1747. Despite everything that had happened over the last few days, the house continued to be her place of escape, her safe haven.

As she let herself in, she scooped up the pile of mail that lay on the mat, and then continued on into the kitchen. Once the wood burner was lit she opened the fridge, wondering what to concoct from the random and somewhat limited ingredients available. She settled on something quick: a pan-fried salmon fillet, couscous and a rocket salad. She also chopped a white cabbage, carrot, and onions, mixing them with mayonnaise, black pepper, and a dab of yellow mustard to make a simple homemade coleslaw.

While she waited for the salmon to cook, Violet selected a bottle of chianti from her wine rack and poured herself a generous glassful. It had been a long, difficult few days. Things could only get better.

She plated up her meal and sat down at the table, where she'd left the pile of mail. There was a leaflet from a local pizza delivery company, a copy of the village news bulletin, and a letter confirming her registration with a local GP. Beneath that was a folded piece of paper.

As Violet scooped a forkful of couscous into her mouth, she opened it out and read the short message that was printed on it. All capitals. Arial font. Plain white copy paper. Three words.

STOP ASKING QUESTIONS

Chapter 29

Violet carefully placed the sheet of paper back onto the table. If this was meant to be a joke, she wasn't laughing.

Someone was rattled – that much was obvious. Was the author of this note the same person who'd left the plant? If so, they were sending a more direct message this time. But was it meant as a warning, or a threat? Or was it another anonymous command from someone who didn't like the way Violet was conducting herself?

Whatever the purpose of the note, whoever wrote it clearly didn't know that Violet wasn't easily intimidated. In fact, her stubborn streak would ensure the note had the polar opposite effect to the one its author intended. She certainly wasn't going to stop asking questions at the behest of a disapproving and anonymous naysayer.

What the note did serve to do was prove how much the questions Violet had been asking had riled someone – so perhaps she was a lot closer to the truth than she'd realised.

She picked up her phone to let DS Winterton know about this latest development. He would *have* to take notice of her now.

'Someone's posted an anonymous note through my door,' Violet said, as soon as the detective picked up.

'Have they now, and what does it say?'

'*Stop asking questions,*' Violet said.

DS Winterton chortled. 'I would imagine there are several people who would like to send a note like that – me included,' he said. 'However, whilst I agree wholeheartedly with the sentiment, I find its anonymity troubling. Is the note handwritten?'

'No,' Violet said. 'It's printed on what looks like an ink-jet printer. It's on a sheet of white A4 paper, and I'd say the font is Arial.'

'When did it arrive?'

'Sometime today. I've been out at work since half past eight this morning. It could have been posted through my door any time after that.'

'And do you have any suspicions as to who might have written it?'

Violet wondered, fleetingly, whether the sender might be Judith Talbot, but dismissed the notion instantly. If Judith had written the note, she would have put her name to it.

'I don't know who sent it,' Violet said. 'But I'm obviously treading on *someone's* toes.'

She told him about the mind-your-own-business plant, which prompted a loud guffaw from the detective.

'I do wish you'd take this more seriously,' Violet told him. 'It proves that I'm on the right lines, doesn't it? I've been asking questions about Helen Slingsby . . . it's not much of a stretch to assume the author of the note also knows something about Martha's death.'

'Not much of a stretch?' DS Winterton said, making no attempt to disguise his scepticism. 'It'll be you who's doing a stretch, Mrs Brewster, if you don't stop messing me about. You can get up to six months' imprisonment for wasting police time, you know.'

'I'm not wasting anyone's time,' Violet said, aware that her voice had risen a couple of octaves. 'I wouldn't do that. I've received an anonymous letter. I'm entitled to report that, surely?'

'OK, let's take stock, shall we?' DS Winterton said. 'The note isn't an overt threat. The wording seems more like a poison pen letter to me, written by someone who's too cowardly to tell you to your face. You've obviously rubbed someone up the wrong way. How long did you say you've lived in Merrywell? It's not taken you long to develop enemies, has it?'

'I realise you find this highly amusing, DS Winterton, but I can assure you that I don't. I'd like the note checked for fingerprints.'

'If they've got any sense, whoever wrote it will have worn gloves,' the detective said. 'However, despite what you might think, I am taking this seriously. I'll send an officer round to collect the note this evening. In the meantime, make sure you don't touch it.'

'I already have,' Violet said. 'My fingerprints will be all over it . . . how was I supposed to know what it was?'

'That being the case, we'll need your prints for elimination purposes.'

'Will I have to come down to the station?'

'No, we can take them digitally in the comfort of your own home these days. The officer will sort it when he comes round.'

'Thank you,' Violet said.

'You're welcome . . . although, I have to say this is all rather convenient . . . you getting a warning to back off. I do hope this note isn't something you've penned yourself?'

'You're not serious?' Violet said.

'It could be your half-arsed way of getting me to look into Mrs Slingsby's whereabouts,' DS Winterton said.

'You don't honestly believe I'd do something like that?'

'No,' DS Winterton said. 'On balance, I don't.'

'Anyway, if I *had* written the note, I'd have made it a lot more threatening,' Violet said, irately. 'It would have said . . . *Stop asking questions unless you want to end up like Martha Andrews.* That would have established a clear link between Helen's disappearance and Martha's murder. But, of course, it doesn't say that because I didn't write the note.'

'OK, keep your hair on,' DS Winterton said. 'Are you in for the rest of the evening?'

'Yes.'

'Then sit tight and I'll ask someone to call round within the next couple of hours. As I say, I don't hold out much hope of finding any prints . . . other than your own, but we will check. What this note does prove is that you've triggered hostility some-where within the community, and I do have to wonder why that is. I'll arrange for someone to check the PNC for Helen Slingsby and . . . what was the name of that other bloke you told me about? The caretaker?'

Helen already knew that DS Winterton would draw a blank with Helen Slingsby, but she couldn't tell him that – otherwise he'd want to know how she'd come by that information. She was in enough trouble already, without incurring Paul's wrath as well.

'His name was Duncan Kirkwood,' she said. 'In 1982, he'd have been about twenty-five. He was Scottish, and he'd worked on the oil rigs, but that's all I know about him.'

'If he's still around, we'll find him,' said DS Winterton. 'Leave it with me, Violet. And in the meantime, be careful. If someone out there is unhappy about you asking questions, it might be wise to take a step back. The last thing we want is for you to put yourself in any danger.'

Chapter 30

A uniformed police officer called at the house just as the ten o'clock news was starting. After placing the note in an evidence bag, he took a digital scan of Violet's fingerprints using a handheld machine.

'This is purely for elimination purposes,' the officer said. 'Don't worry, your prints won't be stored on the police database.'

'How long will it take for someone to examine the note?' Violet asked.

'It won't be a high priority, but we should have the results back within a couple of days. If there are any prints – other than your own – we'll compare them against our database to see if we can get a hit.'

'I don't hold out much hope,' Violet said. 'Anyone nasty enough to write an anonymous note is going to be savvy enough to wear gloves.'

'Either that, or confident enough to know their prints aren't already on the system,' said the officer.

After Violet had seen him to the door, she switched off the television and climbed the stairs. An early night was in order. Whether or not she would get any sleep was another matter entirely.

* * *

The next day was Saturday, and in the absence of anything better to do, Violet decided to open up her MacBook and work from home. She stretched out on the sofa and, with an old episode of *Murder, She Wrote* playing in the background, began to put together a proposal for the youth charity that had contacted her. The project would be another great commission if she could get it, but she knew that competition for the contract would be fierce.

As she sketched out some figures and costings, the doorbell sounded. Violet switched off the television (where Jessica Fletcher was about to reveal the identity of the murderer to the dumbfounded detective in charge), and opened the front door. Joyce Collis was standing on the garden path, holding a cake tin.

'Joyce! Hello, this is a surprise. Would you like to come in?'

'I'm not stopping,' Joyce said, as she handed over the tin. 'But I wanted to bring you this. I know how much you enjoyed my lemon drizzle cake the other day, so I made one for you.'

'Wow! Thank you,' Violet said, smiling as she prised open the cake tin lid and breathed in the tangy smell of lemons. 'This looks delicious. Are you sure I can't tempt you to stay for a slice with a nice cup of tea?'

'I won't have any cake,' Joyce said, 'but a cup of tea sounds just the ticket.'

She stepped inside and followed Violet through to the kitchen. As they waited for the kettle to boil, Joyce enquired how the film was progressing.

'I've got four or five more people to talk to, plus some filming at the school . . . and that's about it as far as the interviews go. Once I have all the raw material, it'll be a matter of selecting the best bits and weaving them together based on a rough storyboard. I've already made a start.'

'That must be the hardest part,' said Joyce. 'Deciding what to keep and what to get rid of.'

'It is. Whittling several hours' worth of interviews down into a twenty-minute film is quite a challenge.'

She made two mugs of tea and handed one to Joyce before cutting herself a generous slice of cake.

'Are you sure I can't tempt you?'

'No, absolutely not,' Joyce said, as she took a seat at the kitchen table. 'I adore baking, but I'm not a big fan of anything citrusy.'

'Whereas I'm an absolute sucker for lemon cake.'

'I realise that,' Joyce said. 'Although, I have to confess . . . when I made you the cake, I did have an ulterior motive.'

Violet sat down and waited, wondering where the conversation was heading.

'I wanted a chance to talk to you,' Joyce continued. 'Matthew came to see us yesterday, and he mentioned your interest in Helen Slingsby . . . I know he's told you about the day she took Matthew.'

Violet almost choked on the piece of cake she was eating. She took a swig of tea to wash it down.

'I don't know what to say, Joyce, other than I'm sorry if I've stirred up a memory you'd rather forget. Matthew told me you don't like to talk about it.'

'He's right.' Joyce nodded. 'I don't. But, please don't apologise. Yesterday, Matthew and I talked about what happened for the first time in years . . . properly talked, and it's done me good. At the time, I chose to bury the memory – it was my way of coping – but I realise now I probably should have talked about it . . . got it out of my system.'

'It must have been an horrendous experience, having your baby taken like that.'

'It was awful,' Joyce said. 'But, with hindsight, I realise the situation could have been a lot worse. Matthew was returned almost immediately. I got him back, unharmed. Not everyone is that fortunate.'

'Thank goodness he was too young to remember what happened.'

Joyce smiled and stirred her tea. 'He slept through the whole thing.'

'Whereas for you, it must have been a waking nightmare,' Violet said.

'It changed me,' Joyce said, nodding reflectively. 'I went from being an optimistic, glass-half-full kind of person, to a nervous worryguts. I blamed myself for what had happened and began to doubt my abilities as a mother. I became afraid of everything.'

'What happened wasn't your fault,' Violet said.

'That's what Brian said . . . but, I didn't believe him. I told myself that if I'd looked after Matthew properly . . . been a good mother, he would never have been taken. I became over-protective . . . excessively so. It drove Matthew up the wall as he got older. The incident also put me off having any more children. I felt I wasn't up to the job.'

Violet reached across the table and squeezed Joyce's hand.

'When something like that happens, a parent's first instinct is to blame themselves,' she said, wanting to comfort Joyce without disregarding her deep-seated fears and insecurities. 'The feelings you had represented your love for your son. They show you took your responsibilities seriously . . . that you *were* a good mother. And Matthew has turned out all right, hasn't he? I'd say you were more than up to the job as a parent.'

'Thank you, Violet. You're right, although it's taken me an awfully long time to realise that. Brian has always been amazingly supportive. He coped a lot better at the time than I did, probably because he didn't have to endure that awful period of not knowing . . . of thinking Matthew had gone forever.'

Holding her mug with both hands, Joyce took a sip of tea to calm herself.

'My baby was only gone for a few minutes,' she said. 'But every one of those minutes felt like an hour. I remember standing there, shaking, convinced I'd never see Matthew again, and trying to work out how to tell Brian that I'd lost our son.'

'Even if the worst had happened, I'm sure Brian wouldn't have blamed you.'

'Thankfully, we didn't have to put that to the test.' Joyce mustered a smile. 'There were no mobile phones back then, and by the time the police managed to get hold of Brian at work, Matthew had already been returned. The first thing they said to my husband, before they told him what had happened, was that Matthew was safe and well.'

'So, unlike you, Brian never went through that terrifying period of not knowing,' Violet said. 'He didn't experience the over-whelming sense of despair you must have felt.'

'That's it exactly,' Joyce said. 'Initially, he was more angry than anything . . . furious with Helen. Absolutely livid.'

'And yet you didn't press charges.'

'No. When we learned about Helen's breakdown, we decided to put it all behind us. Brian hasn't got a vindictive bone in his body, and I just wanted to forget the whole thing. At the end of the day, we had to live in the same village as the Slingsbys, and it didn't feel right to pursue charges. Helen sought treatment for her depression, and life carried on as before, except that we avoided Helen and Nigel. I couldn't bear to be within a hundred yards of the woman.

'When it was time for Matthew to start school, I was reluctant to let him go. I didn't like to let him out of my sight, so sending him off to school was always going to be difficult. On top of that, I had to contend with knowing that Helen Slingsby worked at the school. It was a difficult time for me.'

'I can imagine,' said Violet.

'I'll admit, I was glad when Helen left the village, and I'm sure I'm not the only one who felt that way. For ten years I lived alongside her, keeping quiet about the fact that she'd taken my baby. I did once tell her I'd forgiven her, but I'm not sure that was entirely true.'

'Matthew told me you'd forgiven, but not forgotten,' said Violet.

'That's a good way of putting it,' Joyce said. 'Brian was more magnanimous than me. I saw him once, talking to Helen in the street. I think he felt sorry for her, and I know he felt bad for Nigel. He and Brian were quite good friends once upon a time, but all that ended when Helen stole our son.'

Violet speared another piece of cake with her fork. 'What has Matthew told you about my search for Helen?'

'Not a lot,' Joyce replied. 'He said you'd been helping Nigel to find her, but you hadn't had any luck tracking her down. He said you're concerned something might have happened to her.'

'Did he also tell you my theory that Helen's fate might be tied up with what's happened to Martha?'

'No,' Joyce said, placing a hand on her throat. 'He didn't tell me that. I do hope you're wrong, Violet – although, knowing Helen, I wouldn't be in the least bit surprised if she's still causing trouble, even after all these years.'

Chapter 31

After Joyce had gone, Violet washed the mugs and put the cake away, out of reach of temptation. As she wiped the draining board, she thought about the wall of Post-it Notes in *The Memory Box*, feeling relieved that Joyce would never see the hastily constructed 'incident board'. Goodness knows what she would say if she discovered her and Brian's names among the list of suspects.

She went into the living room, sat on the sofa and placed her MacBook back on her knee. Instead of reopening the Word document she'd been working on, she opened Excel, struck by the vague notion that the police used timelines to help them log key aspects of a case. As she didn't have the faintest idea what an incident timeline looked like, she would have to make do with entering known dates onto a spreadsheet.

? 1972–1982	Helen works at Merrywell Primary as a school secretary
? 1972	Helen has breakdown and takes Matthew from his pram
? 1982	Duncan Kirkwood employed as school caretaker
? June 1982	Helen leaves Merrywell (or does she???)

7 April 2022	Online searches for Helen
12 April 2022	Martha Andrews leaves voicemail, and is later killed in her own home.

Violet wasn't sure what the creation of her spreadsheet had achieved, but there was something reassuring about organising her thoughts. Next, she opened another document in Word and began to create a flowchart of questions.

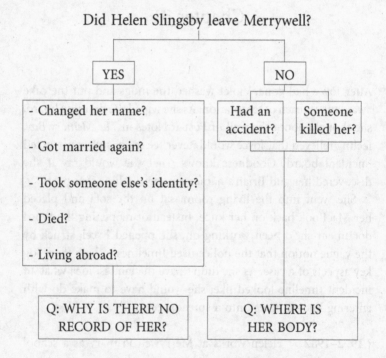

Her next step was to review the six W's she'd been taught to look out for as a journalist, Rudyard Kipling's 'six honest serving men':

☐ who
☐ what

- □ where
- □ when
- □ why

And the last one, which actually began with an 'H':

- □ how

Violet stared at the flowchart, focusing her eyes on the two questions at the bottom. The more she stared, the more obvious the answer to the first question became. The reason there was no record of Helen, was that the answer to the initial question: *Did Helen Slingsby leave Merrywell?* was a resounding *no*.

That left only two possibilities: she'd had an accident, or someone had killed her. And in both of those scenarios, the most pressing of the six W's (aside from the *who*) was *where*.

Where was Helen's body?

If Violet could work that out, then maybe . . . just maybe . . . DS Winterton would start to take her seriously.

Chapter 32

'If you were going to hide a body in Merrywell, where would you put it?'

If Brian Collis was surprised by Violet's question, he didn't let it show. Instead, he stirred his coffee and smiled.

'Is this a theoretical question, or are you planning to bump someone off?'

They were sitting in a quiet corner of the café, which was a lot less busy than usual, even for a Monday.

'It's theoretical-*ish*,' Violet said.

'Interesting.' Brian narrowed his eyes. 'You know, when you offered to buy me lunch in exchange for answering a few questions, I assumed they'd be about local history. What is this? Have you been asked to run a stall at the summer fete, or something? If so, I'd go with the usual *guess the name of the teddy bear*, if I were you. In light of what's happened to Martha, *guess where the body is buried* might be considered in bad taste.'

'Thanks for trying to lighten the mood,' Violet said. 'But, as I'm sure you've already worked out, I'm being perfectly serious.'

'I was hoping I was wrong,' he said, looking more than a little uneasy.

'Sorry, Brian. I should have been up-front with you, but I was worried you might not agree to meet me if you knew what I was going to ask about.'

'I probably wouldn't, but I'm here now, aren't I?' He opened up his ham salad sandwich, removed the tomato, and placed it on the side of his plate. 'I take it this theoretical question of yours has something to do with your search for Helen Slingsby? Matthew told us you'd been digging around, and I know you've already spoken to Joyce on the matter . . .'

'I have, and I apologise if my questions have upset her – or you. But the things I've learned about Helen have convinced me that something awful happened to her back in 1982. Nigel and I have both tried to find her, and a police officer I know has also run a search. There's no record of Helen Slingsby after she supposedly left Merrywell, and the conclusion I've come to is that she's no longer alive.'

'Maybe she fell ill,' Brian said. 'Why assume something awful must have happened?'

'Because if she'd died of natural causes, there would be a record of her death . . . and there isn't. But I do understand your scepticism, Brian. I'm not asking you to agree with my theory, and you certainly don't have to answer my question if you're not comfortable with it.'

'I'm willing to answer your question,' he said. 'As for your theory, I'll keep an open mind about that.'

Violet smiled at him as she stirred her coffee. 'You know the village better than anyone,' she said. 'So, tell me. Where would someone hide a body?'

Brian turned his head left, then right, checking the occupants of the nearby tables.

'Is this really the best place to be having this conversation?' he said. 'Walls have ears, you know. Especially in Merrywell.'

'Good point. Let's finish our lunch, and then we'll go over to *The Memory Box*.'

'Excellent,' said Brian. 'You can show me round – not that there's much to see, I suppose. It's the smallest unit in the shopping village, isn't it?'

Violet's face flushed as she remembered the list of suspects posted on the wall in the back room. There was no way she could let Brian see those.

'You know what?' she said. 'I'll give you the not-so-grand tour another day. It's a lovely, sunny afternoon. When we've finished here, let's take a stroll through the village and you can point out the most likely hiding places.'

'All right,' Brian said, looking at her slightly askance. 'I'll have a think while we eat.' Dropping his voice to a whisper, he added: 'There must be somewhere around here that's suitable for disposing of a body.'

They ended up in the park, sitting on the same bench Violet had used to interview Molly. Over the last few days, the tulip petals had begun to fall, but the auriculas were in full bloom now, their frilly heads huddling together in the sunshine.

'OK, so . . . if I wanted to get rid of a body . . .' Brian casually folded his arms as if they were discussing the weather or the price of petrol. 'I'd choose one of three places. The most obvious is up there, in Trichner Woods.'

He nodded off into the distance, to a nearby hill. It was bare and craggy, with a row of trees lined up along the ridge, like a mohawk haircut.

'That wood has towered over Merrywell for centuries, but surprisingly few people go up there.'

'And that would make it a good place to hide a body?' said Violet.

Brian shrugged. 'Possibly, although I'm no expert in these things.'

Violet grinned. 'That's a relief.'

'Trichner Woods is definitely an option though,' Brian said. 'If you buried someone deep enough, the chances are they'd never be found. The trouble is, the thing that makes it a good choice – its

202

remoteness – is also its biggest drawback. You can't get up there by car, and carrying a body up the side of the hill would be nigh on impossible. It's steep and rough at the best of times. Other than the Incredible Hulk, I can't think of anyone who'd be strong enough to carry a dead weight up there.'

'Unless they had some help,' Violet suggested.

Brian sucked air through his teeth. 'Even then, I wouldn't fancy their chances. There's quite a bit of scree on the hillside. It'd be treacherous, especially if they were going up there at night.'

'You're not doing a very good job of selling option one to me, Brian.'

'Not as a place to *take* a body. But you could lure someone there and then kill them in situ.'

'It doesn't sound like the easiest place to lure someone to either,' Violet said. 'I can't imagine anyone agreeing to meet there without knowing what for.'

'Unless the two people concerned were already in the habit of rendezvousing in Trichner Woods.'

Violet nodded. 'You could be onto something there,' she said. 'Now, tell me about option two.'

Brian paused, watching as a woman approached, accompanied by a small black terrier.

'Mornin',' she said.

'Morning,' Brian replied, giving the woman a nod.

They waited until she was out of earshot before continuing their bizarre conversation. It took a while, because the dog stopped to sniff almost every flower and blade of grass.

'Option two would be one of the old lead mines,' Brian said, when the dog and its owner had finally moved on.

'I didn't realise Merrywell had any lead mines.'

'There are plenty round and about,' Brian said. 'Lead mines have been worked in this area since Roman times. They shut down years ago, of course, and they're a few miles away – but most of them are accessible by car.'

'If they're disused, aren't they closed off?' Violet said. 'You know, boarded up, or whatever?'

'They didn't used to be. When I was a youth, me and my mates would often explore the old mines. But then some unfortunate lad had an accident, and it took the rescuers three days to get to him. After that, steps were taken to make things safe, and the shafts were capped. Mind you, if you know where to look, there are still ways to access them.

'All the locals know about the mines,' Brian continued, slipping into 'local historian' mode. 'There are a few shafts close to some of the footpaths . . . the entrances are usually lined with dry-stone walling, known as ginging, which makes them easy to spot. There are plenty of other, lesser-known shafts as well. If someone dropped something down one of those, it's unlikely it would ever be found.'

'Sounds like a fail-safe way to hide a body,' said Violet. 'What about the village well? Is that an option?'

Brian shook his head. 'You've seen the well for yourself . . . it's nothing more than a water fountain. No . . . for option three, I'm thinking the old air raid shelter.'

'The one on the school playing field?'

'You know about it, do you?'

'Damian Rushcliffe mentioned it during his interview,' Violet explained. 'Although it strikes me as an unlikely hiding place. I'll bet people sneak in there all the time. If there was a body in the old shelter, someone would have found it years ago.'

'People did used to go inside, once upon a time,' Brian said. 'I went down there myself a few times when I was a kid. As a matter of fact, I had my first cigarette in the old shelter. It was my first and my last, actually. It made me sick. I never could face one after that.'

Violet smiled. 'I'm sure your lungs are grateful.'

'For a long time, a lot of young people hung out in the shelter, as well as the odd courting couple. It was all harmless enough . . . until the Seventies kicked in.'

'What happened then?'

'Some youths were caught down there, smoking weed and sniffing glue. A group of villagers got together and complained, and the shelter was eventually locked up for good. A metal gate was installed over the old entrance to keep people out. I don't suppose anyone's been down there since. Why would they want to? It's probably overrun with rats by now.'

Violet shuddered. 'Do you know when it was locked up?' she said.

'I can't remember, exactly. Late Seventies, early Eighties maybe. I can't be more precise than that.'

'Was it before, or after Helen Slingsby left Merrywell?'

'That's the thing,' Brian said, resting his chin in his hand as he considered her question. 'Don't quote me on this, but I think it may have been just after. If you want to know for certain, you should ask Matthew. He might be able to check the council records.'

'OK, I will,' Violet said. 'Although I'm not sure how keen he'll be to help. I get the feeling your son has had enough of my questions to last a lifetime.'

Chapter 33

'I've brought you that coffee I owe you,' Violet said, as she entered Matthew's workshop an hour later. 'I also got cakes. Fiona couldn't remember whether caramel doughnuts were your favourite, or chocolate brownies – so I bought both.'

He stared at her, unsmiling. 'Is this a peace offering?'

'I wouldn't call it that,' Violet replied. 'A *peace offering* suggests we're at war, and we're not. Are we?'

'Not as far as I'm concerned,' Matthew said. 'But, when it comes to conflict, I do try and stay neutral. If I was a country, I'd be Switzerland.'

Violet laughed. 'I get the impression you're more than capable of fighting your corner if you need to.'

He opened up the box of cakes.

'I see you've bought a coffee for yourself. Are you going to stay and drink it here?'

'That was the plan,' Violet said. 'Assuming I'm still welcome.'

'You are.' He smiled. 'Just so long as you don't expect me to share the cakes.'

'That suits me. I've eaten about a year's worth of cake over the last week or so. It's time to rein myself in.'

She followed him into the workshop, and perched on the same stool she'd occupied during her previous visit.

'I'd like to apologise,' she said. 'I should never have accused you of complaining to Judith Talbot.'

'No,' said Matthew. 'You shouldn't. Grassing people up isn't my style. Not at all.'

'I know, and I'm sorry. Can you forgive me?'

'I already have,' he said. 'Life's too short to hold grudges. Is that why you came here? To apologise?'

'That was one of the reasons,' Violet replied. 'The other was to ask for your help.'

He laughed. Loudly.

'So, the cakes *weren't* a peace offering then? Just an out-and-out bribe. You're cheeky, Violet. You really are.'

She gave a sheepish smile and sipped her coffee.

'I've been talking to your dad,' she said. 'He mentioned you might be able to find out when the old air raid shelter was closed off.'

'Did he now? In that case, my dad's got almost as much brass neck as you have.'

'Does that mean you can't help? Or you're just unwilling to?'

'Neither,' he said. 'I'm happy to help . . . providing this is something to do with the film project.'

Violet lowered her gaze and then looked up at him from beneath her eyelashes. 'No,' she admitted. 'It's not for the film. It's something else . . . something I've been discussing with your dad.'

'Are you going to tell me what the two of you have been talking about? It's only fair, isn't it, if you want my help?'

Violet had no choice but to be honest. If *she* didn't tell Matthew the truth about *the-three-best-places-to-bury-a-body* conversation, his dad most surely would.

'You have got to be kidding,' Matthew said, after she'd summarised her chat with Brian. 'I can't believe you're involving my dad in your wild theories.'

'I'm not involving him in anything. I was asking his advice. He knows the village like the back of his hand. If anyone knows where the hiding places might be, it's him.'

Matthew shook his head. 'I suppose I should be thankful you're asking for his help. I assume this means he's not on your list of suspects?'

'What makes you think I've got a list?' Violet said, cursing her cheeks for their blushing betrayal.

'You *have*, haven't you?' He tilted his head and stared at her. 'My dad better not be on it. Or my mum.'

'Neither of them are,' she said, aware that her face was a picture of guilt. 'Not anymore.'

'But they were?'

'Please, Matthew.' She cringed. 'Can we not talk about this?'

'Oh, I think we should,' he said, folding his arms. 'And don't think you can buy your way out of this one with a couple of cakes.'

Violet released a slow breath. 'I'll admit I drew up a list of people who might have had a motive for getting rid of Helen Slingsby, but your parents were never serious contenders.'

'For the role of murderer, you mean?' Matthew scoffed. 'Thanks, Violet. That's reassuring.'

She'd come to Matthew's workshop with good intentions. Laden with coffee and cakes, her sole aim had been to mend bridges – but all she was doing was making things worse. The wisest thing she could do now was walk away, before she completely destroyed what was left of her friendship with the Collises.

'You're angry with me,' she said. 'And you have every reason to be. I should go.'

She stood up and moved towards the door.

'Violet, wait,' Matthew said, when she reached the glass partition. 'Come back. Sit down. Let's talk.'

She shook her head, feeling unexpectedly emotional.

'Please,' Matthew persisted. 'Don't walk away. I'm willing to help, if I can.'

She turned and looked at him, wishing he didn't look so contrite. After all, she was the one who was in the wrong.

'All my life, Helen Slingsby has been the elephant in the room,'

Matthew said, as Violet perched back on the stool. 'Even after she left, her presence was always there, like a ghost. You may be a thorn in my side, Violet, but it's thanks to you that my family are finally talking about what happened.'

'All I'm trying to do is find Helen,' she said. 'It's never been my intention to interfere, or cause problems for you, or your family.'

Matthew took the lid off his coffee and sat down. 'I don't necessarily agree with some of your methods, but I think you're right to be asking questions about Helen. She was a strange, unhappy woman, and nobody liked her very much. For that reason, no one cared when she left. If they had, maybe they would have questioned the suddenness of her departure.'

'It's sad that she didn't have any friends in the village,' said Violet.

'You're right. A friend might have tried to stay in touch and would have known if something was wrong. As it was, nobody knew where she went to, or who she might be with.'

Violet decided to tell him about the pendant. As she recounted what Ged Rivers had told her, a worried expression settled on Matthew's face.

'That certainly rings alarm bells,' he said.

'Do you think she *did* leave?' Violet said.

'That's what I've always believed, but you've done a thorough search . . . and in light of what you've discovered, I'm coming round to your way of thinking. I didn't like Helen, and neither did my parents, but if something happened to her back in 1982, we owe it to her to find out the truth.'

'So, you'll check when the air raid shelter was closed off?' Violet said.

'I'll look into it, but I can't make any promises. The parish council archives are kept at the Derbyshire Record Office. I'll take a drive over there later and see if I can find the information you're after.'

Violet rested her chin in her hands. 'Thanks, Matthew,' she said.

'I'm not sure how I got so enmeshed in all this, or why I even care. If I had my time again, I'd leave well alone and keep out of it.'

'Would you? Really?' said Matthew. 'Can you honestly say you'd pass up the opportunity to help someone and solve a mystery at the same time? I don't think so. That's not who you are, Violet. And you know what? Maybe that's a good thing. The world needs people like you . . . people willing to ask the difficult questions and put their necks on the line.'

'Their *brass* necks, you mean?'

'Absolutely,' he said, nodding his head and laughing. 'Your neck is as brassy as they come.'

Violet arrived home that evening feeling impatient. Matthew had promised to go over to the record office in Matlock before it closed for the day, and by now, she'd expected him to call or text with an update. Perhaps, in the end, something had come up, and he'd been too busy to travel to Matlock. Or maybe he'd gone there and been unable to find out when the air raid shelter was sealed off.

Either way, she wished he'd get in touch, rather than keeping her on tenterhooks.

The whoosh of a text alert finally sounded as she was washing her dinner pots, but the message was from Fiona, not Matthew.

Tom and Darren have descended for a few days, and we're all going over to the pub later. Fancy joining us? xx

Tom was Fiona and Eric's son. He lived on the outskirts of Sheffield with his partner, Darren, and the pair were frequent visitors, regularly spending weekends at the Nash household. Violet had heard a lot about them, but this would be the first chance she'd had to meet them in person. However, she'd planned a quiet evening of reading, and wasn't sure she could muster the energy to get ready for a night in the pub.

As she wondered how to politely turn down Fiona's invitation, another text arrived.

Stop thinking up excuses and meet me at the pub at 8 p.m. You've been meaning to check out the White Hart for ages – this is your big chance. Come ON, Violet. Who knows, you might enjoy it!!

Reluctantly, Violet accepted that this was one invitation she wasn't going to be able to wriggle out of.

OK, bossy boots. I'll be there. See you later. xx

She dashed upstairs and opened the large pine wardrobe in the corner of her bedroom, wondering what on earth to wear for a night out in the White Hart. She immediately ruled out her 'little black dress'. It was months since she'd worn it, and it had always been on the tight side. After all the cakes she'd been eating recently, it was unlikely she'd be able to squeeze into it.

She pulled out a tailored trouser suit in navy blue. Too formal? What about one of her flowery maxi dresses? Too summery?

Another text from Fiona brought her deliberations to an end.

P.S. Don't get all togged up. The White Hart is NOT that kind of place. Dress code is casual i.e. jeans. xx

With a feeling of trepidation, Violet strolled along the street to the pub. In the end, she had decided to wear her smartest black jeans, and a loose-fitting white linen shirt. Hanging around her neck was a vintage, Jorgen Jensen pewter pendant. As it was a mild evening and she didn't have far to walk, she wasn't wearing a coat.

The pub's side door was propped open, and a small crowd had spilled out into the covered smoking area near the car park. Violet made her way to the main entrance at the front of the pub.

When she got inside, she pushed her way to the bar, which was surprisingly busy for a Monday night. Once there, she turned and surveyed the tables, looking for Fiona and the rest of the Nash family.

'What can I get for you?' said the woman behind the bar. She had short, blonde hair and the same shaped eyes as Molly.

'Are you Molly's mum, by any chance?' Violet asked.

'That's right,' she replied, pushing a hand between the beer pumps for Violet to shake. 'I'm Cathy.'

'And I'm Violet.'

'I know. I've seen you around, and Molly's mentioned you a few times. So, what's your tipple, Violet?'

'I'll have half a pint of bitter, please.'

'Nice weather?'

Violet gave a puzzled frown. 'Er, yes. It's quite mild out there.'

Cathy threw back her head and laughed, making her look even more like Molly. 'Nice Weather is our guest ale,' she said. 'From the Dancing Duck Brewery in Derby. I can recommend it. It's a real thirst quencher.'

Violet smiled. 'Half a pint of Nice Weather it is, then.'

Before jostling her way through the packed pub, Violet took a swig of her beer. It was indeed refreshing, with a hint of fruitiness.

Fiona and her family were at a table near the window. Tom and Darren stood up and introduced themselves and made room for her on the window seat. Sophie was there too, sharing a bottle of Merlot with her mum. Eric sat at the end of the table, a pint in one hand and a newspaper in the other.

'Mum tells me this is your first time in the White Hart,' said Tom.

'It is. I've been meaning to call in for ages. I didn't realise it got so crowded in here.'

'It's not usually this busy on Mondays, but there's live music on later,' Eric said, as he put down his newspaper. 'And as the only pub in the village, the White Hart does have the monopoly.'

212

'There's a bar at the Merrywell Manor Hotel, isn't there?' Violet said.

Fiona laughed. 'There is, but you won't catch the locals going in there. It's much too pricey.'

'She's right.' Eric nodded. 'The last time I bought a round of drinks at the hotel, I thought I was going to have to take out a second mortgage. You can get a bottle of wine in here for the price you pay for a glass at the hotel.'

Sophie grinned. 'The prices are high to keep out the riff-raff, Dad,' she said.

'Say what you like, the hotel is superb,' said Darren. 'And the food is exquisite . . . well worth a visit for a special celebration.'

'I'll remember that,' Violet said. 'I might go there for my birthday.'

'That's in January, isn't it?' Fiona said. 'That's ages away.'

Eric had gone back to reading his paper. 'Think yourself lucky,' he muttered. 'It'll give you plenty of time to save up.'

At nine o'clock, a young female singer perched herself at the end of the bar and began to tune her guitar. When she launched into a rendition of 'Africa', by Toto, the chatter in the bar died down.

Violet leaned across to whisper in Fiona's ear. 'It's a while since I've listened to any live music.'

'Then sit back and enjoy it,' Fiona replied. 'I've heard this girl before, and she's good.'

Two half pints later, as Violet listened to the mesmerising notes of 'While My Guitar Gently Weeps' she realised her phone was vibrating in her handbag. She pulled it out far enough to read the screen. It was Matthew.

'Excuse me,' she said, standing up and shuffling around the table. 'I'm going to have to take this.'

Despite the background noise, she answered the call before Matthew rang off.

'Hey, Violet. Where are you?'

'At the pub,' she said. 'Give me a minute . . . I'm going outside. I'll be able to hear you better out there.'

'Sounds like a good night,' Matthew said, as Violet pulled open the front door and stepped onto the street. Maybe it was the three halves of bitter or the blast of fresh air, but she suddenly felt wide awake, even though it was almost quarter past ten.

'It's my inaugural visit to the White Hart. I'm with Fiona and the rest of the Nash clan.'

Why had she told him that? What difference did it make who she was with?

'Apologies for not ringing earlier,' Matthew said. 'I've been at my mum and dad's for a family meal. I've only just got home.'

'Did you manage to get to the record office?'

'I did, yes. It took me a while to hunt down the information you wanted, but I got there in the end.'

'And? When was the shelter sealed up?'

'Are you ready for this?'

'I've been ready since five o'clock this afternoon,' she said. 'Come on, don't keep me in suspense.'

'The first complaint about antisocial behaviour at the old air raid shelter was made in August 1979, but no action was taken. More complaints were made, off and on, over the next few years. Finally, in 1982, it was agreed that the shelter should be sealed off permanently. There was even talk about removing it altogether and filling in the trench, but that solution was deemed to be too expensive. In the end, a security gate was fitted to the old entrance, and then the whole thing was blocked off with a concrete cover.'

'When in 1982?'

'The work was completed in May of that year, and . . . get this. The person who fitted the grid and installed the concrete block was the school caretaker, a Duncan Kirkwood.'

'Duncan Kirkwood?' Violet said. 'You're joking?'

'Why would I be joking?'

She told him what she knew of the school caretaker.

'It must have been one of the last big jobs he did before he left the school,' she said, leaning her back against the wall of the pub and feeling the roughness of the stone through her thin cotton blouse. 'Nigel told me that Helen left him in June of 1982,' she said, pausing to think things through. 'Which means, if she *was* killed here in Merrywell, we can rule out the old shelter as a hiding place.'

'No, we can't,' Matthew said. 'As far as I know, no one's been in the shelter since it was closed off. However, for practical reasons, it had to be left in an accessible condition. The concrete cover over the entrance has a metal hatch in it. It's locked, obviously, but anyone who had a key could have got into the shelter. Or, more to the point, used it to dispose of Helen's body.'

Violet pressed her head against the wall, closed her eyes, and listened to her heartbeat thrumming in her ears.

'Does this mean you're coming round to my way of thinking?' she said. 'Do you agree with me that Helen is probably dead?'

'I honestly don't know what to believe,' Matthew replied. 'But your theory does have merits. More importantly, I know how much the mystery of what happened to Helen is playing on your mind. If I can help you find an answer – one way or another – then I'm willing to give it a go.'

'We could be onto something with the air raid shelter,' Violet said. 'It's got to be more than a coincidence that Duncan Kirkwood left so soon after Helen's departure. Maybe if I spoke to DS Winterton, he'd be willing to organise a search of the shelter.'

She sensed Matthew's hesitation on the other end of the phone. From inside the pub came the intro notes of another song, but it wasn't one she was familiar with.

'Are you sure that's the right thing to do?' Matthew said. 'If you involve DS Winterton at this stage, there's no going back. Depending on the outcome, you'll either be a hero or a villain. If the police search the shelter and find Helen Slingsby, you'll be a hero in their eyes. However, to the people of Merrywell, you'll be branded as the woman who likes to poke her nose into other people's business.'

'And if the police search the shelter and find nothing?'

'Then you become a villain in everyone's eyes – someone who's stirred up trouble for the village, at a time when the community is already dealing with Martha's murder.'

'That sounds like a lose-lose situation to me.'

'You said it.'

'Is that how *you* see me?' Violet said. 'As a woman who likes to poke her nose into other people's business?'

'It doesn't matter what I think.'

'It does,' she said. 'It matters to me.'

She heard him sigh.

'For the record, I believe you've acted with the best of intentions,' he replied. 'But yes, I do think you're sometimes too curious for your own good. Don't take that as a criticism, by the way.'

'How else am I meant to take it?'

'It's an observation, that's all. I worry your curiosity will get you into hot water. The trouble is, you're a strong-minded person, and no matter what I say, I know I won't change your mind.'

'So, as well as being an out-and-out snoop, I'm also deaf to advice, am I?'

He laughed. 'If you *are* willing to listen, I'd suggest you say nothing to the police for now. Not until you know for certain that Helen's body is where you think it is.'

'And how the devil am I meant to determine that?'

'By coming with me to the air raid shelter.'

'How's that going to help? What do you expect me to do? Stand on top of it and use my x-ray vision to look for Helen's body?'

'You have x-ray vision?' He laughed again. 'Is there no limit to your talents?'

'Don't be facetious, Matthew.'

'Isn't that what you were being?'

She shivered in the cool night air. 'Sorry, I didn't mean to be flippant. I just don't see the point in going to the shelter if we can't get in.'

'I agree,' Matthew said. 'But one of the things I discovered at the record office was that the parish council retained a set of keys to the hatch and the grid, in case emergency access was required.'

Violet pushed herself away from the wall. 'There are keys?' she said.

'There are,' Matthew replied. 'And I'm holding them in my hand right now. It required a little subterfuge, but I've managed to take temporary possession of them.'

'You *have* been busy,' Violet said, seriously impressed with what he'd managed to achieve. 'Where did you get them from?'

'They'd ended up in a box of old keys in the clerk's office. I told her I was looking for the key to an old storage area under the stage at the village hall. She handed me the box and wished me luck.'

'How did you know which ones were the keys to the shelter?'

'They were marked with a label. ARS.'

'ARS?'

'Air raid shelter. At least, that's what I hope it stands for. The thing is, I have to return the box to the clerk tomorrow morning. So, if you want to search the shelter, it's going to have to be tonight.'

Violet watched as someone approached the pub and went inside. For some inexplicable reason, she longed to do the same. Suddenly, all she wanted was to go back to the bar, drink more beer and listen to the music.

Why was she being so cowardly? Matthew had gone to a lot of trouble on her behalf, and he was giving her the chance to prove her theory. She should be grabbing this opportunity with both hands.

'Violet?' he said. 'Are you still there?'

'What if I'm wrong?' she said. 'What happens if we go into the shelter and find absolutely nothing? What if my theory about Helen is complete garbage? I'll feel like a fool.'

'Don't you see?' Matthew said. 'That's the beauty of this. If we go into the shelter tonight and find nothing, no one need ever know we've been down there. We can treat it like a covert operation. We'll wait until after midnight, and then make our search. If we find Helen's body, we'll call in the police. If the shelter's empty, we'll lock up again and go home. What have we got to lose?'

Violet liked that he'd said *we*.

'If there's nothing there, you promise you'll keep this between us?' she said. 'You won't tell anyone else?'

'I won't say a word,' he replied. 'I'd only get myself into trouble if I did. Judith Talbot would be spitting feathers if she knew what we were planning.'

'You think she'd disapprove?'

'Definitely.'

'In that case,' said Violet. 'Let's do it.'

Chapter 34

They arranged to meet under the covered gateway at the church at half past midnight. Violet had changed into a pair of old jeans, and she'd put on a checked shirt and an old woollen jumper, assuming it would be cold and damp inside the shelter. She was also wearing a pair of sturdy walking boots, thick socks, and a kagoul. Matthew had instructed her to bring along the best torch she owned. She'd thought about using it as she walked through the village towards the church, but it wasn't necessary – her way was lit by an almost full moon shining in a clear sky. For now, the torch was tucked into her pocket, along with her phone.

When she got to the lychgate, Matthew stepped out from the shadows.

'Are you ready?' he said, keeping his voice low.

'As I'll ever be,' she replied.

Behind him, in the graveyard beyond the gate, hundreds of headstones stood sentinel in the moonlight.

'Let's go,' she said, shivering despite her woolly jumper.

They climbed over the stile by the well and crossed the fields to avoid any possibility of being spotted on the main street. As they passed the rear of Greengage Cottage, Violet got out her phone and played Martha's voicemail to Matthew. She also told him about Helen's pregnancy, the plant, and the anonymous note that had been pushed through her letterbox.

'What are the police doing about it?' he asked.

'They've taken the note away to be fingerprinted, but I get the feeling DS Winterton did that to humour me. He thinks I'm a nuisance.'

'He'll be forced to change his mind if you find Helen's body in the air raid shelter.'

'Don't count on it,' Violet said. 'He'll be seething if I present him with another case to solve.'

They walked in silence for a few minutes, their path lit by the moon. As they traversed the field and curved down towards the school, Violet clutched her stomach, which was fluttering with nerves.

'Do you think we *will* find Helen?' she said.

'I don't know. But whatever the outcome, at least you'll know one way or the other whether she's down there. And even if she isn't, that doesn't mean your theory's wrong. She could be somewhere else.'

'Are you scared?' Violet asked. 'About going into the shelter?'

'I can't say that I'm looking forward to it. It won't be a pleasant experience, especially if we do find Helen's remains.'

'Your dad said it could be full of rats.'

Matthew held up a hand. 'Don't tell me that. If there's one thing I can't stand, it's rats.'

They were approaching the school, which was fenced with metal railings and a locked gate.

'How are we going to get into the back, to the playing field?' Violet asked.

Matthew tapped the side of his nose. 'I know every inch of this village,' he said. 'We'll need to carry on along the lane, and skirt round the back. There's a meadow that abuts the playing field – we'll go through there. It'll mean clambering over a low wall. I hope you're up for that?'

'Lead the way,' Violet said. 'I'm right behind you.'

Chapter 35

'We should have guessed it wouldn't be straightforward,' Matthew said, as he examined the concrete construction that covered the entrance to the disused air raid shelter. Embedded into it was a metal hatch, which was rusty and engrained with dirt.

'When you said a hatch, I thought it would be bigger,' said Violet. 'This looks more like a manhole cover. How on earth are we going to squeeze through that?'

'I'd say that's the least of our worries. We won't be squeezing anywhere unless we can get it open. There's a slot here for the key, but it's pretty clogged up.'

Violet watched as he tried to work the large metal key into the lock. The hills loomed in the distance, dark and menacing, and somewhere in the distance, a creature shrieked.

'What was that?'

'I don't know,' Matthew said. 'An owl, maybe. Or a fox.'

'Doesn't it bother you, being out here at night?'

'Not really,' he said. 'But I guess I'm more used to it than you are. This is the countryside, Violet. A lot of wild animals come out at night. Get used to it.'

She shuddered.

'You're not scared are you?' Matthew said, smiling at her in the moonlight.

'I'm not going to lie. I'd rather be at home, in my bed.'

'Me too,' he said. 'I mean *my* bed, obviously. Not yours.'

He grinned mischievously, prompting Violet to point at the hatch.

'Just get on with opening that,' she said. 'And less of your cheek.'

She watched as he pulled a can of WD-40 from inside the backpack he'd been carrying.

'If this doesn't do the trick, nothing will,' he said, as he sprayed the rusted lock.

While they waited for the lubricating chemicals to do their magic, Violet surveyed the school playing field. The old shelter lay off to the side, its outline still visible as a hump in the grass directly in front of them. Behind it was a walled playground, and in the other direction a football pitch. It was startlingly quiet out here, the only sound the gentle whistle of the wind as it whipped around the side of the school building.

'Let's give it another go,' Matthew said, as he leaned over the hatch and presented the key to the lock. Violet waited, keeping her fingers crossed that the WD-40 had worked, and dreading what would come next, if it had.

She heard a grating sound, followed by a click, and then Matthew punched the air and smiled up at her.

'We're in,' he said, as he removed the heavy metal cover. 'Torches at the ready. I take it you'd like me to go in first?'

She nodded, trying not to think about rats – or, worse, the very real possibility that they were about to find what was left of Helen Slingsby.

Matthew shone his torch into the newly created aperture. She knelt behind him and peered over his shoulder. Beyond the concrete security cover was the original set of steps down into the shelter. At the bottom of those steps was the entrance, which was blocked off by a gridded metal door.

'You do have the key to that door as well?' she asked.

'I've got what I'm hoping is the key,' Matthew replied. 'I'll go down first . . . see if it fits.'

He swung his long legs over the hatch and lowered himself onto the concrete steps below. When he got to the door, he shone his torchlight onto the lock and inserted the key.

Violet held her breath and waited. There was another click, and Matthew pushed the door, which opened inwards.

'That's it,' he said. 'We're in.'

'Wait for me, I'll come down.'

'Are you sure you want to?' he said. 'If Helen's body is here, it's not going to be pleasant. I'm happy to do the search if you'd prefer to stay out there.'

Violet shook her head. 'It's OK. I'm not squeamish. We'll go in together.'

She slid her legs over the side of the hatch and lowered herself onto the steps. Matthew put out a hand to steady her.

'Are you ready?' he said, giving her upper arm an encouraging squeeze.

Fear had stolen her voice, so she replied with a nod and a nervous smile.

Matthew turned, shone his light into the shelter, and disappeared. Violet moved down the steps and followed him inside.

Chapter 36

The first thing that hit her was the dank, musty odour and the stale-tasting air. She clapped a hand over her mouth, wishing she'd brought a face mask.

The interior was smaller than she'd expected. Try as she might, it was hard to imagine hundreds of people crammed inside such a small space. Down one side were the remains of wooden bunk bedframes, lined up against the concrete wall. As she walked further into the shelter, her foot collided with something that clattered across the floor. She pointed her torch in the direction of the sound, and saw that it was an old beer bottle. It spun around, reminding Violet of the old kissing game she'd played as a teenager. She watched it slowing down, and when the bottle stopped, she realised it was pointing at her.

She hurried on, past an old bucket filled with sand, being careful not to brush against the wall on the right, which was fusty and damp.

'You OK?' Matthew said.

She nodded. Then, realising he couldn't see her in the dark, she spoke to him from behind her fingers.

'I'm all right,' she said. 'Apart from the smell.'

'I can't see any rats,' Matthew said. 'Thank heavens for small mercies, eh?'

They crept through the shelter together, edging along the right-hand wall towards the far end. When something dripped from the arched ceiling onto Violet's head, she pressed her hand against her mouth to stifle a squeal.

As they walked, they directed their beams into any possible hiding space. This was an awful, awful place; cold and eerie. The thought of Helen Slingsby being left down here filled Violet with horror.

At the halfway point, the only things their torches had revealed were the bedframes, the beer bottle, and the remains of what appeared to be a man's shoe. And then, as they reached the end of the shelter, Violet's torchlight landed on what looked like a pile of rags laid out on the end bunk. She stopped and grabbed Matthew's arm.

'What's that?'

He directed the beam of his own light at the thing she was pointing to.

'There's only one way to find out,' he said, moving towards the bedframe and blowing air through his mouth.

There was definitely something on the lower bunk, shrouded in an old grey army blanket. Its outline was relatively flat, but at one end, near the wall, was something round and solid.

Violet's fingers trembled as she reached out and pinched the edge of the blanket. Taking a deep breath, she pulled it back to reveal what lay beneath.

Chapter 37

It was a discarded overcoat, and an earthenware hot water bottle.

Violet released the breath she'd been holding on to, and Matthew leaned forward, resting his hands on his knees.

'Thank God,' he said, letting out a huge sigh. 'I honestly thought you were going to uncover a skeleton. Come on, Violet. Let's get out of here.'

They walked back to the exit silently, swinging their torches as they went, double-checking under each of the bedframes, searching for any undiscovered nook or cranny. But other than dust and dirt and gravel, the place was empty. Helen Slingsby's body was not in the shelter.

As she pulled herself back up through the hatch, Violet took in lungfuls of the cold night air. A mixture of disappointment and relief were making her feel nauseous, so she lay back on the grass and stared up at the sky. Orion's Belt was directly above her head: three bright stars more or less evenly spaced in a nearly straight line. She knew that their names were Alnitak, Alnilam, and Mintaka, and that the central star, Alnilam, was more than thirty times bigger than the sun. And she knew that Alnitak at the lower end of the belt, was actually a triple star system, said to be around 1,260 light-years from earth. How could she know *those* things, and yet not fully comprehend what had prompted her to go down into the old air raid shelter? What on earth had she been thinking?

'I'm so sorry,' she said, feeling foolish and silly, and embarrassed about wasting Matthew's time. 'It was stupid of me to think she might be down there.'

Matthew had locked up the shelter door, and he was now sliding the hatch cover back into place.

'You're not stupid, and there's no need to apologise,' he said, as he turned the key to lock it.

'There's every need,' Violet said, propping herself up with her elbows. 'I've dragged you out here in the middle of the night on a fool's errand. What must you think of me?'

Matthew stood up, dusted himself down, and switched off his torch, which was redundant now that they were back under the illumination of the moon.

'You didn't drag me here,' he said. 'I came of my own free will, based on a perfectly reasonable hypothesis. OK, so your hunch was wrong, but that doesn't mean it wasn't valid. At least now we know that Helen isn't here. I'll return the keys tomorrow and no one need ever know we've searched the place. It's a win-win.'

Violet didn't feel like she'd won anything. She'd convinced herself that Helen would be in the shelter, and roped Matthew into an unpleasant and fruitless mission.

And what if it wasn't only the shelter she'd been mistaken about? What if her whole theory about Helen was wrong?

'It's kind of you to try and save my blushes, Matthew, but I feel mortified, and there's nothing you can say to change that. However, I am grateful for your help, and hugely relieved I didn't get the police involved. Imagine what DS Winterton would have said if I'd made him search the shelter? I'd have ended up a laughing stock.'

'You're being too hard on yourself,' Matthew replied. 'I also think you're overrating your persuasive abilities. In the event that DS Winterton had decided to search the shelter, it would have been *his* choice – just as it was my choice to come here with you tonight. And for what it's worth, I'm beginning to think your theory about Helen is spot on. We may not have found her resting place just now – but that's not to say she isn't out there somewhere.'

Violet stood up and walked alongside him, back to the lane.

'Your dad told me there are disused mine shafts around here,' she said, keeping her voice low. 'Maybe that's where Helen ended up.'

He frowned. 'I hope you're not going to ask me to go down one of those with you?'

'No fear,' Violet said. 'Even I know when to draw the line.'

They retraced their steps, back over the stile and across the fields behind Violet's house.

Realising it would be quicker to jump over the low wall and let herself in through the back door, she stopped.

'This is me,' she said, pointing to the rear of Greengage Cottage. 'I may as well leap over the wall, rather than walk all the way round.'

'Righty-o,' said Matthew. 'Good night, Violet. I'd like to say it's been fun, but I'd be lying. It has, however, been interesting. There's never a dull moment with you around.'

His smile reassured her that he was being complimentary, rather than sarcastic.

'I'm going to go in and make myself a hot chocolate,' she said. 'You're welcome to join me, if you want to.'

He glanced over towards her house. 'Thanks, but I'd better go home. I need to get some sleep. I'm out tomorrow, so I've got an early start in the morning.'

He stood and watched as she negotiated the low stone wall, waiting until she'd unlocked her back door. Then, raising a hand in farewell, he continued on his journey across the field.

Chapter 38

Violet switched on the kitchen light, put a pan of milk onto the stove to warm and tried to calm down. At least by coming in through the back, there had been no chance of anyone seeing her sneaking around in the middle of the night.

As she spooned chocolate powder into a mug and stirred in the warm milk, she let her mind wander. Despite the late hour and the ordeal of her night-time escapade, she felt remarkably wide awake. Perhaps it was the walk across the fields, or the adrenaline from the search, but her mind was buzzing and refusing to wind down.

As she'd clambered over the dry-stone wall into her garden, being careful not to dislodge the coping stones balanced carefully along the top, an idea had popped into her head and stayed there as she'd let herself in through the back door. Now, as she sipped her warm drink, she tried to recall what it was.

Perhaps she was more tired than she thought, because try as she might, she couldn't retrieve the memory. Maybe she should follow Matthew's lead and go to bed. If she could sleep, her elusive idea might reappear and be waiting for her when she woke up.

* * *

The next morning, as she made toast and marmalade for breakfast, she turned on the radio and tuned in to the local station. The eight a.m. news included another appeal for information from the team investigating Martha Andrews' death.

They're obviously still short on eyewitnesses, Violet thought. *Why haven't more people come forward? Normally, you can't sneeze in Merrywell without someone knowing about it.*

As she closed the front door on her way to work, the idea that had eluded her in the early hours finally returned, popping into her head unannounced. Climbing over the wall last night and letting herself in through the back door must have triggered a hazy memory, buried deep in her subconscious.

She stopped at her garden gate, pulled out her phone, and found the voicemail from Martha. As she replayed it, she listened carefully as the message reached its conclusion. Yes . . . there it was, a noise in the background, a muffled sound just before Martha said: *I've got to go. There's someone at the door.*

Was she imagining it?

Violet played the message again, and then played it a third time to make absolutely sure. There was definitely something there.

Instead of turning left and going straight to work, she veered right, and then right again along School Lane, holding her breath as she approached Martha's house.

She didn't even need to go into the front garden to confirm her suspicions. It was visible from the gate: a white doorbell button, the same one she'd pressed on the day she'd interviewed Martha.

Her heart was thumping as she called DS Winterton's number.

'It's Violet Brewster,' she said, when he answered the call. 'I've remembered something, although I'm not sure how relevant it is.'

'You can let me be the judge of that,' the detective said. 'I'm happy to listen to anything if it will help me solve the case.'

'Don't get excited,' said Violet. 'I'm not about to unveil Martha Andrews' killer, but what I am going to say might prompt a new line of inquiry.'

'What is it you've remembered?'

'When I visited Martha last Thursday, I went to her front door, rang the bell, and she let me in.'

'I take it she was expecting you?'

'Yes. Yes, she was, but the point I'm making is . . . she had a doorbell.'

'Nothing unusual about that, is there?'

'No, but if you replay Martha's voicemail message and listen carefully, you'll hear a noise just before she ends the call. It's the sound of someone knocking on her door. Why would they do that when there was a perfectly good doorbell?'

'Maybe the bell wasn't working,' DS Winterton said. 'The one I have at home is always playing up.'

'It was working on Thursday when I was there. It was one of those Westminster chimes, and it was extremely loud because I could hear it from outside. If anyone had rung the bell while she was leaving a message for me, it would have been audible in the background. Instead, there's a knock – only a faint one – but a knock nevertheless.'

'So, what is it you're suggesting?'

'That the person who went to Martha's house didn't use the front door. They went to the back.'

'But the house is on a terrace,' said DS Winterton. 'As far as I know, there's no way of gaining entry through the back.'

'No, but the gardens on that row of houses back onto an open stretch of land that leads down to the river. There's a public footpath that runs along the riverbank, and I remember seeing a low wall at the end of Martha's garden. Someone could easily have climbed over it. I did the same thing at my own house last night . . .'

Violet bit her tongue, conscious that it would be better to keep the details of her own wall-climbing antics to herself.

'I suspect the person who called at Martha's house used the back door to avoid being noticed,' she said. 'I may be new to

Merrywell, but even I know you can't walk its streets without someone spotting you.'

'It's true that no one's come forward who saw anyone going into Martha Andrews' house on the day she was killed,' DS Winterton said.

'That's exactly my point. If her attacker went in through the back, he or she would be much less likely to be observed.'

'OK . . . it's possible,' DS Winterton said, although he didn't sound completely convinced by Violet's theory. 'I'll listen to the recording again myself, and if it confirms what you're saying, I'll arrange for the river path to be searched.'

'That stretch of the river is a popular spot for anglers,' Violet said. 'If anyone was fishing down there on the day in question, they may have seen something.'

'We can check the fishing permits to find out if anyone was in the vicinity,' DS Winterton said. 'Thank you, Violet. You can leave it with me now, but please let me know if you remember anything else.'

'I will,' she replied. 'How are things going with the investigation? Are you any closer to solving the case?'

DS Winterton cleared his throat. 'Let's just say things aren't progressing as quickly as I'd like. This *is* a murder investigation, though. That much I can tell you.'

'Have you had the results of the post-mortem then?'

'We have. The pathologist has confirmed that Martha died as the result of a blow to the head. We believe the killer struck her with a rock, although there was no sign of it at the crime scene.'

'Maybe you should check the dry-stone wall at the bottom of Martha's garden. If the killer did climb over it, they could have grabbed one of the stones from the top and taken it up to the house with them.'

'That's a good point,' DS Winterton said. 'The other big mystery, of course, is where the murder weapon is now.'

'The footpath follows the river,' Violet said. 'The killer could have tossed the rock into the water as they made their retreat. If they did, I don't suppose there's much hope of locating it.'

'You never know. It's been a dry spring, and the river's quite shallow along that stretch . . . we might just find it.'

'Good luck with that,' Violet said. 'I'll keep my fingers crossed for you.'

'Thank you . . . and by the way, Violet, before you go, I ought to tell you that we ran a check on Helen Slingsby and Duncan Kirkwood.'

'You did?' Violet allowed herself a smile of satisfaction. 'I wasn't sure you'd bother.'

'I thought we should, after you received the anonymous note . . . which, incidentally, had only one set of prints on it. Yours.'

Running a check on Helen and Duncan. Tick. Checking for fingerprints on the *stop asking questions* note. Tick. Did this mean DS Winterton was finally taking her seriously?

'You were right about Helen Slingsby,' he said. 'We could find no record of her after 1982.'

'And what about Duncan Kirkwood?' Violet said, keeping her tone casual. 'Have you managed to get in touch with him?'

'No, I'm afraid not. He also disappeared off the radar in 1982, exactly like Helen Slingsby. There's no record of Kirkwood at all after that time.'

'What? No way!' Violet experienced a twinge of anxiety. 'Has anyone ever reported him missing?'

'No, apparently not. One of my officers did some checking, and it appears Duncan Kirkwood got into a fair bit of trouble as a youth. Turns out he was brought up in the care system, so it's possible there was no one he was close to . . . no one to miss the fact that he wasn't around.'

'Curiouser and curiouser,' Violet said, relieved that the police were, at last, listening to her. 'What's your take on the situation, DS Winterton? Do you think he and Helen could have run away together? Changed their names? Left the country, perhaps?'

'It's possible, but if they *were* lovers, why go to the trouble of changing their identities? Why not move in with each other and have done with it?'

'Changing their identities . . . relocating to another part of the UK or abroad. You don't suppose they were in some kind of witness protection scheme?' Violet said.

The detective laughed. 'You've been reading too many crime thrillers, Violet,' he said. 'Anyway, do you honestly think I'd tell you, if they were in witness protection?'

'No,' Violet said. 'I assume you wouldn't be allowed to.'

'You assume right,' DS Winterton said. 'Having said that, if I knew they were under that sort of protection, I wouldn't be concerned about them, would I?'

'But you are? Concerned?'

'Puzzled would be a better description. I've asked one of my officers to look into the Helen Slingsby situation. We've also put some feelers out in Scotland . . . to see if we can locate anyone who knew Duncan Kirkwood. I'm not making any promises, mind . . . but, if we do find anything, I'll let you know.'

'If you're going to look into what happened to Helen,' said Violet, 'does that mean one of your officers will be talking to Nigel Slingsby?'

'I'd imagine so. At some point.'

Oh crikey, Violet thought. *I am not going to be popular in the Slingsby household. Nigel will rue the day he got me involved.*

Chapter 39

'Where did you run off to last night?' Fiona said, when Violet called in to buy lunch at the bakery. She'd had a busy morning: interviewing Colin Packer, designing flyers, and filming more infill shots – so she'd worked up quite an appetite.

'I didn't *run* anywhere,' Violet said, hoping the rush of blood to her cheeks wouldn't prompt a cross-examination from Fiona. 'It was well after ten when I left.'

'I'd have put money on you staying until chucking-out time,' said Fiona. 'You were enjoying yourself until your phone rang. I hope it wasn't bad news.'

'No . . . just, stuff,' Violet said, determined to keep her whereabouts the previous evening a secret. 'But, you're right, I did have a nice time at the pub. The singer was excellent. Thanks for inviting me.'

'You're welcome,' Fiona said. 'It's not usually that busy on Monday evenings, but live music always drags in the punters. You'll have to come with us again sometime.'

'I look forward to that,' Violet said.

As she crossed the courtyard and let herself into *The Memory Box*, Violet's phone rang.

'Violet, it's Lionel Pilkington. Colin Packer tells me you interviewed him this morning . . . and I know you have plans to speak to Judith as well. I wonder if you'd like to come over and talk to me sometime?'

Violet's heart sank. The last thing she wanted was for the community film to turn into a campaign vehicle for local councillors. On the other hand, Lionel had given her free access to his photography collection, so she felt indebted to him.

'OK,' she said, laughing nervously. 'Although, I have to warn you . . . the twenty-minute film you commissioned is in danger of turning into a full-length movie.'

'I appreciate that, and I know you can't speak to everyone,' Lionel said. 'But I am a familiar face in Merrywell and I'm sure people will expect to see me in the film.'

'I could do a joint interview . . . you and Judith.'

'Absolutely not,' Lionel said. 'Judith would never go for that. And actually, I'd rather you didn't mention to Colin or Judith that I've asked for an interview. Not until I've had a chance to speak to them. I don't want them thinking I'm trying to steal the spotlight.'

Even though that's exactly what you're hoping to do, Violet thought.

She was aware that politics and ego were often mutually dependent, but she was determined not to let the councillors hijack the film. If necessary, she would leave every one of them on the cutting-room floor.

'So . . .' Lionel said. 'I was wondering if you were free later this afternoon?'

Deciding to give in to the inevitable, Violet agreed to interview him at Fern Lodge at four-fifteen. How much of what he said would end up in the film was anyone's guess.

After she'd ended the call from Lionel, Violet leaned on her desk and thought about the futility of *Operation Find Helen*. She hadn't spoken to Matthew today, although he had sent her a brief text to confirm that the keys to the shelter had been returned to the clerk's office, safe and sound.

Carrying one half of her sandwich, she wandered into the back room and stared at the wall of Post-its. Locating Helen's body was turning into mission impossible, so she decided it was time to consider things from a different perspective. Instead of focusing on the *Where?* question, it was time to reflect on the *Who?* Who had the most compelling reason to get rid of Helen?

Violet scanned the blue Post-its, filling in the blanks for suspect 7 with Duncan Kirkwood's name. Next, she removed Brian and Joyce Collis's names from the wall. As far as she was concerned, they were no longer in the picture, never mind the frame.

Her eye was drawn to suspects 5 and 6: Lionel Pilkington and Damian Rushcliffe. She knew a lot more about Damian than she did about Lionel. Then again, the things she'd learned about Damian had been gleaned from the interview he'd given her – information *he'd* elected to share with her. There could be another side to his character that she hadn't yet discovered. There was also the small matter of the pendant. On the face of it, Damian appeared to have acquired it coincidentally, completely unaware of its history. But was the purchase as innocent as it seemed?

And what of Lionel? He'd been the head teacher at the school when Helen left. He would have known her better than most. What had been the nature of their relationship? Perhaps she should make it her business to find out when she visited him later on.

Lionel had claimed to have no recollection of Duncan Kirkwood. How would he react if she quizzed him about Helen Slingsby? The woman had been his PA: she was one colleague he couldn't misremember.

There was something slightly discomfiting about the way Lionel had summoned her to Fern Lodge. He was one of the few people left on her list of suspects, so perhaps she ought to do some homework before she went dashing off to see him.

As she finished her sandwich, Violet sent a text to Fiona.

If you've got 10 minutes to spare, I'd like to pick your brain about something. Can you pop over? Or I can come over there, if you prefer. xx

The reply came back almost instantly.

Just sorting a catering order at the mo, but will be free in about half an hour. I'll come to you. xx

When Fiona turned up, she was carrying two paper coffee cups.

'There you go,' she said, plonking one of them on Violet's desk. 'One cup of my finest cappuccino.'

'Cheers, Fi. I didn't expect you to bring coffee. I could have made us a drink.'

Fiona wrinkled her nose. 'You won't catch me drinking that horrible instant muck you insist on serving,' she said. 'You really should get yourself a proper coffee maker, especially if you're planning to offer your clients a drink. The quality of your coffee should reflect the quality of the service you provide.'

'I will get one, eventually,' Violet said. 'But I need to start earning some more money before I splash out on an expensive coffee machine.'

Fiona sat down and crossed her legs.

'Are you going to tell me why you've called this conflab?'

'I want to sound you out about something,' Violet said. 'Or rather, *someone*. I'm after information.'

'Well, you've come to the right person. What is it you want to know? Does it have anything to do with the Helen Slingsby mystery, by any chance?'

'Yes and no. I'll admit Helen has been playing on my mind. I can't shake her off . . . and believe me, I've tried.'

'You still think someone from Merrywell could have killed her?'

'I do. I've been trying to work out who that might be, as well as where they might have put her body.'

'Whoa!' Fiona held up a hand. '*You've* been trying to work it out? Shouldn't you be asking the police to do that? They're in a much better position to find answers than you are.'

'They have started to take an interest,' Violet said. 'But Helen Slingsby is old news, and I doubt they'll be in any great rush to find out what happened to her. In fact, the minute they hit a brick wall, they'll probably give up entirely. However, if I can establish a link to Martha Andrews' murder, the police will *have* to take it more seriously.'

'So, by working out who killed Helen – assuming she *was* killed – you think you'll uncover Martha's murderer at the same time?'

'That's the theory,' Violet said. 'Although it's going to be easier said than done. For a while, I had this mad idea that Helen's body was in the old air raid shelter on the playing field.'

'*Eww*! Don't tell me that. You're giving me the creeps.'

'No need to freak out – she isn't there,' Violet said. 'Don't ask me how I know, because I'm not at liberty to say, but you can take my word for it. Wherever Helen is, it's not in the shelter.'

Fiona pinched her lips together. 'Violet Brewster, you can be very secretive when you want to be.'

Violet squirmed. 'I will tell you about it at some point,' she said. 'Once this whole thing is over.'

'Have you considered the possibility that this *thing* might never be over?' Fiona said. 'That despite your best efforts as an amateur sleuth, the whereabouts of Helen Slingsby will remain a mystery?'

'Don't call me an amateur sleuth.' Violet pulled a face. 'It makes me sound like some kind of poky-nosed Nancy Drew character.'

'Wasn't Nancy Drew a teenager?' Fiona smiled. 'I'd say you're more of a—'

'Don't you dare say Miss Marple.'

Fiona closed her mouth and grinned sheepishly. 'So, what's your latest theory?' she asked. 'I hate to say it, but if Helen isn't where you thought she was, could that be because she's alive and well and left Merrywell in one piece?'

'No, something happened to her, of that I'm certain – either *before* she left the village, or shortly after.'

'But without a body, you have absolutely no proof of that,' said Fiona. 'Which, if you'll excuse me saying, does make this whole scenario highly dubious.'

'I know,' Violet said. 'I *know*.'

'Have you thought about bringing in a psychic? Even the police use them sometimes to find bodies and missing people . . . I saw a programme about it once, on telly.'

'Fiona, if I got a psychic involved, the people of Merrywell would think I'd lost the plot.'

'So you've called me in instead, have you? You need me to help you work out whodunnit?'

'Not exactly, but there is someone on my list of suspects that I'd like to know more about.'

'Now I *am* intrigued,' Fiona said, leaning forward. 'Who are we talking about?'

'Lionel Pilkington,' Violet said. 'He's asked me to interview him later this afternoon, but I'm feeling apprehensive about it. The bloke's an enigma. I can't work him out. When I ran into him the other day, he blew hot and cold . . . friendly one minute, aloof the next.'

'He is a hard one to fathom,' Fiona agreed. 'During my time in Merrywell I've made friends with a lot of people, but I can't say Lionel is one of them. He keeps people at a distance, possibly because he has a superiority complex. The only person he's close to is his wife. He and Irene are like that.' She placed the middle finger of her right hand across the top of her index finger and held up her hand.

'So they're happy together?' Violet said.

Fiona nodded. 'They're what is commonly referred to as a *devoted* couple. They stick together like glue . . . never socialise separately. Wherever Irene is, Nigel is one step behind, and vice versa.'

Violet grimaced. 'Sounds pretty claustrophobic to me. Do you think they spend all their time together because they *want* to, or because one or other of them is insecure?'

'I've never really thought about it,' Fiona said, raising her eyebrows. 'I suppose I've always taken them at face value. Come to think of it, I haven't seen them much recently. They're becoming very insular in their old age. As I recall, they didn't even turn up for the Christmas fair at the village hall. They normally run the raffle stall, but apparently Lionel made some excuse or other.'

Violet shifted uncomfortably. The Pilkingtons' disappearance from the village social scene was probably because of Irene's health issues. However, having been told about Irene's condition in confidence, she wasn't at liberty to share that information.

'They don't come into the café anymore either,' Fiona added.

'Did they used to be regulars?'

'Two of our best customers. They used to come into the bakery as well, until Lionel and I had a disagreement.'

'What about?'

'He reckoned my sourdough wasn't up to scratch.'

Violet's mouth fell open. 'What a cheek,' she said. 'Your sourdough is amazing. It's chewy and tangy, just like it should be, and it makes the *best* sandwiches.'

'That's what I told him,' said Fiona. 'I make it properly, unlike a lot of the supermarkets, who use commercial yeast. Anyway, no one disses my bread and gets away with it, so Lionel and I had a minor set-to. He hasn't been in the bakery since.'

'I'd say he's cutting his nose off to spite his face,' Violet said.

'So would I, but it doesn't look like he's going to back down. They continued to patronise the café and bookshop for a while but, like I say, I haven't seen them in there either . . . not for ages.'

'Here's a question for you,' Violet said. 'When I mentioned Lionel's photography collection to Irene, she said the photos were originally her father's. Do you know if that's true?'

'It is. The photographs originally belonged to Irene's father, Edward Theakstone, as did Fern Lodge. Rumour has it, he was quite the eccentric, and a complete egomaniac. His son – his first and, at the time, *only* child – was killed in the Second World War. When the war ended, Theakstone was determined to get himself another heir. He divorced his first wife – who by then was past childbearing age – and married a much younger woman . . . Irene's mother. Theakstone was in his fifties by the time Irene was born.'

'So Irene inherited Fern Lodge from her father?'

'Yes, she's lived in the house all her life. Even after they got married, Irene and Lionel continued to live at Fern Lodge with her parents. The second Mrs Theakstone died a few months after Irene's wedding, but Mr Theakstone lived on into his eighties. The house passed to Irene when he died.'

'And what about Lionel?' Violet asked. 'What's his background?'

'He comes from more humble stock. He grew up in a working-class suburb of Manchester, went to teacher training college, and met Irene when he started working at Merrywell Primary.'

'For saying you're not friendly with Lionel, you seem to know an awful lot about the man.'

Fiona grinned. 'It's amazing what you learn when you keep your ear to the ground.'

'And you say I'm curious,' Violet said, rolling her eyes as she sipped her coffee. 'The Pilkingtons' big house then, the fancy lifestyle . . . that's all courtesy of Irene's family?'

'Without a doubt,' said Fiona. 'Teachers are notoriously under-paid. If it wasn't for the Theakstone wealth, Lionel would never be able to maintain such extravagant surroundings.'

'Did he marry Irene for her money, do you think?'

Fiona laughed. 'How the blazes would I know? I may be the fount of all knowledge round here, but there are some things even I haven't got a handle on. You'd have to ask him yourself, although I wouldn't recommend it.'

Violet chuckled. 'I could always drop the question in at the end of this afternoon's interview. Can you imagine it? *Excuse me, Lionel. Did you marry your wife for her money?*'

'I can guarantee he'd send you away with a flea in your ear,' Fiona said.

'Lord knows what he'd say if he knew he was on my list of suspects.'

'Why exactly *is* he on your list?'

'He's one of the few names left,' Violet said. 'By a process of elimination, I've whittled it down to two or three people. Initially, my main suspect was Duncan Kirkwood, the guy who worked as a caretaker at the school – but now, DS Winterton tells me they can't find any trace of him either. Like Helen, he seems to have disappeared in 1982.'

'You're kidding!' Fiona shuddered. 'Blimey, Violet. What are you getting yourself into? You need to be careful. This is all taking a very sinister turn.'

'Don't worry about me,' Violet replied. 'To be honest, I'm running out of patience with it all. Unless I can work out who Helen was involved with, I'm about ready to give up.'

'You reckon Helen was killed by the same person she was having an affair with?'

'Probably. Or it could have been Nigel.'

'What?' Fiona said. 'No way. Nigel is one of the gentlest, most unassuming men I've ever met.'

'Even nice people have their breaking point. If Nigel found out Helen had been unfaithful, he might have lost his temper and lashed out. He may not have meant to hurt her . . .'

'No, definitely not,' Fiona said, with a firm shake of her head. 'There's nothing you can say that will convince me that Nigel is a killer.'

'What about Lionel?' said Violet. 'Do you think he could have been having an affair with Helen?'

Fiona deliberated for a moment. 'The Lionel of today would never be unfaithful to Irene,' she said. 'But forty years ago . . . who knows?'

'You said Lionel has a high opinion of himself? Maybe Helen pandered to his ego, and he gave in to temptation.'

Fiona seesawed her head, weighing up the odds. 'It could have happened, but if it did, I don't think it would have been a serious thing – certainly not for Lionel. I can't imagine him leaving his rich wife for another woman.'

'Irene did say something strange to me, while I was over at Fern Lodge. She told me that Lionel could be quite a charmer with the ladies. She also said she needed to watch me. What do you think she meant by that?'

'Maybe she was joking,' Fiona said.

'No. I'm pretty sure she wasn't.'

'In that case, maybe she was airing a long-held grievance. If so, it's possible Irene doesn't trust him. Maybe she never has. Who knows, the Pilkingtons might not be quite the devoted couple they would like to have us think.'

After Fiona had gone, Violet thought about Damian Rushcliffe, deliberating about whether to take him off her suspect list. He was a thoughtful and spiritual kind of guy, and those were qualities that were hard to fake. He certainly didn't come across as a potential killer.

Violet wondered what Damian would say if he knew she'd been down into the old air raid shelter.

As she cast her mind back to the previous night's exploration, something Damian had mentioned in his interview began to nag at her. She jiggled her mouse to bring her screen back to life, and opened the document containing the typed transcript of his interview, skipping through to the bit where he'd talked about the shelter. She soon found the section she was looking for.

After the church was damaged, a few people built dugouts in their back gardens. Some of the houses had a cellar they could use, and there was talk of sheltering in the railway cutting over by the station, should the need arise.

Dugouts and cellars. Greengage Cottage had its own cellar, and she'd also noticed a cellar door at *Well View Cottage* when she'd visited the Collises. She wondered how many other houses in the village had one. A huge house like Fern Lodge would, surely? And what about the old dugouts? Were any of them still in existence? Could Helen have been hidden in one of them until such time as her killer could dispose of her body properly?

Violet glanced at the clock. If she hurried, there was just enough time for her to talk to Damian again before she went over to Fern Lodge.

Chapter 40

A few minutes later, Violet paid her first visit to *The Epicurious*, where she bought a dozen of their finest handmade chocolates. She tried not to baulk at the shop's eye-watering prices, telling herself it was money well spent. The chocs were a thank-you gift for Damian for his excellent interview but, more importantly, they gave her a valid excuse to call on him.

It was three o'clock when she knocked on the door of his bungalow. He took a while to answer, but smiled broadly when Violet presented him with the chocolates.

'Come on in,' he said.

Leaning heavily on his stick, he walked back into the living room.

'These look nice,' he said, as he flopped into an armchair and popped one of the chocolates into his mouth. 'What a treat.'

'They're from *The Epicurious*, over in the shopping village,' Violet told him. 'It's a great shop. They sell all sorts of delicious goodies.'

'Aye, I'm sure they do,' Damian said. 'But that stuff sells at tourist prices. My pension doesn't stretch to such luxuries.'

He selected another chocolate and then, rather reluctantly, held the box in Violet's direction.

'It's OK,' she said. 'I bought them for you.'

'And I'm very appreciative,' he said, balancing the box carefully on the arm of his chair. 'How's the film going? Is it nearly finished?'

'I'm getting there,' she replied. 'Actually, there's something you mentioned last week that I'd like to ask you about. You said some of the houses in the village had dugouts or used their cellars as shelters during air raids. Can you remember which ones?'

'I don't know as I can,' Damian said. 'You're asking me to cast my mind back an awfully long way.'

'You told me the other day that your long-term memory was good.'

'Did I? I can't remember,' he said, winking to show he was pulling her leg.

Violet laughed. 'Come on, Damian. Think. Which houses have a cellar and which had an Anderson shelter?'

'Are you going to tell me why you want to know?'

'No,' she replied. 'I don't think I am.'

'You like to keep things under your hat, don't you?' he said, turning down the corners of his mouth. 'You've still not told me why you were asking about Zelda's necklace. Still, you must have your reasons for keeping secrets, and it's not for me to question them. If you're willing to go and make me a nice cuppa to have with these choccies, I'll sit and have a think.'

Damian was delving into the box of chocolates again when Violet returned from the kitchen with a freshly brewed cup of tea.

'Cheers,' he said. 'It always tastes better when somebody else makes it.'

She smiled, wondering how often it was that anyone made a drink for the old man.

'Now,' Damian said. 'I'll start with the Anderson shelters, shall I? There was one at what is now Judith Talbot's house. After the war, it was converted into a garden shed, but I understand Judith got rid of it as soon as she moved in . . . said it was an eyesore. She likes things just so, does that one.'

Violet watched as he put a raspberry cream truffle into his mouth. 'There were also a few families on School Lane that had Anderson shelters, but they were removed shortly after the war ended. I shouldn't imagine folks wanted to look down their gardens and be reminded. As for the cellars, let me have a think . . .'

'There's one at my house,' Violet said. 'Greengage Cottage.'

'Aye, that's right. And I believe the cottage next door to you has one un' all. The Collises' place has a cellar, if I remember rightly, and the corner house on the junction of Church Lane and School Lane. The village shop had one, but it was mainly used for cold storage. Obviously, the pub has a cellar, as does Merrywell Manor and Fern Lodge. The latter has three or four quite sizeable underground rooms from what I've heard.'

'Does it now?' said Violet, her antennae twitching. 'I've been inside Fern Lodge. It's a big, fancy house. Very posh.'

'It's always been a grand sort of place, which puts it out of bounds for most of us,' said Damian. 'Early on in the war, Edward Theakstone was asked if he'd allow the cellars at Fern Lodge to be used as a community shelter – should the need arise. He refused point blank.'

'That wasn't very community-spirited of him,' Violet said.

'Theakstone wasn't known for his compassion,' Damian said, slurping his tea. 'Quite frankly, he was a miserable sort . . . acted like he was lord of the bloomin' manor. He probably thought folks would run off with the family silver if he let them into his home.'

'Not exactly a barrel of laughs, then?'

'Quite the opposite,' Damian said, with a wry smile. 'The only person who ever had any time for old Mr Theakstone was his daughter, Irene. She thought the world of him, and he worshipped the ground she walked on. They had a real mutual admiration society going on.'

'How did Mr Theakstone get on with Lionel?' said Violet.

'He didn't. Theakstone tolerated Lionel, but only because Irene refused to give him up. Lord knows why, but Lionel Pilkington was the one person Irene loved more than her father. I reckon she'd have done anything for him, even turn her back on her family if it had come to that.'

'But it didn't?'

'No, after the marriage, there was an uneasy truce between the two men. The family all lived together at Fern Lodge, so it couldn't have been an easy life for any of them. I dread to think what the atmosphere must have been like. Mind you, it was a big house, so it wasn't like they were living on top of each other – not like most folk around here. There were some big families in Merrywell, back in the day, a lot of them living in tiny cottages.'

'Things have changed a lot since then,' Violet said, glancing at her watch. Time was pressing on. She stood up. 'Anyway, Damian, thanks for the info. I knew you were the man to ask.'

'It's my pleasure,' he said. 'Are you off now, then?'

'Yes, sorry I've got to dash. I've got another appointment to go to.'

'OK, well . . . thanks for dropping by. You're welcome any time. I like having someone to talk to, and I'm glad I could help with your question about shelters and cellars. It's nice to feel useful, even if you are keeping shtum about why you want to know.'

Twenty minutes later, Violet was back in her office. Her camera bag was packed ready for her four-fifteen interview with Lionel, but it was still too early to set off. She would put her time to good use by reading through the final draft of the project proposal she'd been writing for the youth charity. Getting another commission would be a dream come true, but she wasn't going to take anything for granted.

She made a few minor tweaks to the wording, and then submitted the proposal via an online portal. If she got the job, it would mean regular trips to Chesterfield which, although only fifteen miles from Merrywell, was far enough away to get her out of the village for a while. Once the community film was

249

completed, it would be no bad thing to keep a low profile for a few weeks.

As she closed down her computer, her phone rang. It was Matthew.

'Hey,' she said. 'How are you?'

'I'm OK. Yourself?'

'Yes, fine ... although still feeling a bit deflated after our unsuccessful mission last night.'

'At least we didn't blow our cover,' he said. 'The keys have been returned without anyone even realising they were gone.'

'I know, I got your text.'

'I'm sorry I didn't ring earlier,' Matthew said. 'I'm in Manchester today, at an exhibition, otherwise I'd have called in to see you. I know how disappointed you were last night, but I'm glad we tried. As someone famous once said ... *it's better to have tried and failed ...*'

'*... than to live wondering what would have happened ...*' said Violet. 'Alfred Lord Tennyson, I believe.'

'If you say so. It has a ring of truth, no matter who said it.'

'I much prefer the Samuel Beckett quote,' Violet said. '*Ever tried. Ever failed. No matter. Try again. Fail again.*'

'Mmm ... can't say I'm familiar with that one,' said Matthew. 'Should I be worried? Is this your crafty way of telling me you're going to try again?'

'I've not quite given up yet, if that's what you mean. I'm tenacious – you should know that by now. Having drawn a blank at the air raid shelter, I've been thinking about alternative locations.'

Matthew groaned. 'I admire your stamina, Violet, but it's time to call it a day. Leave it to the police.'

'There's not much chance of them finding anything,' she said. 'I'm a lot more willing to stick my neck out than they are.'

'That's because your neck is tougher than theirs, seeing as it's made of brass.'

'Oh, yes,' Violet said, laughing self-deprecatingly. 'That does give me the advantage.'

'On a serious note,' Matthew added, 'you need to watch yourself. You may be tough, but that doesn't mean you're invincible. If you keep poking at a hornets' nest, sooner or later you'll get stung.'

'Don't fret. I'll be careful.'

'Being careful might not be enough. If you insist on chipping away at this mystery, you could end up putting yourself at risk. If someone did kill Helen, they won't want you to expose them, will they? You don't know what kind of reaction you might provoke.'

'The person I've got in mind is less of a danger these days.'

Matthew took a sharp intake of breath. 'You mean you've homed in on a suspect?' he said.

'I have.'

'Is this you taking a shot in the dark, or do you have proof?'

'No, unfortunately, I don't have any evidence,' Violet said. 'My theory is pure supposition. The only reliable thing in all this is my gut. It's never wrong.'

'Didn't your gut tell you that Helen Slingsby's body was in the air raid shelter?'

'All right, clever clogs. My gut is *hardly ever* wrong.'

'And what's it telling you right now?'

'That the answers to this mystery can be found at Fern Lodge.'

Matthew gave a low whistle. 'How the devil did you come to that conclusion?'

'I've been considering the few nebulous facts I've managed to glean over the last week or so, and they're starting to point in one direction. I spoke to Damian Rushcliffe a few minutes ago, and he told me that Fern Lodge has a huge amount of cellarage. I'd say that's as good a place as any to hide a body . . . either on a temporary or even permanent basis.'

Matthew laughed at her. Actually laughed.

'You're letting your imagination spiral out of control,' he said. 'I agree that Lionel might not be the most charismatic bloke in

251

the world, but he's an upstanding member of the community. You can't possibly be serious?'

'I think he was having an affair with Helen,' Violet said. 'And the relationship would probably have run its course if she hadn't got pregnant.'

'But you've no actual proof of this?'

'Not yet,' Violet said. 'But I'm due at Fern Lodge in about fifteen minutes . . . and I've decided . . . I'm going to talk to Lionel.'

'You're going to do *what*? For God's sake, Violet, you can't just march in there and accuse him of murder.'

'I don't intend to,' Violet said. 'You see, I don't think it was Lionel who killed Helen. I think it was Irene.'

Chapter 41

'Whatever it is you're planning, please promise me you won't go to Fern Lodge on your own,' Matthew said. His words boomed through the phone, serving as both a reprimand and a warning. 'I'll be finished here in Manchester in about an hour. I can be back in Merrywell by six. Wait for me, and I'll come with you.'

'Lionel's expecting me in a few minutes,' Violet said. 'I can't cancel at the last minute.'

'Tell him something's come up.'

'He'd smell a rat,' she said. 'If I'm right about Irene, Lionel is bound to know about it. It must have been him who left that plant, and sent the note telling me to stop asking questions. He probably complained to Judith as well.'

'All the more reason to stay away from him.'

'I suspect warning me off is his way of protecting his wife.'

'I don't like any of this, Violet,' Matthew said. 'How did Lionel know you'd been asking about Helen anyway?'

'I didn't think he did . . . not at first. Although, later, I did mention Helen when I asked him about Duncan Kirkwood.'

'You said Martha had also made enquiries about Duncan?' Matthew said. 'Maybe it was Lionel she spoke to. It seems logical, given that he was the head teacher who employed Duncan in the first place.'

'That would make sense.' Violet gripped her phone. 'But did Martha speak to him, or leave a message for him?'

'With Irene?'

'Yes, with Irene.'

'Are you saying Irene killed Martha as well as Helen?'

'I still haven't worked that out,' she said. 'My best guess is that Martha went round to Fern Lodge and talked to Irene, not knowing . . .'

'Not knowing what?'

Violet hesitated. She might suspect Irene of being a killer, but it still didn't feel right to reveal the state of her health.

'I'm really not comfortable telling you this,' she said, 'but given the circumstances, I don't suppose I have any choice . . . Irene is ill.'

'What's wrong with her?'

'She has dementia,' Violet explained. 'Apparently she has good days and bad days. It's possible she was confused . . . got Martha mixed up with Helen. Who knows what was going through her mind.'

Matthew groaned frustratedly. 'This is getting messy, Violet. You could have this all wrong, or you could be bang on the money. Either way, you need to play it safe. Please, wait until I get there before you go round to Fern Lodge.'

'If I turn up with you in tow, Lionel will be suspicious,' she said. 'It's better if I go alone, do the interview and act normally. I'll just have a friendly chat, ask a few neutral questions about the community, and then get the hell out of there. Job done.'

'I still don't like it.'

'I'm not a hundred per cent sold on it myself,' Violet said. 'But I'm expected there in a few minutes. It's too late to back out now. I promise not to ask any awkward questions. In fact, I won't mention Helen Slingsby at all . . . cross my heart.'

* * *

As she made her way down the long driveway at Fern Lodge, Violet paused to take in the details of the house. There was no doubting its grandeur. It was three storeys high, built from local grey lime-stone, with mullioned windows that were dwarfed by the towering façade in which they were set. But despite its impressiveness, there was something undeniably grim and forbidding about the house.

When Violet reached the front door and raised her hand to ring the bell, she remembered Matthew's warning. Was she making a mistake coming here? She lowered her hand, hesitating.

On her right, a gravelled pathway curved around the front of the house and disappeared through an archway of trees. Curious about where it went to, she followed it past the front windows, hoping to scurry by unnoticed. When she reached the trees, she saw that the path snaked down a sloping bank and ended at a small, wooden gate that gave direct access to the public footpath along the river.

Irene could have used this route last Tuesday, Violet thought. *She could have slipped out without Lionel noticing, gone through the little wooden gate, followed the path, and been at the rear of Martha Andrews' house within a couple of minutes.*

It suddenly dawned on her how right Matthew was to be concerned. It wouldn't be wise to go into Fern Lodge alone – not until she'd spoken to the police and let them know her suspicions.

Right now, her phone was tucked inside her camera bag, switched off ready for filming. Rather than dig it out and call DS Winterton, instinct told her to go down the path, out of the gate, and head back to the village along the footpath. She would text Lionel later to rearrange the interview, saying that something had cropped up.

Hoisting her camera bag onto her shoulder, she stepped under the archway of trees, and began her descent towards the gate.

'Violet!'

It was Lionel's voice, coming from somewhere close by. She froze. For one fleeting moment, she considered breaking into a run, leaping over the gate and making her escape, but Lionel was right behind her now. She could hear his footsteps on the gravel. Taking a deep breath to steady her nerves, she fixed a smile to her face and turned.

'I thought it was you,' he said. 'I saw you go past the window. What are you doing down here?'

'I was admiring the view,' she said. 'Your garden is magnificent . . . so many beautiful trees. And you have access to the river . . . how lovely.'

What had she said that for? Why was she drawing attention to the focus of her thoughts? It was a crazy thing to do.

'The grounds are rather special,' Lionel said. 'But they come with a huge amount of responsibility. I can't possibly maintain all of this on my own. I have to employ help, and that can be expensive – but it's worth it. The gardens bring Irene a lot of pleasure.'

'She must love the house very much,' Violet said. 'It's a splendid place.'

She waited, wondering if Lionel would reveal that Irene had inherited Fern Lodge from her father. He didn't.

Instead, he smiled and said: 'Shall we go inside?'

Fleetingly, she thought about making an excuse, but that would only draw attention to her unease, and make Lionel suspicious. At this stage, the best option was to go into the house, do the interview, and act normally.

She followed him back along the path and, on shaking legs, walked in through the front door of the house.

'How's Irene?' she asked, as she stepped into the hallway. 'Is she around?'

'She takes a nap in the afternoons,' Lionel replied. 'That's why I chose this time to invite you over. We won't be disturbed. It's the only part of the day when I get any peace and quiet.'

'It must be hard, caring for someone 24/7, being responsible for them.'

'Not really. Irene likes to potter in the garden, so I do occasionally get some time to myself. Being her carer does have its challenges, and it can be exhausting, but she'd do the same for me if the roles were reversed.'

'I'm sure she would.'

'Shall we go into the study?' he said. 'It's as good a place as any to film the interview.'

She followed him along the wood-panelled hallway and they entered a room in the north-west corner of the house. It was lined with shelves filled with old, leather-bound books, and there was a large mahogany desk in the corner. The two windows had views of the front garden. In the distance, Violet could see the weeping willow tree, its lower branches trailing in the river.

'This must be a lovely room to work in,' she said, making polite chitchat as she hurriedly recovered her composure.

'It certainly *looks* the part,' Lionel replied. 'But it's a little too formal for my liking. This was my father-in-law's domain. I have an office upstairs and, if I have paperwork to do, that's where I tend to go. I've always found this room rather stuffy . . . almost claustrophobic, but it will serve as a good backdrop for my interview.'

At last, he'd mentioned his father-in-law, giving Violet the 'in' she needed to glean more information about the notorious Edward Theakstone.

'Did your father-in-law live with you then?' she said, playing dumb to draw out more details.

Lionel frowned. 'It was the other way around. This was my father-in-law's house . . . it's been in the Theakstone family for generations. My wife inherited it when he died.'

'I see,' Violet said, as she placed her camera bag on the floor and reached inside it for her camera. 'I'm no expert in these things but, architecturally, I'd say Fern Lodge is an important building within the village. Perhaps you'd like to say something about its history for the film? Or would you prefer the focus of your interview to be on another topic?'

Lionel sat on the leather captain's chair behind the desk. 'I have no strong opinions either way,' he said. 'Please sit, Violet, and put your camera down. Before we get started, there's something I want to talk to you about.'

She placed the camera on the edge of the desk and, as nonchalantly as possible, lowered herself into the chair Lionel was pointing to. It was uncomfortable and rickety – exactly like the one she'd sat on at the community centre, on the day she and Lionel had first met. It felt as though things had come full circle. She'd been anxious on the day of her interview with the parish council, but that was nothing compared to how she felt now.

'I've thought long and hard about this conversation,' Lionel said. 'And I've decided it's best to be candid with you.'

Placing his elbows on the desk, he leaned forward and stared at her with cold eyes. 'I understand you've made it your personal mission to find Helen Slingsby.'

Chapter 42

Violet felt her stomach lurch. This wasn't how things were supposed to go. She was here to interview Lionel, not the other way around. She needed to claw back control of the conversation or, better still, get out of here.

'I have asked a few questions about Helen,' she said, schooling her expression into one of calm casualness. 'Nigel's been trying to find his wife . . . I think I mentioned it to you. He thought I might be able to help, but I haven't been able to find any trace of her online, so I've given up. I'm much too busy with the film to get sidetracked.'

Lionel's pale blue eyes narrowed. He'd obviously seen straight through the lie.

'I don't think you're being completely honest with me, are you?' he said. 'I know for a fact you're still asking questions – and not just about Helen. You've now made it your business to track down Duncan Kirkwood – you even asked *me* about him, so don't try to deny it.'

'I thought you said you couldn't remember Duncan Kirkwood,' Violet said, in a rallying display of boldness. 'Has something happened to jog your memory?'

Lionel scowled impatiently. 'I was at the school yesterday.

I spoke to Becky Meads and she told me you'd been asking about some former employees. That's when I remembered . . . about Duncan.'

Violet shrugged, feigning indifference. 'I thought he might know what had happened to Helen. I even considered the possibility that the two of them were involved.'

Lionel gave a dry laugh. 'Helen and Duncan? I don't think so. She had better taste than that.'

Violet shifted uncomfortably, and the chair creaked. She didn't like the way this was shaping up. Not one bit.

'You have no intention of letting this go, do you?' Lionel said, his voice crackling with undisguised anger. 'I did hope you'd see sense and let it drop.'

Violet's heart was pounding. 'Was it you who left me the plant?' she said. 'And sent the note telling me to stop asking questions?'

'Much good it's done,' Lionel replied, making no effort to deny the charges.

Fear was crushing Violet's chest, making it difficult for her to breathe.

'Your stubborn determination has left me no choice but to tell you what you want to know,' Lionel continued. 'As I say, I'll be candid with you, Violet, but only if you promise to hear me out and not go running to the police.'

Violet wasn't going to promise any such thing, but she thought it prudent to keep her counsel. Instead, she gave a noncommittal nod and said: 'Go on.'

Lionel leaned forward to check that the camera was switched off, and then sat back, looking more relaxed. 'The person that Helen was having an affair with, was me,' he said. 'And when I say *affair*, that rather overstates the nature of our relationship. It was more of a brief, inconsequential dalliance.'

Violet experienced a brief moment of vindication – but having her suspicions proved right offered no real satisfaction. The only thing she was feeling now was an overwhelming sense of fear. Her body had gone cold, and she was beginning to tremble. Pulling in a shallow, ragged breath, she eyed the door, wondering how easy it would be to make a run for it.

'Is that how Helen saw it?' she said, aiming for a conversational tone, even though her mouth had gone dry.

'No, sadly, not. The truth is, we worked late a few times . . . fooled around. As far as I was concerned, it was just a bit of fun. I didn't realise Helen was taking it all to heart. She said she was in love with me. She thought I was going to leave Irene.'

'But you had no intention of doing that?' Violet placed her feet firmly on the floor and moved to the edge of the chair.

'Certainly not,' Lionel replied, his voice curt.

'So, what happened next? After you'd had your *fun*?'

As soon as the words were out, she regretted them. Antagonising him was a foolish thing to do, but despite the danger she was in, she was finding it impossible to suppress her anger. Lionel had played with Helen's already delicate emotions and then callously swept her aside when she no longer served a purpose.

'Please don't take that judgemental tone with me, Mrs Brewster,' he said. 'Believe me, I tried to let Helen down gently, but she wasn't having any of it. She was like a limpet. Rather than break things off, she expected me to divorce Irene. She had this silly notion that we were going to run away together, leave Merrywell. I told her it wasn't going to happen, that I had a wife and son who I loved.'

'And Helen was unhappy about that?'

'Unhappy? She was livid,' Lionel said. 'She barged into my office one afternoon, demanding that I tell Irene. When I refused, she stormed out and didn't speak to me for the rest of the day. I worked late that evening . . . I only wish I'd left on time . . . things might have turned out differently if I had.'

He tilted his head and turned away.

'What happened?' Violet said, doing her best to hide the tremor in her voice.

'Helen came round here, to Fern Lodge, and told Irene about the affair. I'm not sure what her motivation was . . . spite probably, or revenge. Or perhaps she thought she could get her own way by ruining my marriage. Whatever her reasons, Helen had underestimated my wife.

'Irene always gives the impression of being a calm, serene person, but you know what they say about appearances being deceptive. Helen made a fatal mistake in coming here. She didn't realise that Irene has been plagued by jealousy all her life – and when the green-eyed monster pays a visit, it plays havoc with her personality.'

'What are you saying?'

Lionel put his hands behind his head and leaned back. 'Helen told my wife a cock-and-bull story about how she and I were going to run away together. It was all nonsense, of course, but Irene wasn't to know that. She was furious. She lashed out . . . struck Helen hard, and knocked her off balance. She fell down . . . banged her head.'

The matter-of-fact way he was relating such appalling details made Violet's blood run cold.

'I arrived home to find Helen lying on the floor of the drawing room,' he continued. 'She was dead. Irene was in a state of shock . . . standing there, pale and shaking. I had no choice but to help her . . . you understand that? Irene is my *wife*. I'd do anything for her.'

Violet cast a sly glance over Lionel's shoulder, towards the door. She had to find a way to get out of here.

'I know you and Irene are close,' she said, placating him with fake empathy. 'Husbands and wives . . . they look out for each other, don't they?'

'Irene has always relied on me . . . *leaned* on me,' Lionel said, a note of complaint creeping into his voice. 'There's no way I could have betrayed her to the police, and there was our son to think of. He was away at boarding school at the time. He knows nothing about any of this.'

'What did you do with Helen's body?' Violet said, knowing she was putting herself in danger by asking the question, but needing to know the answer.

'It's here, in the cellar,' Lionel said, his voice cold, almost business-like. 'There's a network of underground storage rooms below the house. I put Helen's body into the smallest of them, bricked it up and whitewashed over it. It seemed like a reasonable solution.'

Reasonable? Violet was screaming inside. *There's nothing reasonable about killing an innocent woman and hiding her body beneath the house that you live in. And* whitewashed? *That word is very apt, because that's exactly what this was: a whitewash. You were concealing a crime to protect your own reputation.*

'Fern Lodge will pass to our son eventually,' Lionel continued. 'The house will stay in the family, so I know there's no chance of Helen's body being discovered, not in my lifetime anyway. You must realise that none of this was my doing. I was simply helping Irene.'

You can't exonerate yourself completely, Violet thought. *It was your 'dalliance' with Helen that set this whole sorry story in motion.*

'It's what you do now that matters,' she said, using every ounce of control she had to stay calm. 'You have to tell the police.'

'I can't do that,' he said.

As she opened her mouth to object, Lionel held up a hand.

'Please, hear me out. I'm asking you to be compassionate. I don't want to involve the police. Irene is ill and not fit to stand trial. What good would it do to drag all of this out into the open?'

Was he seriously expecting her to keep this a secret? Or was he sounding her out before deciding what to do next?

'Be reasonable, Lionel,' she said, praying he still possessed a shred of decency she could appeal to. 'Helen should be properly laid to rest, and Nigel deserves to know what happened to his wife.'

'Nigel doesn't deserve anything,' said Lionel, dismissively. 'He and Helen were miserable in their marriage. And anyway, he's survived for forty years not knowing where Helen is. Why the sudden interest?'

'I think he's hoping to get married again,' Violet said, breaking a confidence in one last-ditch attempt to influence Lionel's better nature.

He scoffed. 'At his age?'

'There's no age limit to love.'

Lionel smiled pityingly. 'You're obviously a caring person, Violet, and I admire that, truly I do. But I need you to see things from my point of view. I didn't kill Helen, but I did dispose of her body. If I'm thrown into prison, who will look after my wife?'

'I think you're overlooking the fact that Irene will be facing charges of her own,' Violet said. 'The judge may take her illness into account when it comes to sentencing, but she was young and healthy when she killed Helen. She'll be answerable for her actions based on her physical and mental state at the time the crime was committed.'

'And do you think that's fair? It was a crime of passion, a spur-of-the-moment act . . . Irene had no intention of killing Helen. She's had to carry the guilt of what she did ever since.'

'Are you expecting me to keep quiet about what you've told me?' Violet said. 'Am I supposed to say nothing to the police? How can you justify that?'

'I realise it's asking a lot,' Lionel said, 'But the truth is, Helen wasn't a very nice person. I know we're not supposed to speak ill of the dead, but the reality is, she was manipulative and selfish, and she treated Nigel shabbily.'

Violet felt light-headed. The conversation was taking on a dreamlike quality, as though she had fallen into an outlandish, alternative world, where nothing was quite as it should be.

'That still doesn't justify what your wife did,' she said, clenching her fists and reminding herself of the very real danger she was in. 'Did Irene know that Helen was pregnant? Did she know that in killing Helen, she was also killing her unborn baby?'

Lionel's face twitched. 'Pregnant?' he said. 'How could you possibly know that?'

'How I know doesn't matter. What I'm asking is, did Irene know? Did *you*?'

'Absolutely not. I have no idea what you're talking about. Whoever told you that must have been misinformed.'

If Lionel was putting on an act, it was a convincing one – but Violet didn't trust him. In fact, she couldn't shake the feeling that there was something here that wasn't adding up.

She stood and reached for her camera bag. 'I should go,' she said. 'I hope you do the right thing, and report this to the police, Lionel. If you don't, I'll have no choice but to tell them myself. For your sake, and Irene's, it's better that it comes from you.'

Lionel pushed himself up from the desk, moving so quickly that the chair rolled away from him.

'Please,' he said, coming to stand in front of her. 'Don't be hasty. There must be a way we can work this out . . . come to an arrangement?'

'Arrangement?'

He placed his hands on Violet's upper arms to prevent her from grabbing the bag.

'Please don't go yet,' Lionel said. 'Not until you've heard what I have to say.'

'Let go of me,' Violet said, wriggling to free herself from his grip.

Instead of letting go, Lionel tightened his fingers and pressed his thumbs into her biceps.

'*The Memory Box*,' he said. 'I take my hat off to you, Violet. Setting up a new business is a brave thing to do, especially in the current economic climate. Did you know that twenty per cent of businesses in the UK fail in their first year? Sixty per cent fail by year three. It's a tough world out there. I'm in a position to help you.'

'Help me how?'

'I have contacts at other councils,' he said. 'I also know a lot of businesspeople locally. I can put in a good word for you. I'm even happy to give you a chunk of money to see you through the first six months of trading. That's always the hardest period in terms of cash flow. How does twenty thousand pounds sound?'

'Is that how much my silence is worth?' Violet said. 'Twenty thousand?'

'All right, fifty thousand then.'

Violet tore herself away. Abandoning her bag, she dashed towards the door, but Lionel moved faster, blocking her way.

The atmosphere had become toxic. She felt like a canary in a coal mine – exposed and vulnerable. The only way out of this situation now was to go along with Lionel – pretend to accept his hush money. Much as it pained her, she needed to convince him that she was willing to play the game – and then she'd get the hell out of Fern Lodge and go to the police.

'Do you know you have a very expressive face, Mrs Brewster?' Lionel said. 'It gives you away. I can see exactly how your mind's working. You're going to pretend to go along with my plan, aren't you? But then you'll go running to the police.'

'No, I'm not going to do that . . .'

'Don't *lie*,' he said. His voice was an angry bellow, and his face was quivering with fury and desperation. 'Do you really think I'm stupid enough to let you leave here? I will not let you ruin my life.'

As Violet stared at his face, the scales fell from her eyes and she realised she had made a terrible mistake. The smokescreen that Lionel had manufactured was slowly parting, and everything was becoming clear. After days of speculating, the pieces of the puzzle had fallen into the right order. Finally, Violet knew and understood the truth.

'Is that what you said to Helen?' she asked, demanding honesty, even though it meant flying in the face of danger. 'And to Martha?'

She chastised herself as she spoke, wondering how she could have got things so horribly, dreadfully wrong. She had arrived at Fern Lodge believing that Irene was the killer, and Lionel had done a credible job of convincing her of his wife's guilt. But there was something about the way he was telling his story that didn't ring true, and Violet's gut was urging her not to believe a word of it.

'You're trying to blame your wife for something *you've* done, aren't you?' she said. 'You're setting her up . . . using her confusion to your advantage and letting her take the fall for crimes *you* committed. You killed Helen, didn't you? What about Martha? Did you kill her as well?'

Instead of answering her question, Lionel pushed her backwards, towards the rickety chair.

'Sit down,' he said, his voice a hiss. 'It's time you shut up and started to listen.'

Chapter 43

Rage had transformed Lionel's face, twisting it into a malicious scowl.

'You only have yourself to blame for what's going to happen next,' he said. 'You should have done as I asked and stopped asking your confounded questions.'

A surge of adrenaline was urging her to fight or take flight – but right now, neither of those things were remotely possible because she was riveted to the spot, fear gripping her muscles. Coming here was one of the most stupid, reckless and foolhardy decisions she'd ever made. She should have taken Matthew's advice. Instead, she'd blundered in here alone, driven by stubborn impetuosity and a misguided sense of invulnerability. She only hoped it was a mistake she lived long enough to learn from.

Naively, she'd been taken in by Lionel's web of lies. If she'd been smarter, seen through his act, and worked things out earlier, she wouldn't have landed herself in this mess – a mess there seemed no way out of.

Her chances of escaping from Fern Lodge were diminishing with every second that ticked by. To have any hope of surviving this, she would have to do as Lionel demanded: sit down, keep quiet, and listen. Having broken the silence he'd maintained for four decades, he seemed determined to talk and let all of his sordid secrets crawl out of hiding. Violet's one glimmer of hope was that the truth might put things into perspective for him. Make him see sense.

On the other hand, when Lionel revealed the details of what had really happened back in 1982, the words would be impossible to take back. Violet shuddered. Once the truth had been aired, the only way to keep her quiet would be to silence her forever.

He dragged the captain's chair around the desk and parked it next to her, wedging her into a corner. Then he sat down, positioning himself between her and the door.

'I had a fling with Helen,' he said, his voice wheedling and oily smooth. 'It was stupid, and it meant nothing, but then the silly woman came to me and told me she was pregnant. When I asked what she expected me to do about it, she told me we should go away together, leave Merrywell.'

He leaned closer, fixing her with an icy-blue stare. Violet resisted the urge to recoil, afraid it would provoke him.

'But you didn't want that?' she said, desperate to keep him talking.

'Of course I didn't. The woman was deluded. I wasn't going to give up my job, my wife and son . . . my *home* for someone I didn't even like very much.'

'Did you tell Helen that?'

'Not at first,' Lionel replied. 'Initially, I tried to play nicely . . . shake myself free of her amicably, but she clung on like a leech. She was like you, Violet . . . determined and persistent, and unwilling to listen. Helen paid the price for her stubbornness, and so will you.'

'I'm listening now,' Violet said, her voice barely a whisper.

'Good, because this may be the only chance I get to tell someone the truth of what happened . . . the *real* story, as opposed to the fictional version I've been peddling for the last few minutes.'

'There are elements of truth, even in fiction,' Violet said.

'Be quiet,' Lionel said. 'I don't want any comments or questions from you . . . this is going to be a soliloquy, not an interview.

However, if you don't have the patience to sit quietly and listen, we may as well get out of here.'

'You'll let me go?'

Slowly, he shook his head. 'I can't do that. Not now.'

Violet shivered. Fear had weakened her. Even if she could manage to get out, she wasn't sure she had the strength to run.

'No one will believe it if I disappear,' she said, flailing verbally for a lifeline. 'Unlike Helen, I have friends . . . people who know that I've come here.'

'I don't believe you,' Lionel said.

A vein was pulsing in his temple, and there was a wildness in his eyes, as though he'd lost all sense of reason.

Violet decided to play for time. If she could keep Lionel talking long enough, maybe Matthew would make it back from Manchester and turn up here at *Fern Lodge*.

'I do want to hear what you have to say,' she said, doing her best to sound attentive.

It was the sound of the clock on the wall chiming the half hour that quashed any hopes of being rescued by Matthew. It was only half past four. Matthew had said he would be back by six. There was no chance that Lionel's confession would last for an hour and a half.

'Please,' she said, stalling while she racked her brains for an alternative escape plan. 'I'll be quiet. I'll sit and listen. Ever since I heard about Helen, I've wanted to know what happened to her. I really would like to hear your story.'

Lionel stared at her for a moment, and then nodded.

'Helen and I weren't on the same wavelength,' he began. 'Frankly, there were times I wondered whether we were even on the same planet. She kept wittering on about leaving our spouses, moving south, and starting a new life together with our baby. When I reminded her that I already had a wife and son here in Merrywell, she dismissed that as irrelevant. The longer I refused to co-operate, the more determined and nasty she became. She threatened me . . . told me if I didn't go along with her plan, she'd go to see Irene and tell her everything. I couldn't let that happen. Irene would have divorced me. I would have lost everything . . . financial stability, *Fern Lodge*, my position here in the community. I'd worked damned hard to escape my poverty-ridden youth and make something of myself. I wasn't going to let Helen Slingsby strip away everything I'd achieved.

'I knew I had to play smart. I gave in to her demands . . . agreed that we'd go away together. I even told her that I loved her, although I nearly choked on the words.'

Violet watched him shudder at the memory.

'Helen promised to keep everything a secret until I could get some money together,' he continued. 'I told her I needed a few days to move some cash to a new account, money that would see us through until I could get a new job and we found somewhere to live. What I was really doing was using that time to work out a plan . . . deciding how best to rid myself of Helen once and for all.'

From somewhere in the house came the sound of a door closing. Had Lionel's shouts woken Irene? Would she come to the study to find out what was going on?

'I suggested to Helen that we should just go . . . disappear overnight and say nothing to anyone . . . but she insisted on leaving a note for Nigel. She said she owed him that much. I helped her write it, dictated some wording that was suitably vague. The last thing I wanted was for her farewell letter to mention me.

'Helen packed a suitcase and left one evening while Nigel was out playing bowls. I told her to come here, to Fern Lodge. I instructed her to go round to the side of the house, where the car would be parked. What she didn't know was that I was waiting for her in the shadows. When she arrived, I hit her with a spade and knocked her out. Once she was unconscious, I put a hand over her face and smothered her. I can assure you . . . she didn't suffer.'

And is that supposed to make things all right? Violet thought, sickened by Lionel's lack of remorse, his calm casualness.

'There's an old coal chute on that side of the house,' Lionel said, as the clock began to chime the quarter hour. 'Years ago, the coal merchant used it to drop off his delivery. It was an easy way to get Helen and her suitcase into the cellar.'

Even though he had, quite literally, treated Helen like a sack of coal, there was no hint of regret in his voice.

'I'd already bought a supply of bricks,' he said. 'That night, I sealed Helen's body into one of the little storage rooms while Irene was asleep. She didn't have a clue.'

'I did. I knew what you'd done.'

Violet jumped. She'd been so absorbed in listening to Lionel's story that she'd failed to notice that Irene had slipped into the room behind him. How long had she been standing there? How much had she heard?

At the sound of his wife's voice, Lionel's face blanched. Violet thought about using the distraction to make a run for it – but the Pilkingtons were blocking the only exit.

'Irene, what are you doing here?' Lionel snapped. 'You're supposed to be taking a nap.'

'I didn't want to sleep today,' she replied. 'So, I didn't swallow the tablet you gave me.'

When he spoke again, Lionel's voice had taken on a softly persuasive tone. 'The doctor said you need lots of rest, Irene. You need to go and lie down. Go on . . . I'll come and check on you in a little while.'

'You think I go around with my eyes closed, don't you?' Irene said. 'But I saw you that night . . . I did. I watched you go out into the garden. I wondered what you were doing, so I followed you. I saw you kill that woman.'

'You're confused, Irene,' Lionel said, putting an arm around his wife's shoulders and ushering her through the door. 'You need to go and lie down. Violet and I have some business to conclude. I'll come and find you later.'

As Irene turned to go, Violet locked eyes with her.

'He's going to hurt me as well, Irene,' she said. 'Please, ring the police. Tell them what's happening.'

272

'Ignore her, dear,' Lionel said, his voice stern. 'Go back to the drawing room. There's nothing for you to worry about.'

Giving her husband one last look, Irene lowered her head and walked into the hallway, taking Violet's last shred of hope along with her.

The only option now was to postpone the inevitable, and the best way to do that was to keep Lionel talking.

'Tell me about Martha,' Violet said, after Irene had left the room. 'I know I'm not supposed to ask questions, but I'm not willing to settle for a half-truth. You promised to tell me the whole story. Did you kill Martha as well? And what about Duncan Kirkwood . . . what happened to him?'

Lionel closed the door and stood in front of it with his arms folded.

'Martha came round here last week when I was at a council meeting. She spoke to Irene, and started asking questions about Duncan. Irene told her to write me a note and, as soon as I read it, I knew I had a problem. There was nothing Martha liked more than stirring things up. When she worked at the school, she was the one who always thought she knew best.'

'What did her note say?'

'That you were looking into Helen's whereabouts, and that she was trying to recall the name of the caretaker who'd left the school around the same time as Helen. She couldn't remember Duncan's name, but she thought I'd be able to.'

'You told me you couldn't remember Duncan.'

'I lied,' Lionel said. 'I didn't want you looking for him. You might have been willing to accept there being no trace of Helen, but I knew the game would be up if you found out that Duncan Kirkwood had disappeared as well.'

'I don't understand . . . What happened to him? And what about Martha? Why did you have to kill *her*?'

Violet was engulfed by a groundswell of sadness and guilt. If she hadn't asked so many questions, Martha might still be alive.

'Because I was angry,' Lionel said. 'With her, and with you. Between you, you were prising open something I'd managed to keep a lid on for years. Martha always was a bleeding heart . . . always looking to champion someone else's cause. When I read her note, I knew it had to be nipped in the bud.'

'So it was you who went round there?' Violet said. 'You went over the back wall and knocked on Martha's door.'

'I did. She seemed to sense danger the minute she saw me. She turned and ran towards the front door, trying to get away . . .'

'But you hit her,' Violet said. 'With a rock? One you'd taken from Martha's own garden wall?'

He smiled. 'Quite the sleuth, aren't you, Violet? You know, you could have become a real asset to this village. It's a crying shame you won't be around to enjoy life here in Merrywell.'

'Tell me what happened with Duncan,' she said, desperate to keep Lionel talking.

'Duncan?' Lionel gave a dry laugh and leaned back against the door. 'He was a wily sort, and he guessed something was afoot when Helen left so suddenly. I told everyone she'd given me a few days' notice, but of course she hadn't. Duncan came to see me and told me he knew about me and Helen. Apparently he'd seen us together in my office in . . . shall we call it a moment of intimacy? Duncan was a troubled man. He had massive gambling debts – which is why his girlfriend in Matlock had given him the elbow.'

'Did he know that you'd killed Helen?'

'I doubt it. I think he thought I'd sent her away . . . paid her off to keep her quiet. Duncan had got himself a job on the rigs, so he was leaving anyway, but before he went, he was hoping to grab himself a bonus by resorting to a spot of blackmail. He told me he wanted five grand, otherwise he'd tell Irene about my affair with Helen. I agreed to pay him, and asked him to meet me at the side of Fern Lodge. It was exactly the same routine as Helen. Same spade, same chute. Different storage room. I hadn't anticipated having to deal with Duncan, so I had to buy more bricks pretty sharpish.'

'And what now?' Violet asked, sounding braver than she felt. 'Am I to become your fourth victim? Do you have another spot in your cellar lined up for me?'

'Not this time,' Lionel replied. 'I need to make this one look like an accident.'

'And how are you going to do that?'

'We'll take a walk down to the river,' he said. 'The bank can be very slippery at this time of year. It would be so easy to stumble, hit your head and fall face down into the river. It's quite shallow at the moment, but you can drown in as little as an inch or two of water.'

'I told you,' Violet said. 'There are people who know that I'm here. You won't get away with this, Lionel. You can't hide the truth forever.'

'If I'm going to go down,' he said, 'I'll go down fighting. Now come here, and let's get going.'

For a moment, she thought she might have a chance to break away, but as she reached the door, he pulled something from beneath the desk. It was a long piece of cord, which he threw over her head before wrapping it around her body, pinning her arms to her sides. Running was still an option, but sprinting at speed would be impossible without her arms to propel her.

The clock in the hallway said five to five. Matthew would only just be setting off from Manchester. Fiona would be in the bakery, prepping for the following morning. As Violet thought of Amelia and her mother and her new friends, a hard lump lodged itself in her throat. Was she going to stand by and let this happen? She loved her family and new life here in Merrywell. Surely those things were worth fighting for?

Lionel held on to her by the knot of rope at her back, propelling her forward, down the hallway and into the drawing room. A discarded throw suggested Irene had been sleeping on the sofa, but there was no sign of her now.

'We'll go out through the French doors,' Lionel said, pushing her roughly in the small of her back.

The second they stepped outside, Violet began to scream, shouting for help at the top of her voice.

Lionel hit her across the back of the head with what felt like a fist. 'You're wasting your breath,' he said. 'No one will hear you. We're well out of earshot of the village.'

Even so, he reached around and covered her mouth with his hand and pushed her towards the bottom end of the garden, to a small grove of beeches.

'Through there,' he said, propelling her towards a gate beyond the trees. 'We have our own private stretch of the river here. And when I say private, I mean no one will see us or hear us. You can struggle all you like . . . no one's going to come to your rescue.'

As they descended a stony bank towards the river, Violet used all her strength to break free of Lionel's grip. Pulling in a deep breath, she tried to run, but it was impossible to balance with her arms strapped to her body. As she began to build up speed, her left foot slipped on the wet, rocky shore of the river. At the same time, she felt Lionel's hands shove her hard in the back, pushing her over.

Unable to use her arms to break the fall, she toppled, full-length – the side of her face smashing onto the riverbank. She lay for a moment, her head throbbing painfully, her feet scrabbling for leverage on the river shingle as she tried in vain to get up.

'Stay down,' Lionel said.

She turned and looked up at her tormentor. Lionel was towering over her, the sun haloing behind his head. In his hand, he held a large rock.

'This time,' he said, 'I'm going to put an end to your questions once and for all.'

He raised his right arm, lifting the rock high for maximum impact. Violet squeezed her eyes shut and waited.

There was a swishing sound, followed by the thud of something hard colliding with bone.

Chapter 44

When she opened her eyes, Lionel's towering presence was gone. Instead, she was shocked to find Irene standing above her, holding a cricket bat. The initial sense of relief Violet felt at being rescued was quickly overtaken by fear. What would Irene's next move be? Did she intend to wield the bat a second time – in her direction?

Rolling onto her stomach, Violet tried frantically to tuck her legs beneath her so that she could get onto her knees.

'I wasn't going to let him do it again,' Irene said, as she stroked the bat's smooth willow wood. 'What he did before was wrong. He thinks I don't remember things, but that's not always true. Some days . . . like today . . . I feel like my old self. But then I recall what happened all those years ago, and I realise I'm better off living my life in a fog.'

As Violet struggled to her feet, she glanced over to where Lionel was lying, face down at the edge of the water.

'Irene, can you please untie me?' she said. 'We need to turn Lionel over. We don't want him to drown, do we?'

'You can drown in as little as an inch or two of water,' Irene said, as she continued to run her hand up and down the bat. 'I heard Lionel say that just now. I was listening in the hallway . . . that's what he was going to do, isn't it? Drown you.'

'Yes,' Violet said. 'Thanks for saving me. Now, we need to help Lionel.'

Carefully, Irene leaned the bat against a rock and went to stand behind Violet, fumbling with the knot Lionel had tied. Violet gave a sigh of relief as the cord began to loosen, moving her elbows to hasten the process. When, at last, she had untangled herself, she threw the rope aside and ran over to Lionel's prostrate body. A lump was already forming on the back of his head where Irene had whacked him with the cricket bat, but when she turned him over, Violet was relieved to see that he was breathing.

Automatically, she reached into her pocket for her phone, but of course it wasn't there. It was in the house, switched off and zipped up inside her camera bag.

'Irene, do you think you can help me carry Lionel into the house?' she said. 'We need to ring for an ambulance, and the police.'

Violet put her hands under Lionel's arms and locked her fingers across his broad chest. Irene went to stand at his feet. She was holding the cricket bat again. Gently, reverentially, she balanced it along the length of Lionel's body, before bending her waif-like body and grabbing his feet.

'I need to look after the bat,' Irene said, as they half-carried, half-dragged Lionel back towards the house. 'It's Daddy's. He scored a record innings at Merrywell Cricket Club with that.'

Lionel was heavy, and it took them a while to reach the house. As they stumbled through the French doors and placed him on the sofa, Violet realised he was beginning to come round.

'Stay with him, Irene,' she said. 'I'm going to go and get my phone and ring for help.'

Violet's legs were shaking as she raced into the hallway and turned towards the study.

That's when the doorbell rang.

* * *

278

As the sound chimed through the house, it was accompanied by a frantic banging. Someone was hammering a fist on the wooden door.

Violet dashed through the hall and fumbled with the latch. When she opened the door and saw who was standing there, she thought the blow to her head was causing her to hallucinate.

'Violet? What the hell happened to your face?'

She touched her right cheekbone, only now aware that it was sore and grazed and swollen.

'Matthew?' she said, engulfed by an overwhelming sense of relief. 'What are you doing here? I thought you were in Manchester.'

'I left early,' he said. 'I was worried about you, and I can see now that I had every reason to be.'

He stepped into the house, a deep frown of concern on his face. When he put an arm around her waist, she leaned into it, testing to see whether he was real, or just a figment of her imagination.

'Let's sit you down before you pass out,' he said, guiding her towards the drawing room.

'Not in there,' she said, reluctant to encounter Lionel Pilkington again so soon. 'I need my phone . . . it's in the study . . . I need to call the police, and an ambulance.'

Matthew pulled his own phone from his pocket. 'I'll make the call,' he said. 'And then, I think you'd better tell me what's been happening.'

Having summoned the police and an ambulance, Violet and Matthew went in to check on a semi-conscious Lionel. Irene was holding her husband's hand, relishing her role as nursemaid, having seemingly forgotten that she was one who had inflicted his injuries in the first place.

Having reassured himself that Lionel's life didn't appear to be in danger, Matthew turned and gently examined the bruise that was forming on Violet's face.

'I thought you said you were going to come in here, act

normally, and then get the hell out,' he said. 'Are you going to explain how that plan was so spectacularly derailed?'

'I was wrong about Irene,' she said, keeping her voice low so that Irene couldn't hear. 'It was Lionel all along. He killed Helen, and he also killed Martha and Duncan Kirkwood. I'll tell you the rest in the study. I need to go in and get my camera bag.'

'Never mind about your camera,' Matthew said. 'By the look of that bruise on your face, I'd say you've taken quite a fall. You could be concussed. You should sit down and wait for the paramedics.'

'I'll sit down when I get to the study,' Violet said. 'Come on. There's something I need to do.'

After she'd checked the contents of her camera bag, Violet sat on the rickety chair in the study and told Matthew what had happened with Lionel.

'So he confessed?' Matthew said. 'To three murders?'

'He did,' Violet said. 'The plan was to kill me too, of course. He didn't expect me to survive long enough to tell the police where the bodies are.'

Matthew gave a shuddering sigh. 'Thank God you're all right,' he said. 'I would never have forgiven myself if anything had happened to you. I should have left Manchester even earlier, driven faster . . . arrived before it all kicked off.'

'You got here a lot quicker than I thought you would. And you did warn me about coming here. I should have listened to your advice.'

'Yes.' He nodded. 'You should.'

'Then again, my coming here did get Lionel to confess.'

'True, although he'll probably deny everything, and go back to blaming Irene for his crimes.'

'He can try,' Violet said. 'But he won't get away with it.'

'I hope you're right. But without any real evidence, it's going to be your word against his.'

'No, it's not.' Violet lifted her camera bag onto her knee and pulled a small electronic device from the front pocket. 'This is my digital audio recorder,' she said. 'I use it all the time because it provides better sound quality than the microphone on my camera. When Lionel brought me in here, something told me to switch it on. It was in my bag all the time, recording everything Lionel said.'

She pressed a couple of buttons, placed the recorder on the desk, and played a snippet of Lionel's confession.

Matthew grinned. 'Violet Brewster,' he said. 'You are full of surprises.'

'I am,' she agreed.

'You're also going to be flavour of the month with DS Winterton.'

'Let's wait and see, shall we?' she said, as somewhere in the distance, a siren wailed. 'That sounds like him now.'

Chapter 45

'You're late,' Fiona said. 'I didn't think you were coming.'

It was the following Thursday, and Violet had agreed to take part in her first quiz night at the White Hart.

'You can blame DS Winterton,' Violet said. 'He called just as I was leaving the house. He wanted to give me an update.'

She sat down, next to Fiona, and glanced around the crowded pub. Groups of four or five people were gathered around almost every table, and sheets of paper were being distributed by Billy Gee, the landlord.

'What's the latest, then?' Fiona said, giving Violet a gentle nudge. 'I hope Lionel's not still trying to blame Irene?'

'No, he soon changed his tune when he was told about the voice recording. He's made what DS Winterton called a *full and frank confession*.'

'So he's been charged?'

'He has,' Violet said. 'And remanded in custody. I don't suppose he'll ever be a free man again.'

'Serves the beggar right,' said Eric, who had arrived at the table carrying three glasses of beer on a tray. 'Three innocent victims . . . and you, Violet, could have been his fourth.'

'I would have been if Irene hadn't stepped in. If it wasn't

for her and Edward Theakstone's cricket bat, I wouldn't be here now.'

'Irene always was a good sort,' Eric said. 'I wonder what's going to happen to her now?'

'I've heard she's gone to stay with her son and daughter-in-law in Bristol,' said Fiona. 'I gather they're putting Fern Lodge up for sale. Edward Theakstone would be spinning in his grave if he knew that ownership of the house was passing out of the family.'

'Or maybe he'd just be glad to know that Irene is safe, and being well looked after,' Violet said. 'What about everyone else in the village? How have they taken the news?'

'Everyone's in shock,' Eric said. 'The thought of a killer living among us all these years . . . it's hard to get your head around that. And poor, old Martha. If she'd known what Lionel Pilkington was really like, she would have steered well clear of Fern Lodge.'

'I still don't fully understand why Lionel killed Martha,' Violet said. 'He said it was to stop her asking questions and nip things in the bud, but I suspect there was more to it than that.'

'Perhaps Martha had guessed the truth,' said Eric. 'Maybe she accused Lionel outright and put him on the back foot.'

'Possibly,' Violet said. 'Although Lionel went in there carrying a rock, so he had every intention of killing her. I get the impression there may have been some history between the two of them, but I don't suppose we'll ever know what was going through Lionel's head.'

Violet sipped her drink.

'You know, I feel terrible about what happened to Martha,' she said. 'She wouldn't have gone to Fern Lodge at all if I hadn't asked her about Helen.'

'I hope you're not still blaming yourself for what happened,' Fiona said. 'None of this was your fault.'

'It's kind of you to say so, Fi, but I can't help but feel guilty – which is why I've taken steps to make amends.'

'What do you mean by that?'

'I'm driving over to Ashbourne tomorrow, to collect Rusty from the Cats Protection,' Violet said. 'I'm adopting her.'

'You mean Martha's little tortoiseshell?' Fiona said. 'You've kept that quiet.'

'I didn't want to say anything until I'd paid her a visit. I needed to check that Rusty and I were a good match. I think we'll get along all right. Turns out she's a really sweet cat. I'm picking her up at ten o'clock in the morning.'

'I hope you're not taking her on just to try and atone for what happened to Martha,' Eric said.

'I'd be lying if I said that wasn't a factor,' Violet replied. 'But it's not the only reason. I've always wanted a cat, but it was never an option when I lived in London. I worked long hours, and the traffic on my street was horrendous. When I moved here, I planned to get a cat once I'd settled in. It's just happened a bit quicker than I thought.'

On the other side of the pub, another group of people had pushed their way to the bar. The residents of Merrywell obviously took their quizzing seriously, because the place was packed.

'Do you know if a date's been fixed yet for Helen Slingsby's funeral?' Eric asked.

Violet shook her head. 'No, that's one of the things I asked DS Winterton about. The police haven't released her body yet . . . or what's left of it. It could be several more weeks before Nigel gets to say his final goodbyes. I spoke to him yesterday. He said when it does happen, it will be a quiet service . . . just himself and Sandra. He doesn't want a fuss.'

'That's very sensible,' said Fiona. 'I hear they're going to pay for Duncan Kirkwood's funeral as well.'

'They will if no one else comes forward to claim his remains,' Violet said. 'Nigel and Sandra said it was the honourable thing to do. They're good people. Let's hope they can put all of this behind them and enjoy the rest of their lives together.'

'Talk of the devil . . .' Fiona said.

The pub door had swung open and, for a moment, the ambient chatter ceased as Nigel and Sandra walked over to the bar.

'It's not like them to come in on quiz night,' Fiona said, when the background rhubarb rhubarb sounds had returned to their previous level.

'I'll go over and have a word,' Violet said. 'They're bound to feel awkward with everyone talking about Helen and Lionel and the whole shebang.'

'Sandra won't be bothered,' Fiona said. 'This is her daughter's pub, after all – but Nigel might be a tad uncomfortable. He'll appreciate you having a word with him. While you're there, you can get me a bag of crisps.'

'All right, bossy boots. What flavour?'

'Cheese and onion.'

Violet weaved her way around the packed tables and went to stand at the bar, where Cathy Gee was pulling a pint of bitter for Nigel. Sandra was already sipping a large glass of white wine.

'How are you both doing?' Violet said, giving them her friendliest smile.

Nigel patted Violet's shoulder. 'Not so bad,' he said, sounding remarkably chipper. 'Don't you worry about us, Violet. It's been a rotten week, but we've come through it. We know the truth now, and we've you to thank for that. Let me buy you a drink to show our appreciation.'

'Thanks, Nigel, but I'm all right for now. Eric's just got a round in. I only came over to say hello and check you're OK. Are the two of you joining in the quiz? If you are, we could do with a couple of extra team members.'

Sandra laughed. 'We never do the quiz,' she said. 'I'm rubbish at general knowledge. Nigel's very good, but he's not allowed to take part because he helps Billy out with some of the questions.'

'I compiled the sports questions for tonight,' Nigel said, tapping the side of his nose. 'Billy's going to let me be question master for that round, so make sure you stick around.'

285

'Sport isn't really my forte,' said Violet. 'I'll be relying on Fiona or Eric for those questions.'

'We Collises always score highly in the sporting round,' said a voice in her ear.

She turned to find Matthew standing behind her, sipping a pint of beer.

'Hello,' she said. 'I didn't realise the Collis family were pub quiz devotees.'

'Every week, without fail,' Matthew said. 'Me, Mum, Dad, Rhys. Our team name is the Collis-see-ums. Get it?'

Violet groaned. 'For your sake, I hope your quizzing skills are better than your puns.'

Matthew smiled. 'I've been meaning to call in and see you,' he said. 'How are you, after your ordeal?'

Matthew had waited at *Fern Lodge* as the ambulance crew had checked Violet over, and sat with her afterwards, as she made a statement to the police and handed over the voice recording. Then later, he had driven her to Greengage Cottage and organised a takeaway, which they had eaten together at the kitchen table.

'I'm fine now,' Violet said. 'Apart from my bruises.'

Matthew examined her face. 'They seem to have faded to a delicate shade of yellow.'

'It's an improvement on bluish-purple, I suppose,' she replied.

'Bluish-purple . . . mmm, like a sort of violet colour, you mean?'

She rolled her eyes. 'Very funny. You're quite a punster, aren't you?'

'I'll make that the last one. Promise.' He held up his hands in surrender. 'Apart from the bruises, are things back to normal?'

'Yes, thank goodness. I've got a couple more days' worth of editing to do on the film, but it's nearing completion, and I've also got a few new jobs lined up. I'm hoping life is going to return to a nice, steady pace.'

'Does that mean you'll be putting your sleuthing skills into mothballs?'

'To be honest, Matthew, on this occasion, my sleuthing skills let me down big time. I was wrong about the air raid shelter, and I was wrong about Irene. My fervid curiosity landed me in a very tricky and dangerous situation. So . . . maybe it's time for me to quit snooping altogether and focus on my business. After all, that's what I came to Merrywell to do.'

Matthew winked. 'We'll see,' he said. 'With you around, I get the feeling anything could happen. See you later, Violet. Good luck with the quiz.'

There were six rounds of questions in all. At the halfway point, Billy Gee called a break to allow people to replenish their glasses.

'It's the sports round next,' Fiona said, as she swigged a fresh glass of beer. 'I hope you're good on sport, Violet, because Eric and I are useless – both at playing, and answering questions on the subject.'

Violet laughed. 'If you brought me onto the team for my sporting knowledge, you're in for a disappointment.'

With his customers supping fresh drinks, Billy Gee picked up his microphone and leaned on the bar.

'Let's get started again then, ladies and gentlemen,' he said. 'We're going to move on to sport now. The questions in this round have been compiled by Merrywell's very own Nigel Slingsby. And for this week only, I'm going to ask Nigel to come up and ask the questions himself.'

As Nigel accepted the microphone from Billy, the crowd in the pub gave him a rousing round of applause. Violet smiled, touched that the people of Merrywell were showing him their unconditional support.

'Hello—' The microphone gave an ear-splitting squeal as Nigel wandered too close to one of the speakers. Looking flustered, he stepped back towards the bar.

'Sorry about that.' He laughed apologetically. 'You can see why Billy's only letting me do this as a one-off. As you've already heard, the next set of questions are all sporting-related, but before we start the round, I have a question I'd like to ask Sandra. As a general rule, she doesn't do quizzes, but I'm hoping she'll make an exception today and give me the right answer.'

He smiled at Sandra, and beckoned her over.

'What are you up to, Nigel?' she said, fanning the fingers of her left hand across her breastbone as she stood up. 'If you're going to ask me a question, you'd better make it multiple choice.'

'No need,' Nigel said, as Sandra walked over and stood by his side. 'Because this is one question only you know the answer to. You'll have to forgive me for not getting down on one knee – but as you know, that's not an easy feat when you've had knee replacements . . .'

He grasped Sandra's hand and smiled at her.

'Sandra Feddingborough, will you do me the honour of becoming my wife?'

Violet held her breath and waited for Sandra to reply.

Epilogue

Four weeks later, Nigel and Sandra were married at the registry office in Matlock. It was a simple and quiet ceremony, with only close family in attendance, but they threw a big, noisy party afterwards at the White Hart.

The members of Merrywell Bowls Club were there to raise a toast to the happy couple, as were Violet, Eric, Fiona and dozens of other villagers. Nigel and Sandra made a special point of inviting Matthew and his parents, and Violet was pleased when all three Collises turned up to join in the celebrations.

It wasn't long before Matthew sauntered over to where Violet was sitting.

'Are you all set for tomorrow?' he asked, as he sipped his celebratory glass of bubbly.

'As I'll ever be,' Violet replied.

The 'premiere' of the community film was to be held in the village hall the following evening. The councillors and interviewees had been given priority seats, and Judith Talbot had borrowed a 'red carpet' from the Merrywell Manor Hotel. The event was to be a celebration of the village, and attendees were being encouraged to dress in their finest clothes for the occasion.

'I will admit to a few nerves,' Violet said. 'I'm not sure what the locals will make of the finished film.'

'I think they'll give it their seal of approval,' said Matthew, who had already viewed the final draft. 'It definitely gets a big thumbs-up from me. You've done a great job.'

'Thank you. It's certainly been a memorable project, in more ways than one.'

'I must say, it has been something of a baptism of fire for you,' Matthew said. 'But you can be proud of what you've achieved – both with the community film, and finding out what happened to Helen.'

'Thanks, Matthew. And thanks for your help . . . with everything. You'll be pleased to hear that my latest project is proving to be much more straightforward.'

'No investigative skills required with this latest one then? No murder to solve?'

'Absolutely not,' said Violet, with a firm shake of her head. 'I mean, what are the odds of me stumbling across another mystery?'

Matthew drained his champagne and smiled.

A Letter from Jane Bettany

Thank you so much for choosing to read *Murder in Merrywell*. I hope you've enjoyed meeting Violet Brewster and the other residents of Merrywell as much as I've loved writing about them. It's been an absolute pleasure to develop a new cast of characters, and create a community for them to inhabit. Although Merrywell is a fictional village, it combines the best features of several places in my home county of Derbyshire, bringing them all together in one location (if Merrywell was a real village, I would *definitely* want to buy a house there).

If you enjoyed *Murder in Merrywell*, please consider leaving a review. I love hearing what readers think of my books, and reviews also help me to connect with new readers.

If you would like to be the first to know about my future releases, including the next book in the Violet Brewster series, please follow me on Twitter or Facebook:

Twitter: https://twitter.com/JaneBettany

Facebook: https://www.facebook.com/JaneBettanyAuthor

https://harpercollins.co.uk/blogs/authors/jane-bettany

Best wishes

Jane

In Cold Blood

No secret can stay buried forever . . .

As the Whitworth family begin renovations on their new
home, their plans are brought to an abrupt end when they
discover a body buried in the back garden.

DI Isabel Blood and her team are called to investigate,
but as she approaches Ecclesdale Drive,
a feeling of unease settles in her gut.

The property cordoned off is number 23.
The house she used to live in as a child . . .

The forensic team estimate that the body has been
in the ground for up to forty years – coinciding with
the time Isabel's family lived in the house.

Isabel's father vanished without a trace when
Isabel was fourteen years old. And with her mother
remaining tight-lipped about her father's disappearance,
Isabel can't escape the unnerving sense of dread that
it's his body, buried in the garden.

**Fans of *Vera*, Val McDermid and Elly Griffiths
will love *In Cold Blood*!**

Without a Trace

**You can cover up the truth,
but every murder leaves a trail . . .**

The rain was relentless. It stung **Ruth Prendergast's** face as she
dashed towards her house, desperate to escape the cold and
settle down for an early night. But upon entering her bedroom,
she finds a man, lying on her bed – a knife buried in his chest.

When **Detective Isabel Blood** and her sergeant arrive
on the scene, Ruth claims she's never laid eyes on the
victim before. But with no sign of a break-in,
how did the killer gain access to the house?

Then Ruth disappears, leaving Isabel and her team
to fear the worst. Has their lead suspect escaped,
or is Ruth in danger herself?

Forensic evidence at the crime scene is sparse,
and it's proving impossible for Isabel to make a breakthrough.
With Ruth still missing, time is running out.

But how can you catch a killer that doesn't leave a trace?

Last Seen Alive

When **Anna Matheson** fails to collect her son from the babysitter after a works party, the police are swiftly called. Anna is a stickler for time and a good mother – she would never abandon her baby. Her disappearance is totally out of character and **DI Isabel Blood** and her team soon suspect foul play.

CCTV footage shows Anna was last seen at precisely 11.11 p.m., as she collected her coat to leave the party. But the cameras outside the venue have failed to pick up her exit from the car park – how could she have vanished in plain sight?

Rumour has it that Anna was set to make big changes in the workplace, and Isabel can't help but think someone wanted her out of the way.

Everyone at the party is a suspect, **and all the clues point to murder . . .**

Acknowledgements

A heartfelt thank you for reading *Murder in Merrywell*, the first book in the Violet Brewster series.

I've had immense fun adding a dash of 'cosy' to my crime writing. It's provided the chance to weave warmth, friendship and humour into my storylines, and create a protagonist who isn't constrained by police procedures. Violet's curiosity does land her in trouble from time to time, but it also allows her to do things that a police detective wouldn't be able to get away with.

Writing this new series would not have been possible without the support and commitment of the brilliant publishing team at HQ. Special thanks go to my talented editor, Audrey Linton, whose feedback and suggestions have not only improved the book, but also made Violet a nicer person.

Sending love and thanks to my family and friends – for putting up with me and being kind enough to read my books. A special shout out to fellow author and friend Charlotte Baker, in appreciation of the writerly chats and words of encouragement. Thanks, Char!

I'll end by thanking my lovely husband, Howard, who is always on hand to offer support. He doesn't read my books until he has a finished paperback copy in his hands, but – with this novel – I decided to talk through a plot snag with him. That meant giving an overview of the story (including the biggest spoiler of all – the identity of the murderer). So, I hope you've still enjoyed the book, Howard, even though you already knew 'whodunnit'! Kudos to you for suggesting that a piece of jewellery could solve my plot problem. I hope you approve of how I used your idea.

Dear Reader,

We hope you enjoyed reading this book. If you did, we'd be so appreciative if you left a review. It really helps us and the author to bring more books like this to you.

Here at HQ Digital we are dedicated to publishing fiction that will keep you turning the pages into the early hours. Don't want to miss a thing? To find out more about our books, promotions, discover exclusive content and enter competitions you can keep in touch in the following ways:

JOIN OUR COMMUNITY:

Sign up to our new email newsletter: http://smarturl.it/SignUpHQ

Read our new blog www.hqstories.co.uk

🐦 https://twitter.com/HQStories

f www.facebook.com/HQStories

BUDDING WRITER?

We're also looking for authors to join the HQ Digital family!
Find out more here:

https://www.hqstories.co.uk/want-to-write-for-us/

Thanks for reading, from the HQ Digital team

ONE PLACE. MANY STORIES